a place
in time

JoAnn Ross

1

THERE WAS NO turning back.

After studying the holodiscs in the secret government archives, after charting and recharting his destination, after spending five long solar revolutions designing and constructing his transporter, Logosian astrophysicist and hopeful intergalactic explorer Sebastian Blackthorne was on his way.

Lights—red, green, yellow, and blue, flashed. The lights were a medley of wavelengths, surrounding him, radiating in all directions. His body felt as if it were being stung by a hundred, a thousand angry nitrowasps.

Employing the centuries-old meditation techniques the Ancient Ones had brought with them from the planet Janos on Stratum Eleven, Sebastian focused his thoughts, directing his mind to his destination: the planet Earth in the Milky Way galaxy.

Sebastian had chosen Earth because its atmosphere and gravitational pull were remarkably similar to that of Logosia. Also, although he'd been a child at the time, he could remember in vivid detail the excursion he'd taken with his parents and sister in the family spacecraft.

The occasion had been the quadricentennial of his mother's homeland, and although four hundred years of a nation's existence was a mere blink of an eyelash to a Logosian, the Americans, his mother included, had considered it quite an accomplishment.

Sebastian had chosen California for his destination because he remembered the western state in North America to be a harmonious and eclectic location. Venice, specifically, he recalled, was a place where a stranger's sudden appearance amidst the amazingly diverse mix of natives would not cause alarm.

There was another reason he'd chosen Earth as his destination. A highly inappropriate, vastly un-Logosian, particularly human, emotional reason.

This trip was a personal pilgrimage to the planet of his mother's birth. And although hope was heretically anti-reason and entirely irrational—therefore diametrically opposed to every aspect of Logosian philosophy—in some deep, secret place inside his heart, Sebastian hoped that somehow, by understanding the planet his mother had willingly left behind but had never forgotten, he might come to better understand himself.

In preparation for his journey, his mother had told him everything about her planet that she could remember. Unfortunately, with the exception of that one visit, Mia Vardanyian had been away from her home for more than forty years. Sebastian needed more detailed, up-to-date information than she could provide.

Although it was technically against confederation regulations, Logosian government officials had found an arcane loophole in the inter-galaxy treaty and placed, out of sensor range, intelligence satellites whose cloaking devices had allowed them to go unnoticed around Earth. For more than two hundred solar revolutions, the satellites had been beaming back pictures and audio tapes of the planet.

Scores of clerks—females, whose duty it was to handle the mundane, mindless tasks that were the hallmark of government bureaucracies throughout the universe—transferred the electronic data onto holodiscs, which were filed away in the government archives.

Sebastian's younger sister, Rosalyn, a highly placed government xenoanthropologist and the sole female professor at the Logosian Science Institute, had originally professed grave doubts about both Sebastian's theory and his motive.

When she couldn't convince him to give up his perilous plan, Rosalyn relented and, risking her own career, provided him with classified government datachips far more detailed than the holofiles he'd been permitted to check out from the Logosian National Library.

This wealth of information enabled Sebastian to learn the language and customs of the place called California.

And now, utilizing his unproven theory of molecular astro-projection, Sebastian intended to be the first intergalactic traveler without the encumbrance—and protection—of a space vehicle.

Rosalyn was seated at the computer, her expression grave as her fingers tapped over the touch-plate, turning complex mathematical algorithms into scientific visualization.

Her blond hair was arranged atop her head in its usual tidy braided coronet, and she was wearing a softly clinging silver gown, its patch revealing her to be a fifth-level

Academician on her breast.

Although everything about his sister—her hair, her classically styled gown, her studious demeanor—was carefully calculated to portray formal restraint, an aura of uncharacteristic excitement surrounded her like a shimmering alpha field.

Outside the clear quartzalite windows, moonlight cast a rosy glow over Logosia. Inside, Sebastian and Rosalyn watched the screen as the computer scanned its way through billions of miles.

Four-dimensional visuals of the universe burst forth in a dazzling display of furious fireworks: stars flaring, dying in cold black voids while worlds were being reborn from exploded remnants, whirling galaxies hurling heated gases in all directions, glittering stardust, blinding fireballs, and speeding, spinning, flaming quasars.

Planets were scattered about like comet-tail dust. Matter and light disappeared, sucked up by devouring black holes, disappearing from the screen, never to be seen again.

"We're coming up on the Milky Way," Rosalyn announced unnecessarily as the glowing, spiraling band of starlight appeared on the screen.

That shared feeling of expectation was making the air crackle around them. It crossed Sebastian's mind that he could use a Valdox.

Not that he would have resorted to taking one of the popular tranquilizer tabs. Because if there was ever a time when he needed to keep all his wits about him, this was definitely it.

Spiral arms extended outward from the mass of light, like an Earth child's pinwheel.

A pleasant, long-ago memory flashed through his mind.

Sebastian's lips curved into a faint smile as he recalled his mother purchasing the whimsical red-and-white toy for him at some fantastical kingdom Earthlings had inexplicably named Disneyland.

His memory of that halcyon afternoon was as clear as if it had been yesterday. He could feel the warmth of his mother's gaze, smell the evocative scent she always wore, the perfumed oil created from the moonflowers she cultivated in her greenhouse garden. That same scent was repeated in the potpourri Mia Vardanyian had insisted on keeping in every room of their home.

And although none of his friends' mothers would have ever done anything so frivolous as growing flowers, Sebastian had secretly thought them wonderful. Indeed, he could never think of his mother without seeing those bright crimson blooms.

His smile turned to a frown as he also remembered returning to Logosia and having Hotek Venturian, a mean-spirited green-blooded bully, grab the pinwheel away and crush it beneath the heel of his crokogator-skin boot.

Nothing was free, Sebastian had learned. Eidetic memory, as useful as it was, did not come without its own high cost. All experiences—good and bad—were automatically, indelibly stored in his memory banks, waiting only to be recalled.

Sebastian sighed and returned his attention to Rosalyn's screen, studying the glowing orb inside one of the galaxy's spiral arms.

He and his sister exchanged a meaningful look. The glorious flaring body was Earth's sun.

"It won't be long now," he said.

Rosalyn's lovely face, schooled since infancy to appear

serene, was anything but. Her normally smooth, pale brow was furrowed, her clear amber eyes—a legacy from their mother—revealed inappropriate concern, and worry lines bracketed her lips.

"There's still time to change your mind," she advised him.

Sebastian didn't answer. There was no need. Although Rosalyn was mindblind, lacking Logosian telepathy, he knew that it was not necessary for her to read his mind to know what he was thinking. Because she also possessed the terran blood of their mother, his sister could appreciate the driving need that had gnawed at Sebastian for as long as he could remember.

From this vantage point, Sebastian was able to see all the planets: Pluto, a brief speck, seen, then dismissed. Icy Neptune, with its eight moons and clouds of methane ice; blue-shrouded Uranus with its twin moons, Oberon and Titania; enormous, stormy Jupiter; be-ringed Saturn; and Mars, its dark red landscape appearing, from this distance, so like his own planet.

Then there she was. *Earth*.

Sebastian's studies allowed him to recognize the land masses floating in the blue seas, the glittering white of the polar ice caps, the jagged snow-topped ridges of the Himalayas, the Alps, the Andes, the Appalachians, the Rockies, the Cascades.

He drew in a breath and leaned forward, taking in a thin gray ribbon that curled across the Asian landscape, and realized that he was looking at the Great Wall of China. He remembered his mother telling him the enormous man-made barricade had been erected to repel intruders, but at the time, he'd been too young to fully comprehend the concept of armed, deadly enemies.

Logosia had been peaceful for generations. Indeed, it had been more than six hundred solar revolutions since his planet had experienced war.

Sebastian's heart picked up its beat as he stepped into the imaging circle. He tightened his fingers around the compact quantum accelerator. It had taken years of fine-tuning, but he'd finally succeeded in shrinking the molecular accelerator down to a size small enough to be held in a man's palm. It was also small enough to include a miniature ecumenical translator. The voice module for the translator was implanted in his middle ear. No properly prepared space traveler would think of leaving Logosia without his ecumenical translator or his hologram credit disc.

Sebastian concentrated all his energies on his extrasensory perception, one of the few genetic traits he shared with other Logosians. In order to fully understand the people who populated his mother's planet, he must appear to be one of them. If he were to walk among the inhabitants of Earth without drawing undue attention to himself, he must make certain that his features blended harmoniously with the natives.

And since his own clothing was created from fabrics not available on Earth and fashioned in current Logosian style, he needed to ensure that he was properly attired. For that, he required a model drawn from the mind of a terran.

Utilizing the mental imaging that was as natural to every Logosian as breathing, Sebastian imagined he could feel the warmth of the sun on his body, he could hear the ebb and flow of the Pacific Ocean tide along the Venice, California, shoreline. He could smell the salt on the warm summer breeze.

Sounds rose up from the spinning blue-green orb that was Earth, reverberating inharmoniously in his ear like voices from the ancient Tower of Bukh. Images flashed before his eyes like a laserfilm, glowing in the shimmering, ghostly beam of white light.

He had just managed to separate one feminine Earthling's thoughts from the others when Rosalyn's startled voice interrupted his concentration.

"What do you mean we miscalculated?" he shouted as he was pulled faster and faster toward the light.

Sebastian felt a pulsing deep inside his body, the increasingly strong beats synchronizing with the flashing lights that were now the entire spectrum of the rainbow.

He was breaking apart.

Disintegrating.

Dissolving in the sparkling golden light.

"And where the sweet nirvana is Rum Runner Island, Maine?"

It was the last thing Sebastian would say before vanishing from his laboratory.

And his planet.

2

I T HAD BEEN snowing for five days.

More than twenty-two inches of the wet white stuff had been dumped on the island, and if the weather forecast was even close to the mark, another ten inches would pile up before the series of storms, dubbed the Canadian Express, had passed. As much as Kirby Pendleton could appreciate a white Christmas, she did have her limits.

Although she'd grown up on the remote island off the rocky Maine coast, five years spent in Southern California had made Kirby forget how cold her home state could get.

She was sitting in a high-backed leather chair, her feet up on the old, scarred desk that, like the chair, had belonged to her father. After blowing on her coffee to cool it, she watched the white flakes of snow being blown against the window.

Even as she reminded herself that she'd become bored with California's unrelenting sunshine and that her nostalgic desire for seasonal changes had been one of her reasons for deciding to leave the L.A. Police Department to pin on her father's badge here on the island, Kirby wouldn't mind if Mother Nature pulled the plug on the snow machine. At least until after the New Year.

Leaning her head against the back of the chair, she closed her eyes and allowed her mind to drift. She imagined herself back on Venice Beach, lying on the sun-warmed sand. Instead of the unappealing, dark blue winter-weight wool uniform she was currently wearing, in her fantasy she was clad in a hot pink bikini—skimpier than she'd ever actually dare wear—soaking up the golden rays of the sun while a movie-star-handsome man in surfer jams and no shirt rubbed sun block all over her body.

She sighed as she imagined his wide, clever hands stroking their way across her shoulders, down her back, along the soft skin at the insides of her thighs, spreading oil and sensual warmth at the same time.

When he turned her in his arms, a lock of sun-bleached blond hair fell over his dark forehead, and Kirby pictured herself reaching up to brush it away.

No. Not blond, she corrected. Steve had blond hair, and if there was one person she definitely didn't want to invite into her daydreams, it was her former husband.

He'd be dark, she decided. The man of her dreams would have hair as black as midnight. And his eyes would be dark, as well, the color of obsidian, only softer. His nose wouldn't be pug, like Steve's, but strong and straight as an arrow.

His lips would be full but firmly cut, not the least bit feminine, and always tinged with a private smile just for her. Focusing on those enticing lips before moving down to take in his bold square jaw, Kirby drifted back into her fantasy.

She drank in the tropical scent of the coconut oil his

dark hands were rubbing on her body. She heard the ebb and flow of the tide, the soft sigh of the salt-tinged summer breeze, the chime of bells.

Bells?

Jerked back to reality again, Kirby dropped her feet to the floor and grabbed her phone.

"Don't you dare tell me you're not coming to dinner," she greeted her twin brother after seeing his name on the screen. "Not when I've gone to all the trouble to fix your favorite. That's right, Grandmother Pendleton's pot roast."

She laughed off his professed alarm. "I'll have you know I got the recipe from Emily."

Of the three Pendleton daughters, Kirby's eldest sister, Emily, had always been the domestic one. Kirby was not.

"She promises that it's foolproof, so you don't have to worry about ending up in the ER." Kirby lifted her feet to the desktop again and leaned back in the chair. "So, if you haven't called to back out on my pot roast, what's up? Another explosion in the brain factory?"

Nate Pendleton spent most of his waking and sleeping hours ensconced in a laboratory out in a remote site in the Maine island's woods. After meeting a few of her brilliant brother's equally brilliant but frighteningly loopy co-workers, Kirby had stopped asking what they were doing out there.

As Nate went on to explain the reason for his call, Kirby's smile faded.

"No, I haven't heard a thing. You're the first person to call since Mr. McCarthy wanted to file a complaint against John Allen's snowplow blocking his driveway. What kind of lights?"

She switched the phone to the other ear and, reaching

over, turned up the police scanner. It was set to the State Police frequency, and over the buzzing static, Kirby could hear numerous voices, all claiming to have seen something strange in the sky over Rum Runner Island.

"If one of you eggheads set off another experimental rocket without notifying me ahead of time, so help me, Nate—"

He cut her off with a rapid-fire spat of denial.

"All right. I believe you. You don't have to bite my head off. It's probably just the aurora borealis," she decided. "I know it's a little late in the year, but the weatherman on Channel Four said that it's because of the solar flares, and, after all, you're the one who told me the flares are what are causing so much chaos with the radio and television frequencies.

"So, although I'd love to have a spaceship land in the town square, just to liven things up around here, I don't think it's going to happen."

They both laughed, but Kirby couldn't help noticing that her brother's laughter was not quite as robust as hers. *What did he know that she didn't?*

"Well, whatever it is," she said, "there's undoubtedly a reasonable explanation. There always is."

After making him promise to drive carefully on the way to the house, she hung up.

She'd no sooner disconnected the call than the phone chimed again.

And again.

An hour later, after it seemed that she'd talked to nearly all six hundred and forty of the island's full-time residents, Kirby was left wondering what on earth had gotten into everyone.

Their stories varied, but everyone, from the mayor to Matthew Kelly—whose wood carvings had made him a celebrity among summer visitors who were willing to pay big bucks for a life-size porcupine made out of tooth-picks—to Agnes Adams, the town's librarian for forty-five years, all insisted that aliens had landed on the island.

The descriptions of the alleged spaceship ranged from a shimmering blue light to a white light shaped like a cigar to a silver saucer-shaped spaceship.

Johnny Kelly, Matthew's son and paperboy for the weekly *Rum Runner Island Yankee Observer,* reported that he'd seen a gang of seven-foot-tall men dressed in what looked like Reynolds Wrap walking down Main Street, while seventy-nine-year-old Scott MacIntyre, who'd run the Shell station on Maple Drive since long before Kirby had been born, reported that three-foot-tall little green men with a single flashing eye in the middle of their foreheads had dug a hole in the football field at Evergreen High School.

And a hysterical Mildred O'Connor, owner of Mil-dred's Shear Pleasures Beauty Emporium, was certain she'd seen a filmy, smoke-like entity going down her neighbor's chimney.

"Do you think it could possibly be smoke coming *out* of the chimney?" Kirby asked mildly. She smiled as Mildred's machine-gun-quick babble quieted.

"Don't worry about it," she said after the beautician apologized for calling. "That's what I'm here for."

"It must be the full moon," she decided after the phone had been silent for twenty minutes. "That, along with the flares and the storm. Five straight days of staying indoors can make anyone stir-crazy."

Kirby knew it was certainly getting to her.

Making a mental note to ask Nate if he knew of any instances where solar flares had caused mass hallucinations, she pulled on her gloves, put on her coat, switched the landline to ring at her house, and waded through the drifting snow to her Jeep Grand Cherokee.

✧   ✧   ✧

IT WAS AS cold as the glacial plains of Algor.

Sebastian rubbed his bare arms briskly with his numbed hands, trying to get the frozen human blood circulating in his veins.

Wherever he was, he'd definitely plotted the coordinates wrong. Because if this was indeed Venice, California, someone in the archival agency had played a Jupitorian practical joke by exchanging holodiscs. As for proper clothing, for some unfathomable reason, he found himself clad in nothing but a pair of brief orange trousers printed with flowers that left his chest, arms, and most of his legs bare.

Damn it to Hadean, despite all reason, regardless of all the years he'd dedicated to planning this mission, somehow, he must have seriously miscalculated.

Sebastian knew that the entire Logosian scientific community thought him crazy for asking why propelled vehicles must be the only way to bridge the gap between solar systems. Why couldn't it be that physics, not technology, held the ultimate answer to space travel?

After all, as he had pointed out at the annual meeting of interplanetary astrophysicists, any first-level Logosian was perfectly capable of sending thoughts for hundreds, even thousands of junctures.

By the fourth level, the average Logosian could send

those same thoughts in three-dimensional holographic form. And by the time a Logosian reached the eighth level of maturity, he was able to utilize telekinesis to move around effortlessly beneath the planet dome.

So why couldn't a person, aided by a pocket-size anti-matter accelerator device, travel through the galaxies in an astral or ethereal body?

Why couldn't the component atoms that made up Sebastian Blackthorne be taken apart, transported through space, utilizing the theory of quantum electrodynamics, and be put back together when they'd reached their destination? Indeed, why couldn't they be rearranged to resemble some entirely different life-form?

Despite continued opposition from first the scientific community and then, when his heretical views became more widely known, from the Logosian ruling council itself, Sebastian had steadfastly refused to abandon his theory.

Displaying a dogged tenacity and drive that was consid-ered, in his secular society of intellects, to be unseemly, he threw himself into his work.

Such inappropriate behavior resulted in his dismissal from his much sought-after position as head of the space council. Although the outcome had not been a surprise, Sebastian had never expected his peers—those very same scientists who'd once proclaimed him to be one of the most brilliant males on the planet—to shun him.

But they had.

And after he'd published his treatise asking what was wrong with rewriting the laws of physics if they didn't do what you wanted them to, rumors suggesting that lower-class Janurian warrior blood had somehow slipped into his family's gene pool—a gene pool already compromised by Xanthus Vardanyian's marriage to an Earthling—had begun to circulate.

Sebastian was accustomed to having his parentage held against him. And all his life, first as a student, then as a teacher at the science institute, he'd worked overtime to prove himself a true Logosian.

But, although he'd always done his best to adhere to the Logosian way, not once, in all his thirty-one years, had he ever considered denying his humanness.

To do so would have been to deny his mother, and since every Logosian child was brought up to respect and revere his elders, such behavior would have been totally without reason.

Sebastian also knew intuitively that such denial would have pained him in some intrinsic way he could not quite understand. Still, the rumors tarnished his family's name and endangered his sister's already tenuous position at the institute.

Although Sebastian didn't give a freebooter's damn what anyone thought of him, he was furious at those who couldn't find anything better to do with their time than to criticize Rosalyn for her brother's actions.

Cursing violently, evoking the names of ancient, forgotten feudal gods long removed from the official Logosian calendar, Sebastian forged his way through the driving snow, teeth chattering violently, his near-naked body turning to ice.

There were times, and this was definitely one of them, when he almost wished he'd taken his parents' advice and become a twelfth-level Sage, like his father, grandfather, and every one of his other male relatives before him, all the way back to Flavian Vardanyian—one of the original Ancient Ones.

"Well, it's too damn late now," Sebastian muttered, wondering how long he could last in such hyperborean conditions.

Having chosen California as his destination, he hadn't paid proper attention to the ways Earthlings had adapted to their planet's more frigid climes. Such behavior had been shortsighted, unreasonably careless, not to mention potentially dangerous.

It had also been undeniably human.

The deep-seated stubbornness that had caused him so much grief on his home planet rose to assert itself, keeping his feet doggedly moving forward.

He passed what he suspected was, in warmer seasons, a brook. Now it was a sparkling, shimmering sheet of ice. Water froze on Earth at zero degrees centigrade, Sebastian remembered. He didn't need a thermoscan to know that the frigid winter air surrounding him was a great deal colder than that.

Unfortunately, his body—like that of his terran mother—was seven-tenths water. Did this mean that he was destined to end up crystallized, frozen in place like this glistening stilled creek?

No. This couldn't be his fate, Sebastian told himself over and over again. His labored breath was a wavering white ghost in front of him, freezing on his face.

His last thought, as first his limbs and then his mind went numb, was that he'd be damned if he'd die before proving that he'd been right.

3

THE SNOW BLEW against the windshield, piling up almost faster than the wipers could sweep it away. Drifts blew across the roadway, and county snowplows had made high walls of snow along the shoulder. It was dusk, that suspended time between day and night when the world turned a deep purple.

Kirby sat hunkered over the steering wheel, peering through the swirling white curtain, when she suddenly saw something or someone lying in the center of the road.

Slamming on the brakes, she skidded sideways, missing the snow-covered object by inches. Her heart pounding, she jumped from the Jeep and raced toward what she could now see was a man.

He was unconscious and nearly naked. Wondering what on earth had happened to cause him to be out here in the middle of nowhere, wearing only a pair of hibiscus-printed orange jams, she took his pulse, frightened when she found it dangerously weak.

"Hey!"

She ran her hands over his body, feeling for broken bones. Then she checked out his hands and feet and ears, searching for any dead white tissue that would indicate frozen skin.

When she didn't find any, she began briskly rubbing his arms, his face, his outstretched legs. Ice crystals coated his dark hair and eyebrows. Although he looked vaguely familiar, Kirby couldn't place him.

Pressing both her gloved hands against his tanned chest, she began to administer CPR, breathing and pushing, breathing and pushing.

Breathe.

Push.

Breathe.

Sebastian felt the sweet warmth against his lips first. Then the hard, rhythmic pounding against his chest.

"That's it," the female shouted when his rigid chest began to rise and fall of its own accord. "You're doing it! You're breathing. Come on, don't give up now! Keep going."

Sebastian read her mind and discovered that she was frightened. The idea that she could care so deeply for another of her kind, especially one who was a total stranger to her, was something he'd have to think about, later, when he was no longer hovering on the dark abyss of human death.

As she continued to pound painfully but surprisingly effectively on his chest, shouting at him all the while, Sebastian decided with a detached sense of wonder that she was every bit as stubborn as he.

He wondered if such a discordant personality trait made her an outsider, too. The idea that two individuals from such dissimilar planets might have something intrinsically in common was pleasing. Nearly as pleasing as the taste of her mouth.

When she placed her cheek against his chest, his heart kicked.

"That's better," she said. "But I can't lift you by myself. And I certainly can't leave you here to freeze to death. So, you're going to have to help me."

Sebastian opened his eyes and found himself looking straight into hers. Which were as blue as the rare blue diamazimans mined in the alluvial river plains at the base of the mountain range located far outside his climate-controlled domed city. His father had spent a small fortune to have one of the precious stones set in a pendant for his mother for their last anniversary.

"Help you?" he asked, dragging his mind back to the problem at hand.

Since his mother had long ago, due to pressure from the Elders' ruling council, given up her native tongue, Sebastian had been forced to practice his Earth dialect from Rosalyn's audio discs. Hoping that his accent was appropriate for wherever this was he'd landed, he was relieved when she seemed to find nothing wrong with his speech.

"We need to get you to the truck." Her voice had a much more melodic quality than the computerized tones he'd studied. "Do you think you can stand up?"

"Of course."

He might no longer be on Logosia, but Sebastian was not about to abandon eons of scientific dogma proclaiming the female of the species to be the frailer sex.

Having this Earthling discover him half-dead was bad enough. To continue to display weakness in front of a female would be a shame he'd never live down. Shaking off her touch, he pushed himself to his feet with a sudden burst of energy.

A mistake. Stars swam in front of his eyes, his legs trembled, and his head went light as a flitterfly.

She caught him in mid-sway.

"That's what you get for trying to be Ironman," she muttered, putting her arm around his waist to steady him. "Take a few deep breaths. It'll help you get your land legs back."

It crossed Sebastian's whirling mind that she was surprisingly strong for someone of her small stature. The top of her head barely reached his shoulder.

"My land legs?"

"Just an expression," she answered in unison with the ecumenical translator embedded in his middle ear. "You must not be from around here."

"No." Of that he was certain.

"I didn't think so. Feeling better?"

Amazingly, the deep breathing had helped, immediately clearing his head like a whiff of straight paradoxygen.

"Yes. Thank you," he said with formal politeness drilled into him from childhood.

She glanced around into the swirling white snow. "Are you all alone?"

"Yes." He wondered what she'd say if he told her precisely how alone he was at this moment.

"You're shaking badly." Her eyes were filled with unexpected concern. "Let's get you warmed up. Then you can tell me what happened."

Her ground machine appeared to be an older model than those pictured on the archival holodiscs. As he made his way gingerly toward it, Sebastian wondered if he'd somehow gone back in time as he passed through space.

Not knowing how to ask such a question without drawing any more undue attention to himself, he decided that
explanations could come later.

"Fortunately, I always keep blankets in the Jeep," she
told him with a surprising amount of cheer, considering
that her own thick lashes were covered with icy white frost.

He climbed into her machine, as she indicated, then sat
passively as she wrapped the thick red blanket about his
frozen body. He was light-headed, his hands and feet were
numb, and the rest of him felt unreasonably clumsy.

"There you are." She tucked him in as if he were a
child, fastened a belt across his chest, then shut the
passenger door. He watched as she went around the front
and climbed into the machine.

"What's your name?" she asked.

"Sebastian." Spots were spinning in front of his eyes
again. Sebastian tried to blink them away and failed.
"Sebastian Blackthorne."

That said, he surrendered to the whirling darkness.

✦   ✦   ✦

"OH, HELL."

Kirby cursed under her breath as he crumpled onto the
bench seat, his dark head landing in her lap. Reaching over
him, she picked up the radio microphone and pressed a
button.

"Rum Runner to Evac Eagle One, Rum Runner to
Evac Eagle One. Do you copy, Eagle One?"

There was a crackling static, then, "Ayuh, I copy ya,
Rum Runner. What's the problem?"

"I've got a patient for you," she said.

"An emergency?"

"Yes. Exposure, possible hypothermia. He's a male, approximately six foot, two hundred pounds." She didn't add that the weight was very excellently distributed on his deeply tanned masculine frame.

"Age, around thirty. I found him lying out in the snow."

"How're his vitals?"

"His pulse is thready, but his heartbeat's reasonably strong."

"Conscious?"

"He wasn't when I found him a few minutes ago, then he was, but now he's passed out again."

"Trauma? Broken bones, anything like that?"

"Not that I could tell, but like I said, his pulse isn't as strong as it should be."

"Frostbite?"

"None that I could see. But I've only had basic paramedic training," she said. "This man needs to be checked out by a physician. And Doc Merryman is in Bangor visiting his daughter."

"Ayuh, I heard Mary had a baby. Boy or girl?"

"A girl. Eight pounds, six ounces. What about my patient, Eagle One?"

"Sorry, Rum Runner," the disembodied voice said over the crackling static, "but it's a no-go."

"What?"

"There's a blizzard blowin'. I can't send out a chopper until the weather clears, Kirby. It's too much of a risk."

"I know," she said on a harsh huff of breath as she glared at the driving snow that had been making her life increasingly difficult.

"But what am I supposed to do with him? The damn

ferry's not running because of the choppy water."

"Get him somewhere dry and warm and cover him up to keep him from losin' any more body heat."

"I've already done that. I've got him in the Jeep right now, wrapped in a blanket, and the heater's going full blast."

"See? Ya don't need me at all."

"Dammit, Mac, this is a serious situation."

Just because Joe MacGregor had been her father's best friend and had known her all her life, he still seemed to think that gave him the right to tease her, despite her badge, the same way he had when she was seven.

"Sorry," he said. "But I have faith in you. The thing ta do is keep him warm. Since ya can't stay in the Jeep all night, you'd best take him to jail. Or back to your place."

Her place was closer. And jail wasn't an option unless she wanted to stay there all night with him. "Then what?"

"Didn't they teach ya about hypothermia in California?"

"They brushed over it in the police academy, but there's not much need for it on the beach," she countered. Which wasn't precisely true. Occasionally a winter sailor or surfer would get into trouble in the colder season's water. She'd just never been on duty when it had happened. "Want to compare notes on heatstroke, sunburn, or near drowning in riptides?"

"You're in a rotten mood today, ain't ya, Kirby Pendleton?"

"You wouldn't be at your best, either, if you'd had the day I've had."

"Ayuh. I heard about your little green men."

"There *weren't* any little green men. So, if you don't

mind, I'd like to get home before my patient and I get carbon monoxide poisoning from sitting in a car with the motor running."

"Take his temperature. At ninety-four degrees, ya got confusion. At ninety, an irregular heartbeat, at eighty-six, muscle strength gives out and the patient gets drowsy, maybe falls unconscious."

"That's where we are now, I think," Kirby said, glancing down at the man sprawled on the seat. He'd given standing up a pretty good shot but hadn't been able to pull it off.

"Ayuh. That's what ya said. If he wakes up and can swallow, give him some warm, nonalcoholic drinks."

"No brandy?" She could certainly use some right about now.

"That's in the movies," he advised drily. "We don't do that in real life."

"Somebody ought to tell all those Saint Bernards, running through the Alps with kegs around their necks," she muttered. "Okay, so I give the guy some tea. Then what?"

"Like I said, keep him covered. Don't take a chance on burnin' his skin with heatin' pads or hot-water bottles, don't leave him alone, and keep checkin' his vitals. That's about all ya can do for now."

"Okay. I think I can handle that."

"Who ya got there, by the way?"

"He said he's Sebastian Blackthorne."

"Name doesn't ring a bell."

"It didn't for me, either. Although he looks vaguely familiar, I can't place him, and since we don't have any Blackthornes living on the island, he's obviously from the mainland."

"Well, let me know how he's doing. If this dang storm ever blows over, and you still need an evac, I'll fly to the island myself."

"Thanks, Mac."

"Oh, and one more thing."

"What's that?"

"They did teach ya CPR at that hotshot California police academy, didn't they?"

"Yes, and I've already used it."

"Good. Keep a real close eye on those vitals, Kirby. 'Cause if your patient's temperature drops to seventy-seven degrees, ya can expect cardiac arrest. Then death."

In her line of work, working in an urban environment, she'd seen plenty of bodies, but never one that she'd been personally responsible for. She did not want this stranger to be the first.

"Don't worry, Mac," she vowed. "I didn't go to the trouble of saving him to have him die on me."

"Ayuh. You're a good girl, Kirby. Your pa would be right proud of ya." It was the same thing he'd told her the first time she'd baited her own fishing hook. "Good luck."

"Thanks. I think I'm going to need all I can get. Rum Runner over and out."

She released the button on the radio and looked down at him. "Okay, buster. Let's get you home. And if you even dare try to have a heart attack, I swear I'll toss you in a cell and throw away the key."

When she pushed him off her lap, Sebastian stirred. It took an effort, but he managed to open his eyes. "A cell?"

"Oh, good, you're awake." Her relief was so palpable that Sebastian felt as if he could reach out and touch it. "Don't worry," she assured him. "I'm taking you home with me. You're going to be fine."

She patted his arm reassuringly. Then, shifting the machine into gear, she resumed driving.

"How far is it to your home?" Sebastian asked, checking for the accelerator he'd slipped into his pocket at the last minute. Stored warmth radiated from its core.

"It's only about five more miles. We should be there in about fifteen, twenty minutes. I'd go faster, but I don't dare with all the ice on the road."

Twenty minutes to go a mere five miles! Sebastian shook his head in mute disbelief, then wished he hadn't when boulders crashed around inside it. Reminding himself that he had come to Earth to learn, not to judge, Sebastian conceded that there was one thing about this planet that was far superior to anything on Logosia.

And that was the marvelously sweet scent emanating from the woman. If all Earthlings smelled like this, Sebastian decided, it would certainly make up for a great many of the planet's other failings.

With that intriguing thought in mind, he passed out again.

4

H E MANAGED TO rouse long enough to remain upright as she led him into her house. They'd no sooner walked in the door, when a huge orange ball of fur suddenly blocked their path, its howling demand sharp and strident.

"Don't worry," she assured him. "It's only Darcy."

"Darcy?"

"My cat. He's a Maine Coon. I named him after Mr. Darcy. From *Pride and Prejudice*?" Her voice went up, turning her explanation into a question. "I guess you never read it."

"No."

"Nor seen all the movies?"

"I don't believe so."

"I guess you're one of those guys who don't like chick flicks," she said with a shrug. But her friendly face did seem to fall a bit.

"Anyway, he's just reminding me that dinner's late." When she reached down and patted the cat's head, it began to purr. The sound reminded Sebastian of a small motor.

"Try to be patient," she advised the cat. "I'm told it's a virtue."

"You own this animal?" Sebastian asked incredulously. He tried to remember the last time he'd seen any animal inside a home and came up blank.

"Obviously you don't know much about cats," Kirby said. "*You* don't own them. *They* own you."

Eyeing the animal with distrust and trying his best not to cringe, Sebastian realized that this creature must be the woman's pet. On Logosia, pets—considered an unnecessary nuisance—had become extinct several hundred solar revolutions ago.

Because he couldn't seem to stand without swaying, she put her arm around him again and led him out of the small entryway, across another room, and down a hallway to what he took to be a bedroom. But rather than a thin pallet on the floor, the bed was large with a covering of red flowers stitched on a white background.

"You're going to be just fine," she said as she pushed him down gently onto the bed, then stripped off the short pants that, despite the heat that had been blasting from the dashboard of her machine, were still damp. "You're safe now."

Sebastian knew he was anything but safe, but his head was too muddled and his body too weak to think about his situation now. The mattress felt as soft and fluffy as summer clouds created beneath his city's dome by the department of meteorology and climate control, and as he luxuriated in its warm embrace, he slipped comfortably back into the void.

✧   ✧   ✧

WHEN EMILY HAD turned the old whaling captain's house they'd all grown up in into a B and B, she'd passed down a few pieces of the furniture that held too many personal memories to have strangers using it to Kirby.

After stripping the shorts off the sleeping man lying in the antique sleigh bed, the cop in her took a quick survey. He was six feet, approximately one-hundred-and-eighty-five pounds, dark hair, eyes the color of the deepest espresso beans at the Coffee Corner next door to her office. The colorful tattooed sleeve on his arm, extending across his left shoulder, was the only identifying mark she could see without rolling him onto his stomach.

Because she was female, and human, and, hello, he just happened to be really, really cut, the woman in her took a longer look at the lean, hard muscle, his broad chest, the ridges of a six-pack that went into that deliciously sculpted V where his lower abs met his hip flexors. Then—because, well, how could she not?—Kirby let her gaze slide south to an impressive package that certainly wasn't showing any signs of snow-induced shrinkage.

If one of those nerds over at her brother's brain factory had programmed every physically perfect male into a computer, then printed it out on one of their fancy 3-D printers, the result would be her naked stranger.

Not that he was really hers. She was, after all, the police chief, and he was merely another civilian she'd promised to protect and serve. But the thought of serving this particular civilian sent a sexy shiver through her that had nothing to do with the blizzard blowing snow against the bedroom windows.

Get a grip! You're a law enforcement officer, not someone who gets weak-kneed at the romance novel naked-chest covers on the racks at Mayhew's Market. Romances which, okay, she bought on a weekly basis. But that didn't mean that she couldn't tell fantasy from reality. Not only was she very clear on the difference, she'd also decided that fictional romance beat the real thing hands down.

Taking a deep breath, Kirby dragged her gaze away from the naked guy sprawled on his back in the center of her bed and returned to the problem at hand, which was keeping him warm. After lighting a fire in the corner fireplace, she piled every quilt she could find in the house over the top of his supine body, then retrieved the thermometer from the bathroom medicine cabinet.

Although it required her to touch his deliciously roughened jaw again, which was—she couldn't lie—no hardship, she managed to slip it between his lips and under his slack tongue. It beeped at just below ninety-two degrees, which was encouraging.

"Not great," she said as she checked his pulse and found it stronger than when she'd first discovered him lying in the roadway. "But better."

After assuring herself that he wouldn't die in the next two minutes, she finally took off her coat and returned to the kitchen, where she served up a can of cat food. Growling happily, Darcy signaled absolute bliss with the chopped chicken livers.

That little domestic chore taken care of, Kirby made a mug of tea, then went into the living room and opened the cupboard where her brother had stashed a bottle of cognac. On the table next to the cupboard, the red light was flashing on her answering machine. Although it might be old-school technology, due to cell service being so iffy here on the island, everyone she knew had hung on to their landlines.

Hitting play, she took off her Glock, locked it away in

its metal box, then retrieved the liquor.

"Hey, sis," Nate's deep voice rang out, "I know you're gonna kill me, but I think I had a breakthrough on my quantum jump theory, and I need to stay here and run some programs."

"Surprise, surprise," she muttered.

"How about breakfast tomorrow morning instead? I'll pick up some cranberry and orange muffins and bagels you like and see you about nine. I really am sorry. But I think I'm finally on the right track, and I promise to dedicate my Nobel Prize to you. Sleep tight, kiddo. And don't let any little green men bite."

"Cute, Nate," Kirby muttered. "Real cute." She'd heard all she wanted to about aliens landing on her island. Opting to refrigerate her planned dinner once it finished cooking in her crockpot, she opened the fridge and retrieved half of a saved leftover lobster roll from yesterday's lunch.

"Maybe you don't need any alcohol," she said to the mystery man sprawled in her bed when she returned to her bedroom with the sandwich, tea, and cognac. "But I do."

She managed to rouse him long enough to pour the tea down his throat. Then, as his head sank back into the feather pillow, she changed from her uniform into a navy blue University of Maine sweatshirt and a pair of blue-and-green-checked flannel pajama pants.

Finally, pulling the rocker her grandfather Pendleton had made for the birth of her sister Emily up to the bed, Kirby put on her earphones and turned on the TV atop the dresser. When she moved to California, in order to maintain her holiday spirit in the land of sunshine and beach days, she'd started watching a Christmas movie every night of December. So, she settled in to watch *Love Actually* for the umpteenth time while sipping the cognac, eating the lobster roll, and keeping an eye on her patient.

Having finished his dinner, Darcy joined Kirby in the bedroom, leaping onto the bed with feline hope, where he settled down for the night, nestled against the stranger. Whom, she remembered, had shown all the signs of being one of those guy cat haters, but what he didn't know wouldn't hurt him.

Her vigilance was rewarded when, sometime in the middle of the long, weary night, after she'd managed to get another two mugs of tea down him, his temperature approached normal and his breathing became deep and steady. She pressed her fingers against his dark neck and felt the strong, steady beat of his blood.

"I think you're going to make it," she decided, touching his forehead as she had been doing for hours. "No, I take that back. You're definitely going to make it."

She'd just given into temptation to brush her fingertips against his scruff-roughened cheek again when she heard a sound in the other room. Going absolutely still, she drew in a breath and concentrated.

Nothing.

Then, the soft, recognizable tone of her brother's computer being shut down.

"Nate?" Her purposely low voice sounded like a shout in the stilled hush of the room. Her patient, muttering inarticulately in his sleep, rolled over.

"Nate," she repeated, "is that you?" It wasn't unusual for her brother to come and go at all hours, but that didn't stop a strange uneasiness from shimmying up her spine. Not helping matters was Darcy suddenly arching his back and bristling his tail.

The cat hissed. Kirby's breath quickened as she crossed the room and made her way silently, carefully, down the hallway.

The rest of the house was as dark and silent as a tomb.

"Damn it, Nate," she said as she flicked the switch for the overhead light in the living room. Nothing happened. "This isn't funny."

Making her way carefully across the room, she found the drawer where she kept the flashlight. The batteries were low, the light a faint, stuttering yellow beam, but as she swept it around the room, she couldn't see anyone.

With Darcy weaving through her legs, the cat's bushy tail twitching nervously, Kirby walked over to the old, scarred pine desk that had been her grandfather's and put her hand atop the computer. It was shut down. But warm.

Which was, of course, absurd. She was all alone in the house. Except for her patient. And he hadn't moved.

"You're going as crazy as the rest of the town," she muttered. Next she'd be seeing little green men raiding her refrigerator.

Still, experience had taught her never to disregard her intuition. Taking the Glock out of its box, Kirby started checking the rest of the house.

5

IMAGES FLICKERED ON the far reaches of Sebastian's consciousness. Something treacherous was lurking in the darkness, something as deadly as a Janurian pit viper.

She's in danger, some distant voice warned him. *You must save her.*

Who? From what? He tossed and turned, struggling to rise above the fog. He tried to lift his eyelids and found, to his frustration, that they'd turned to stone.

"Must rescue her," he mumbled. "Danger."

His hands curled into fists at his sides, and with a mighty groan, he attempted to rise from whatever bonds were holding him in check. But the effort proved too much, and even as he cursed his damnable weakness, he sank once more back into the dark mists.

✧　✧　✧

THE FRONT DOOR was bolted, just as she'd left it. The back door, and all the windows, were also locked. The house was totally secured. If an intruder had gotten in, he would have had to come down the chimney, which, considering the fact that the fire had died down, he possibly could have done. But there was absolutely no way he could have escaped the same way. Unless he was Spiderman. Or Saint Nick arriving early.

The electricity being out wasn't a serious concern given that loss of power was commonplace on the island during storms. Which was why Nate had installed a battery backup on his computer.

So, the obvious, only rational answer was that her imagination had simply gotten the best of her. Reminding herself to ask her brother about solar flares when he showed up with the muffins in the morning, she returned to the bedroom. Darcy followed, leaping onto the bed and, after pawing at the quilts, settled back down with one last warning hiss.

Something had changed.

Her house, always pleasantly cozy, was now strangely alien. As Kirby rocked in the chair, the Glock in her lap, her unease grew. She remained on edge for a very long time, filled with an impending sense of awareness mingled with uncharacteristic restlessness and a dark feeling of foreboding.

It was only her imagination, she assured herself over and over again as she continued to observe the man claiming her bed. She was only responding to a long, nerve-racking day. Eventually the events of that day began to catch up with her, and her eyelids became heavier and heavier. Unfortunately, the maple rocking chair, while comfortable for short periods, had not been designed for sleep.

She tried borrowing one of her patient's quilts and lying on the pine plank floor beside the bed, but the braided rug and quilt were not enough to keep her from becoming chilled by the cold floor.

There was always the sofa in the other room. But Joe MacGregor's warning about not leaving her stranger alone flashed through her mind like the red, white, and blue police lights atop the Jeep. And although she'd rather throw herself into icy Rum Runner Bay before admitting it, something about the living room made Kirby uneasy. Besides, without heat, it would soon be freezing in there, and she simply wasn't up to building another fire.

"For heaven's sake," she complained, "it's your damn bed. And it's not as if you're wearing some filmy do-me Victoria's Secret baby-doll nightgown." She seriously doubted her flannel pants, sweatshirt, and heavy wool ski socks would inflame any male's libido. "Besides, he's unconscious. What can he do?"

And even if he was capable of trying any funny stuff, she reminded herself that she was, after all, a detective who'd been awarded a commendation for her undercover work back in California. If she could handle the big-city bad guys, she was certainly safe from one near-frozen male who kept passing out on her. Wrapping her mother's quilt tightly around herself, she pushed the cat aside and lay down beside him.

She was asleep the instant her head hit the down pillow.

✧   ✧   ✧

SEBASTIAN WAS HAVING the sweetest dream. He was somewhere in Stanza Five, on one of the more hospitable planets. Veneitan, perhaps, lying in a bed of fragrant flowers.

A woman, warm and soft, was wrapped around him, her lips pressed against his throat. Her long curls were the color of a Logosian sunset, bright and burnished reds and golds. He brushed his cheek against the silky, fragrant strands.

It had been a very long time since he'd been with a woman. Unfortunately, his work on the quantum accelerator had precluded sufficient time for pleasure.

But now, as he slipped his hand beneath the hem of her tunic, ran his fingers lazily up the delicate bones of her spine, and was rewarded by her soft, yielding sigh, Sebastian decided he'd been a Haldon-headed idiot not to make time.

It was only a matter of setting priorities, he told himself, enjoying the feel of her warm flesh against his palm. Or, as Zorana was constantly saying, of utilizing proper time management.

His future bondmate was renowned throughout the galaxy for her time-management seminars. The woman was an expert at setting up schedules, organizing her day—her entire life, for that matter—into a series of color-coded time blocks that flashed and buzzed continually on her wrist computer.

Sweet Valhalla, how he'd hated that trigging computer! Especially when he wanted to linger with its owner and the damn thing kept clicking away the time, a digital stopwatch dictating his performance.

Still, he had to admit that Zorana was efficient at fitting myriad activities into a single lunar period. Perhaps it was time to acknowledge that her criticism of him had merit and ask her to organize him.

If it gave them more time to lie together like this, it would be worth listening to her disparaging comments.

Conveniently forgetting that Zorana had coldly broken

their bond promise after he'd lost his prestigious position at the institute, Sebastian vowed to turn over a new leaf.

He drew her closer. When he pressed his lips against her temple, her breathing quickened.

"Ah," he sighed. "You're so soft. So warm."

He continued stroking her, enjoying the quiet, inarticulate sounds of pleasure that were a distinct contrast to his bondmate's usual prickly attitude toward anything the least bit emotional.

"I want to make love to you, Zorana. So very much."

It was when his hand moved to her chest that the dream began to waver. Her breast fit into his hand so perfectly that it might have been designed with him in mind.

But how could that be? As she was always so quick to point out, Zorana was a perfect Logosian female. A superb product of genetic engineering, the woman he'd been promised to at age seven was blond, blue-eyed, and slender as a Genetian reed. Since the only logical reason for breasts was to feed a child, Logosian women—who had utilized either replicants or surrogates from off-planet for the unpleasant task of childbearing for the past two centuries—no longer possessed them.

His numbed mind worked through the logistics problem with the lumbering mental speed of a Janurian preschooler:

Zorana was a perfect Logosian.

Logosian women were all flat-chested.

The woman in his arms possessed exquisite breasts.

Therefore, utilizing the most basic deductive reasoning, this woman was not only not Logosian, she was not Zorana.

The logic was flawless.

There was only one problem.

Who the blazing Hadean was she?

KIRBY'S SUN-DRENCHED BEACH fantasy of the day before had given way to a dream of an isolated ski lodge, somewhere high in the Alps. She'd spent the day schussing the steep, powdery runs with a French count who possessed more titles, charm, and money than any one man had a right to.

She knew, from the admiration in his flashing dark eyes, that she looked spectacular in her new, outrageously expensive lipstick-red ski outfit. The brilliantly clever design of the outfit somehow managed to maintain its sleek fit while successfully camouflaging the extra ten—well, if forced to tell the truth, the whole truth, and nothing but the truth, more like *fifteen*—pounds she was always vowing to shed. That alone made it worth every penny.

After a last exhilarating run, they'd returned to the quaint lodge that resembled a giant cuckoo clock. Inside, they joined the other guests—Rhianna, Chris Pine, Hugh Jackman, and Taylor Swift—for brandy in the lounge.

But rather than enter into the spirited argument about the importance of quantum physics in overcoming hypothermia the others were engaged in, she and her count were content to exchange long, lingering looks.

Outside, an Alpine blizzard raged.

The voices of the others gradually faded while the room grew uncomfortably warm. They could have been the only two people in the world.

Finally, just when she felt in danger of melting from the

lambent flame in his sexy bedroom eyes, the count suavely suggested that they retire to his room.

His obedient manservant, clad in the red livery of the Swiss Guard, had laid a fire in preparation of their return. The valet struck a match to the kindling, gave a low, sweeping bow, then backed out of the room, leaving them alone.

At last! The moment she'd been waiting for all day had arrived.

His devilish jet eyes didn't move from her own adoring ones as he pulled her down onto the white fur rug in front of the fire. He pressed a kiss against her temple. Then slowly, tenderly, he began to undress her, his strong, dark hands doing wonderfully wicked things to her body.

"Ah, you're so soft," he crooned as his fingers caressed her breast, creating a glow deep inside her. "So warm. I want to make love to you, Zorana."

Zorana?

Kirby's eyes flew open.

And found herself staring directly into the all-too-familiar eyes of her dream lover. But these dark eyes didn't belong to a French count any more than they'd belonged to that beach boy she'd fantasized about yesterday afternoon.

"Oh, no," she groaned. Covering her face with her hands, Kirby prayed for strength. "It's you."

6

A MEMORY FLASHED on the view-screen of Sebastian's mind. A vision of white and cold and dark. Other memories returned. Memories of driving through the snow, the scent of flowers blooming in the warmth of her machine.

Sebastian realized that this was the woman who'd brought him in from the storm. Another vision, of her pounding energetically against his chest, flashed in his mind's eye.

"I remember thinking—no, knowing—that I was going to die," he said. "And I would have, were it not for you. You saved my life," he remembered.

"Yes. I suppose I did." She glanced down, causing him to realize that his hand was actually beneath her tunic.

"I'm very sorry," he said, pulling it away before she could say a word. "I didn't mean to offend you." He tried giving her a reassuring smile. "I believe I must have been dreaming."

And what a dream it had been! His fingers practically itched with the desire to slip back beneath that bulky material.

"No problem," she said, even as the flush on her

cheeks suggested otherwise. "You were very ill. Close to death, I believe. It would make sense that you might be a little delirious."

"A logical deduction," Sebastian agreed. "But I'm afraid that I've upset you."

"Not really." She was not a very good liar. But he appreciated her intention to reassure. "I'm just not accustomed to waking up in bed with a strange man." As she untangled her legs from his and left the blissfully comfortable bed, Sebastian experienced a tinge of regret.

He knew that the masculine pleasure he'd received from learning that she slept alone was decidedly human. He'd learned from his studies that terran males were accustomed to claiming women for their own in much the same way they claimed their other prized possessions.

In that respect, they were not so different from Logosian men. The marriage collar worn by Logosian wives—a collar his sister had sworn never to wear—was a much-revered tradition. Sebastian wondered if this woman was claimed.

"You're looking better," she said as she studied him judiciously. The slight flare of her pupils when her gaze paused on his chest suggested her interest wasn't merely medical.

"I'm feeling a great deal improved," he agreed. One particular part of his body more than others as that dream flashed back into his mind. "Thanks to you."

"It's my job."

"It was your kindness," he corrected. "And your tenacity. I will be forever in your debt."

"Like I said, it's my job. A simple thank-you will be more than sufficient."

Sebastian took her literally. "Thank you," he said with grave formality. "I do not know your name."

"It's Kirby. Kirby Pendleton."

"I am honored to meet you, Kirby Pendleton." He held out his right hand in the manner prescribed by an ancient Earthling text on manners Rosalyn had unearthed in the archives. Although the origin of such a custom was not clear, his sister had surmised that it had something to do with showing that the extended hand carried no weapon. "My name is Sebastian Blackthorne."

"Yes." She held out her own hand. "I know. You told me last night. It's good to meet you, too, Mr. Blackthorne."

"Please, call me Sebastian."

What Rosalyn had assured him was merely a social, almost impersonal, touch proved anything but. A jolt of energy crackled between them, making his palm burn. When she jerked her hand free and crossed her arms beneath those beautifully formed breasts he had not imagined, Sebastian knew she'd felt it, too.

"So, where are you from, Sebastian?" Her voice was not as steady as it had been. Yet another sign he hadn't been the only one affected.

Not quite knowing exactly where he'd landed, he said the first Earth city that came to mind, the one that had been his destination. "Venice. In California."

"Pricey," she murmured. "How long have you lived there?"

"Not long," he hedged. "Why?"

She shrugged. "It's just a coincidence, that's all. I worked in Venice for five years before coming back to the island. I guess our paths never crossed."

"It appears not."

"So, where are you staying?"

"Staying?"

"Where's your motel? Or inn?"

"I don't know."

"My sister runs the Pendleton Point Inn overlooking the ferry terminal. Perhaps that rings a bell?"

"I'm afraid not. Though I would assume it's named after your family?"

"It is. Two of my ancestors were sea captains out of Searsport, on the mainland. Others were boat builders who started out with schooners in the 1800s, then moved here during the nineteen twenties…

"I suppose, if you don't know where you're staying, then you also don't know where the rest of your things are, either?"

"No."

"Nor what you were doing out in the middle of a Maine island's woods nearly naked."

A memory flashed through his mind—the sound of Rosalyn shouting something about Maine.

"I'm in Rum Runner, Maine?"

Frown lines furrowed her smooth, lovely brow. "That's right. It's an island, off the coast. It was named for the smugglers my family built boats for during Prohibition."

When the translator gave the meaning of the island's name, he wondered if, since Kirby Pendleton had come from a family of rebels and risk takers, the two of them might actually have something in common.

"What's the date?"

Her frown deepened. "December sixteenth."

At least he'd gotten something right. "What year?"

When she told him the date, revealing he'd miscalculated by one-hundred-and-eighty-three solar revolutions, Sebastian was stunned. The magnetic field must have altered time. He'd have to make the necessary adjustments before returning to Logosia. He certainly wouldn't want to land back on his home planet during the brutal Resistance Wars.

"How much do you remember?" she asked.

"The last thing I remember, I was at home."

"In California."

"That's right. Venice."

Lying was extremely uncommon behavior for a Logosian. It wasn't that there was any specific moral prohibition, per se, but the Ancient Ones, in the Book of Laws, had correctly pointed out that one lie inevitably led to another until soon the entire situation had become untenable.

Reason is truth, the elders had written. *Truth, reason. All else is irrational.*

Being half-human, Sebastian had found that shading the truth, on occasion, under proper circumstances—such as now—was not that irrational a solution.

"Then," he continued, "the next thing I knew, I was walking down the road—"

"In the middle of the worst snowstorm in fifty years." Her frown deepened. "With hardly any clothes on. If you're not completely off your rocker, I'd say you must have received one helluva knock on the head."

From the way she was looking at him, Sebastian had the strangest feeling she could see inside his head, which was ridiculous, since he knew that Earthlings—even those existing in his own time—were too primitive to possess the ability to enter another's mind.

Still, rather than risk her spotting an out-and-out lie, Sebastian opted for not saying anything.

"You probably have temporary amnesia, from the shock of whatever happened," she diagnosed.

"That is logical." Sebastian thought it was time to change the subject before she decided to take him to whatever passed for the authority in these parts. "Do you have a lav?"

"A lav? Oh, the bathroom." That appealing color rose in her cheeks again. "Of course. I spent the night pouring tea down your throat, which you might not even remember, being so out of it...

"Well, anyway, it's right in there." She waved her hand toward a door cut into a wall covered with bright yellow flowers. "You'll find an extra toothbrush in the cabinet. You're free to use my razor, so long as you're not one of those chauvinistic men who complain that women's legs dull the blade.

"Oh, and you'll need some clothes to wear until we track down whatever happened to yours."

She walked over to another door, opened it, and began pulling things from hangers. "Nate, my brother, spends a lot of time here, and fortunately, you're just about the same size."

When she turned around, he was standing beside the bed, looking far too virile for a man who'd been hovering on the brink of death only a few hours earlier.

As good as he looked lying down, upright, he was magnificent. His shoulders were wide, and the mahogany-hued skin of his chest was drawn tautly over sleek, smooth muscles. He must work out, Kirby considered. There was not an ounce of excess flesh on his body. His broad shoulders and chest tapered down to a narrow waist and hips. His stomach was as flat as her grandmother Pendleton's old washboard and—

Oh, Lord.

She was obviously not the only one suffering lingering arousal from a sensual dream.

Lifting her gaze, she found him watching her with unblinking interest. Embarrassed at having been caught blatantly staring, Kirby dumped the pile of clothes on the mattress, turned, and left the room.

IT WAS HIS fault, Sebastian considered. For some reason he would think about later, her slow, studied appraisal had made his body behave in a most un-Logosian way. But why should that cause her such distress? After all, his reaction had merely been a biological response to the same human arousal he'd read in her mind. Although rare for a Logosian, such a reaction was supposedly normal for an Earthling. So why had she suddenly turned as red as a Logosian moon and raced out of the room as if all the dogs of Garn were on her heels?

Such behavior was highly illogical.

Unable to solve the equation, Sebastian reminded himself that Rosalyn had warned him that he'd be dealing with a most illogical race. Heaving a weary sigh, he gathered up the clothing and went into the bathroom.

A mirror took up most of one wall. Sebastian stopped in front of it and was relieved to see that outwardly, at least, he remained physically unchanged. His relief was short-lived when he remembered he was going to have to somehow discover what had caused a serious time and location destination miscalculation without Rosalyn's assistance.

Deciding to tackle that problem later, once he'd acquired sufficient scientific data, he glanced around, taking in his surroundings. Flowers bloomed on the walls in this room, as well, delicate purple flowers with dark green leaves.

If all terran homes were like this one, it explained why his mother had spent so much time in her greenhouse. Obviously flowers were more important to Earthlings—at least to the females—than the holodiscs had indicated.

A crystal dish shaped somewhat like the geometric Golden Spiral held dried petals that Sebastian easily recognized. Although the potpourri carried a different, spicier scent than that Mia Vardanyian made from her beloved moonflowers, the idea was the same.

Vowing to create flowers on at least one wall in his mother's home as soon as he returned to Logosia, Sebastian stripped and, after emptying his bladder of all the tea she'd been right about him not remembering drinking, stepped into the shower, held out his arms—and waited.

Apparently, rather than sense his needs, words were required. "One hundred and ten degrees," he instructed.

Nothing.

Realizing that he was dealing with extremely primitive plumbing, he turned the shiny metal knob. And was suddenly hit by a blast of frigid water. Having expected a sonic shower, he'd not been prepared for water. And certainly not water that felt as if it came from an Algorian glacier.

Belatedly he noticed the black letters etched into the knob. Reaching out, he turned toward the *H,* rewarded when the water began to warm. Experimenting, he twisted the knob even more, until the streaming flow was as blessedly hot as the sulphur geysers on Ontarian.

Glancing around, he found an alcove cut into the tile. In the alcove was a pink rectangle he suspected was a cleansing bar. He wet it, then rubbed it between his palms. The resultant fragrant froth reminded him of his rescuer.

Tilting back his head, Sebastian closed his eyes and reveled in the glorious feel of the hot water pelting his skin, sluicing over his shoulders, running down his legs. Ten minutes later, the small room was engulfed in a cloud of steam, and he'd never felt more relaxed in his life.

It crossed his mind that if there were such showers on Logosia, the pharmaceutical company that made Valdox would go out of business.

He stepped out of the ceramic cubicle and stood there on the fluffy white rug, legs and arms outstretched again, waiting. When he realized that no unseen light or warm breeze was going to dry him, that he was actually expected to do it himself, he looked around the room, saw the stack of flowered purple towels, took one, and began rubbing it against his skin to soak up the moisture.

After drying his body, he opened a metal cabinet and found the toothbrush she'd mentioned, wrapped in some sort of crackly transparent wrapping and thankfully labeled, or he wouldn't have recognized its purpose.

The toothpaste, too, was labeled. As he spread the blue gel onto the bristles, then scrubbed them over his teeth, Sebastian wondered how the woman maintained such a dazzling smile using such primitive dental care.

That task out of the way, he brushed his wet hair into reasonable order, decided to pass on the treacherous-looking razor, and dressed in her brother's clothing. Then, following an unfamiliar-but-alluring scent down the hallway, he found himself in a warm and cheery room.

The room was a virtual treasure trove of wood products. The walls were covered with warm, rich golden planks that gleamed like a sunrise over Galactia. Interspersed among the planks were dark knots. The floor was wood, as well, but a darker hue than the walls and roughly scraped. In the corner was the same sort of tree he'd been stumbling through last night, covered in twinkling white lights.

The cat he vaguely remembered was lying on a rug with a design that displayed three trees draped in the icy snow he'd been stumbling through last night, eyeing him with unblinking yellow eyes.

Walking over to the window—real glass, Sebastian realized, pressing his fingers against the panes momentarily—he saw Kirby Pendleton standing a few meters away from the house, at the edge of a stand of yet more coniferous trees that reached up toward the sky.

It was still snowing, although instead of blowing sideways in gusts, the hexagonal ice crystals were floating down from the slate sky like drifting feathers.

She was wearing that hooded coat again, a bright splash of scarlet against the white snow, gray sky, and dark green trees. Her mittened hands were scattering something over the ground.

He watched, intrigued as a flock of birds descended from hidden branches and began snapping up what he recognized to be a variety of seeds and bread crumbs. They were, as birds were throughout his own galaxy, unreasonably greedy.

They chattered loudly, pecking at one another, fighting

over the brown and black seeds as if their lives depended on it. Which, Sebastian considered, gazing around at the glistening white world, was undoubtedly true. He had a feeling that the feathered gluttons were dependent on this woman for survival.

As was he.

He noticed with surprise that she was actually talking back to the flocking birds. Since none of his studies had shown that Earthlings possessed the ability to communicate with other species on their planet, he was forced to mark this down as yet another irrational aspect of human behavior.

He made a mental note to pass his observation on to Rosalyn, who had made quite an illustrious career for herself studying alien social behavior. His sister had risen like a comet through the stuffy ranks of the xenoanthropology department at the science institute, overcoming both her dual heritage and her gender.

Apparently finished both with the feeding and the conversation, Kirby headed back to the house, trudging through the knee-deep snow. When she saw him standing in front of the window, she stopped momentarily in her tracks.

Their eyes met through the clear pane of glass.

And the awareness that flashed through his mind staggered him.

For that single heart-stopping moment, Sebastian Blackthorne felt every bit as disoriented as he had last night while stumbling blindly around in that frozen white alien world.

7

ALTHOUGH IT TOOK an effort, Sebastian recovered quickly. By the time the door opened, he was feigning interest in the fire blazing in the large stone hearth. There had been a fire in his bedroom, too, he recalled.

Although such method of heating a room was distressingly primitive, not to mention being an almost sacrilegious waste of rare wood, he couldn't deny that the fragrance of the burning log and the way the heat waves radiated against his outstretched hands were most pleasing.

"Well, you definitely look as if you're going to live," she greeted him as she entered the kitchen.

"I believe I am. Thank you for letting me use your shower. The hot water was very enjoyable."

"I'll bet it was, after yesterday." She shrugged out of her thick red coat and hung it on a hook.

Her woven blue trousers were identical to the ones she'd given him. They fit her a great deal better than his, he decided, taking in the way they hugged her very feminine hips. She was wearing that same tunic, which, for some reason, had a growling animal he recognized from pictures of extinct Earth animals to be a bear. Beneath the dark blue material, her breasts were softly rounded. He jammed his hands into the pockets of his trousers to resist the urge to touch them again.

"You said your sister runs an inn?"

"Yes, Emily. She's the eldest and was working for the Boston Winfield Palace Hotel when she decided to come home and turn our old family house into a B and B. My other sister, who's eleven months older than me, is Shelby. For some reason—my dad always blamed pregnancy brain fog—my mother seemed to get stuck on names ending with y when naming her children.

"My twin brother was going to be either Ridley or Bradley, but my father put his foot down and insisted on the right to name his only son, which was awfully lucky for Nate, don't you think?"

What he thought was that her eyes were incredible. Looking into them was like looking into two shimmering pools from the tropical neighboring planet Roshinia. Pools he'd be more than willing to drown in.

"That's my brother's name," Kirby continued cheerfully. "Nate. Well, technically, Nathaniel after Nathanial Hawthorne, who's supposedly a cousin of the Pendletons several times removed. My father, who was a big reader, loved his allegories. Especially 'The Minister's Black Veil,' where Hawthorne points out how Puritanism deprived people of joy and encouraged the sin of pride by showing off their rigid idea of morality.

"Despite him having referred to women writers as a 'damn scribbling mob,' which really irritates me, I have to admit that Hawthorne's work turned out to be timeless. His themes, especially in *The Scarlet Letter*, remain relevant today, over a hundred and fifty years later. How many authors can you say that about?"

Fortunately, her question appeared to be rhetorical, because Sebastian had no idea what she was talking about. He also didn't want her to stop. Her voice reminded him of music. He could listen to it for hours.

Small talk was an alien thing to Logosians. They were far too reserved to engage in idle conversation. Also, due to a highly developed intellect and need for exactitude, they preferred choosing one singularly appropriate word when other species might use two or three less perfect ones. The terrans who visited his parents' house had always been fairly talkative, as were the Freemasians, that alien group responsible for construction and repair on the planet.

And, of course, the gregarious shuttlecraft agents from Blarninian were infamous for being able to talk a blue streak when trying to convince you to purchase a shiny new model of transportation, even when your current one was quite sufficient. But even the most loquacious outlanders would have appeared taciturn when compared to Kirby Pendleton.

As her words came at him like pulsars, Sebastian tried his best to keep up, but even with the ecumenical translator decoder working at full speed, he couldn't comprehend half of what she was talking about.

A slight grinding sound caught his attention. Sebastian glanced over at the wall where a small replica of a house hung. As he watched, a door opened, and a toy bird popped out of the house, chirped a few times in a ridiculously artificial voice, then disappeared behind the door again. Belatedly he realized that the foolish-looking little bird had counted off the hour. *What a strange, illogical way to tell the time.*

"What of your parents?" he asked after the door had

closed behind the bird. "Are they living in their home that your sister turned into the inn?"

"No. My father died a few months ago."

Although it was irrational, since he'd had no way of knowing, Sebastian could have kicked himself for having been responsible for the light fading from her remarkable eyes.

"I'm sorry," he said quietly.

"So am I." She shrugged. "He was a wonderful man. Everyone loved him."

"My father was most revered, also," Sebastian heard himself saying.

"Oh? Is he—"

"He passed on as well," Sebastian said. "Last year. I am just coming to grips with the idea that he's gone."

Death on Logosia was not a time for grief. It was, Sebastian had always been taught, merely the natural order of things. The old giving way to the new. However, when his father had ceased to exist during the last solar revolution, Sebastian had experienced a startling deep feeling of pain and an even stronger sense of loss that were distressingly, and distinctly, human.

"Grieving takes its own time," Kirby agreed gently. "How is your mother taking it?"

"She doesn't say very much, but I suspect that she is still grieving, because she has immersed herself in her work a great deal more than she did when Father was alive."

"That's the same thing my mother did. The day after the funeral she was off to Tahiti, where she's currently painting natives like Gauguin. Some people might consider her taking off to the tropics to be self-centered, but it's because she cared so much about Dad that she couldn't bear to stay here without him."

She shook her head slightly, as if to shake off painful memories. She walked over to a clear glass container and poured a dark liquid into a mug, causing fragrant steam to rise.

"Would you like some coffee?"

Having no idea what he was agreeing to, but anxious to please, Sebastian said, "Yes, thank you."

He curled his fingers around the container she was holding out toward him, took a tentative sip, and found, to his surprised pleasure, that it tasted rather like the caffoid tablet he chewed each morning. But much, much better. And a decided improvement over the herbal teas his house droid prepared. Teas that tasted like chlorophyll.

"This is wonderful."

Kirby rewarded him with a smile. "What a nice thing to say. Unfortunately, coffee is the apex of my culinary skills. Of course, even that took a lot of practice. In fact, on my first night working the graveyard shift at the Venice Police Department—oh, no!"

She slammed her cup down on the counter. "I forgot all about it," she moaned.

Pulling on an oversized yellow mitt that looked like one of the gloves worn by members of the confederation fleet's decontamination team, she opened the lid of a red container on the counter.

"Oh, damn. It's ruined."

He studied the blackened contents of the pot. "So it seems. May I ask what it was?"

"Grandmother Pendleton's pot roast." Kirby's shoulders slumped. "It was supposed to cook for ten and a half hours at two hundred degrees."

He studied the arcane dial he took to be a thermostat. "The temperature is set at two hundred degrees."

"But I was supposed to turn it off last night. Nate was coming to dinner."

"It was my fault," he offered in an attempt to soothe the lines etching her brow. "You were distracted."

"No, it's not your fault." She dragged her hand through hair that this time Sebastian mentally compared to the gleaming hue of the copper silicate ore mined on the planet Orionas. There were so many different colors it appeared almost to change hue depending on the light.

"I'm too much of a Yankee at heart to spend the money on a newer model with a programmable turn-down control. Not that it would matter all that much, because unlike my sister, who's the Martha Stewart of Maine, I'm a lousy cook," she muttered.

Although he had no idea who this Martha Stewart person might be, her obvious distress tugged at something elemental inside Sebastian. "But you make very good coffee. I believe you were telling me about when you first learned to make it so well," he reminded her, irrationally wanting to make her smile again.

He was partially successful. Although her faint smile lacked the dazzle of her earlier grin, Sebastian found it no less appealing.

"You're just trying to get my mind off my failure."

"Yes," he responded with absolute Logosian honesty. "I am."

She looked at him curiously for a moment, then shrugged. "Well, getting back to my days in California, you have to understand that I really wanted to fit in, to become part of the squad."

"Highly understandable," he agreed. "Teamwork is often preferable to individual effort."

She gave him another brief, inquisitive glance. "Yes. Well, anyway, I offered to make coffee for the men, which I realize would make most feminists, my sister Shelby and my mother included, hit the roof, but it seemed like a good idea at the time."

Her sister and mother sounded like Rosalyn, who was constantly lecturing about female rights. Although Sebastian could understand his sister's frustration, and he could even admit that she was the one woman who was probably intellectually equal to a male, he could not, in good conscience, agree with her desire to abolish the rigid structure of what was a very efficiently run patriarchal society.

"One taste and the desk sergeant threatened to lock me up and throw away the key if I ever poisoned his police force again."

"You poisoned the police?"

"Not really," Kirby assured him. "I was only speaking figuratively. But I did decide right then and there not to put the sergeant to the test.

"So, I called my sister Emily—"

"The Martha Stewart of Maine."

"Exactly." She nodded her bright head. "I got her recipe for coffee, and after working my way through nearly an entire can of beans, I finally got it right. Emily makes perfect coffee, but then, she always does everything perfectly," Kirby said without rancor. "I also got this recipe for the pot roast from her. You can bet that Emily never turned a piece of chuck roast into charred shoe leather."

Sebastian couldn't understand her concern about the

pot roast. It was obviously ruined. So why dwell on something she could not change?

This woman was quite possibly the most illogical being—other than the gossamer-winged flitterflies on Evian 4—he'd ever come across. But she was also vastly, unnervingly appealing.

"You were a clerk on this police force?"

From the way her soft curves molded the trousers and bear tunic, Sebastian had the feeling that she'd look pleasingly attractive in the thigh-high dark blue tunics worn by the Logosian police clerks.

"I was a cop," Kirby corrected.

"A what?"

"A cop," she repeated.

In his ear, the ecumenical translator told him the unfamiliar word was a colloquialism for a law enforcement officer.

"Actually," Kirby said with discernible pride, "I'd made detective before I quit to move back here."

"You were a police officer?" He didn't even try to conceal his disbelief.

"Detective third class. And now I'm the police chief of Rum Runner Island, which truthfully isn't that big a deal since the entire force consists of a part-time deputy, Danny Mayfair, and me."

"A police chief," he murmured, failing to understand what type of skewed logic could allow a female to work at such a dangerous post.

"That's right." Her eyes narrowed, and red warning flags that did not appear to be embarrassment, but annoyance, waved in her cheeks. "Do you have a problem with that?"

The ecumenical translator had never failed him. Logic told him that it was operating properly. Still, Sebastian could not believe he was understanding her correctly.

"What were your duties in Venice? When you were a detective third class?"

"I worked in the rape and domestic violence section and spent a month undercover, which resulted in the arrest and conviction of the Venice Surfer Rapist, a serial creep who'd been terrorizing women on L.A. beaches for over a year. Okay?"

"That sounds dangerous." He wondered why her father, who obviously would have been alive at the time, would permit her to hold such a risky position.

She shrugged. "So is running around in a blizzard in shorts. You might be all the fashion rage on the beaches of Venice, Blackthorne, but you were definitely underdressed for Maine. And speaking of last night's little adventure, we probably should get you to a clinic for a checkup."

"I don't want to go to a clinic."

"I don't really care what you want," she shot back in a way that no properly acquiescent female on Logosia would ever dare to do.

He folded his arms and attempted to stare her down. "And if I refuse?"

She lifted her chin and met his challenging glare head on. "I wouldn't advise putting me to the test."

Gone was the blithe spirit who'd chattered on like a brightly plumed jabberkeet. In her place was a brisk, take-charge law enforcement official who could have held her own with any uniformed, stun-pulsar-carrying policeman on Logosia.

"But you're in luck," she said. "For now. Because until

this snow stops, there's no way I can get you to the mainland."

Her obviously reluctant decision caused a cooling wave of relief to flow through Sebastian. He'd had no intention of allowing her to take him to the hospital, where they would perform a series of tests on him. What he hadn't determined was how far he was willing to go to stop her.

"Whatever you say."

His mild tone had Kirby shooting him a quick, suspicious look. "We need to unravel the mystery of what happened to the rest of your clothes," she said. "It's really strange. We never have muggings here on the island, and theft is almost unheard of."

The orange flames of the fire were warming the room. The coffee was spreading through him, soothing his body even as it stimulated his brain. He was relieved that although his body might be that of a terran, his mind had remained reassuredly Logosian.

All the archival data described the residents of Earth to be a benign, if unpredictable and occasionally violent, race. Which was perfectly explainable when you considered that the planet itself was still in its adolescence.

Eons from now, if they could avoid destroying their world with their careless pollution and unending territorial disputes, they would, as his own people had, evolve to a point that such problems as war and disease and poverty would be a distant memory. Something to be taught in ancient history classes.

"Oh, my God." Grabbing hold of the back of a chair, Kirby sank onto the rush seat.

Sebastian recognized the name of one of Earth's deities, but from her startled tone, he knew she was not praying.

"What's wrong?"

She was looking at him, her gaze wide with shock.

"I suddenly realized why you look familiar."

"Why is that?" Sebastian asked with a great deal of trepidation. What if he resembled someone she knew? Someone she disliked? Perhaps even someone she had arrested in Venice.

What would he do if she threw him back out into that icy white stuff to fend for himself?

"You're the man in my fantasy."

8

HER VOICE, WHICH had remained as strong and steady as catonium during their crisis last night, was now soft and unsteady. "I was dreaming about you."

"Dreaming?"

"Well, technically it was a daydream. Right before all the UFO calls."

So he *had* been seen. Sebastian had hoped that the lights of the aurora borealis would have allowed him to slip in undetected.

"UFO calls?"

"Don't worry about that." She brushed off the question with a wave of her hand. "We always get a few crank calls during a full moon. I've got a feeling that the solar flares are somehow involved, too," she confided. "But I don't know if there's any scientific data backing me up."

He knew the answer, of course, but decided there was no logical way to reveal it without also having to explain that the definitive study proving solar flares intensified feelings of excitement and anticipation was still five solar revolutions in the future.

Something clicked in Sebastian's memory banks. "Did you say your brother's name is Nathaniel Pendleton?"

The benchmark study of solar flare arousal, which was still being taught in Logosian astrophysical psychology classes, had been developed by a scientist named Nathaniel Pendleton. Not only that, Galileo, Copernicus, Newton, Darwin, Einstein, Pendleton, and Pournelle were the only Earthlings who'd ever earned mention in the Logosian textbooks.

And even then there were footnotes pointing out that these seven men were not considered representative of their species. They were, the textbook writers had felt it necessary to stress, highly exceptional.

"That's him," Kirby said. "Is that what you're doing here? Have you come to recruit him, too?"

"Recruit him?"

"Every university and think tank in the country—the world, actually—has been after my brother since he was nine. He graduated from medical school at fifteen," she said. "Then he went to MIT and earned his doctorate in physics in two years. That's when things got really crazy.

"After weighing all the offers, he went to work at a famous think tank in Boston, but he didn't stay there very long."

"What happened? Wasn't the work challenging enough?" It would take, Sebastian knew, a great deal to challenge Nathaniel Pendleton's remarkable intellect.

"Nate would never tell me. All I know is that he left abruptly after an unpleasant disagreement with Dr. Defour, the man who ran the place. Something about twisting data to falsify results.

"You've no idea how viciously competitive the scientific community can be," she informed Sebastian earnestly. "Anyway, after Nate left Boston, he established his lab out here in the middle of nowhere. It gives him more privacy. And independence."

Sebastian knew firsthand exactly how brutal the supposedly lofty, idealistic world of scientific exploration could be. But his lingering frustration over his dismissal from the science institute was overridden by the discovery Nathaniel Pendleton was actually living here, on Maine's Rum Runner Island. Being in proximity to such brilliance more than made up for his arriving in the wrong time.

"I did not come here to meet your brother." That was the absolute truth. No way could he have imagined such an opportunity.

"Good. Because I'd hate to have to call him and tell him not to come to breakfast because another headhunter is after him."

"I'm not a headhunter." Sebastian had no idea what such a man might be, but considering the propensity for violence of this planet's inhabitants, he didn't want to dwell on the possibilities. Especially not some of the ones currently being provided by the translator.

"Maybe you were working at the lab with Nate," Kirby suggested. "That might explain why you were dressed so weird."

In quest of a comfortable lap, the cat left the warmth of the fire and leaped onto Sebastian's thighs, draping itself bonelessly over him.

"Just push him down," Kirby advised.

"He's fine," Sebastian said, despite being decidedly uncomfortable with the idea of bringing wild creatures into the house. "Why would my clothing make you think I was working in your brother's laboratory?"

"Well, I certainly don't want to hurt your feelings, in

case you are working at the lab, but most of the people I've met from out there are definitely living in their own little worlds."

Having devoted the past six years of his life to this particular project, Sebastian could identify with that. "Including your brother? Is he working in his own little world?"

She laughed at that, a soft, musical sound that Sebastian liked. A great deal.

"Oh, Nate's the worst of the bunch. In fact, my twin brother lives so far out there he has to have his mail delivered by space shuttle."

Knowing that the first colony of terrans in space was forty-eight-point-six years in the future, Sebastian decided she must be speaking figuratively again.

"Oh, damn," she cried out as the cat suddenly dug its claws into Sebastian's legs and catapulted onto the lighted tree. "I hate it when he does that!"

The branches rustled as the animal appeared to be crawling to the top, where a small, blond, winged replica of a woman dressed in a glittery white dress stood. As he watched, a huge paw reached out and threw a small yellow wooden boat off the tree. It hit the floor with a clatter.

"Darcy!" Kirby stood beneath the tree, her hands on her nicely rounded hips, and glared up at the cat. "Stop that! Now!"

The animal's response was to send a small red item flying.

"Not my lobster," she complained, ducking as it flew by her head. "That's brand new."

She shook her head as what Sebastian recognized as a lighthouse was the next to go. She looked back over her shoulder at him. "This is why I had to buy all non-breakable ornaments this year," she said. "Last Christmas it took him all of ten minutes to break every glass ball on the tree."

Even as the translator struggled to come up with an explanation, a memory stirred. His mother celebrating the solstice each winter. She'd told him that when she'd been a girl, they'd adorn a tree in the forest with ornaments, light a fire, and dance and sing around it. Apparently, before her time, residents of this planet had brought their trees indoors. He wondered if they'd ceased the practice due to the type of destruction currently taking place.

"That must have been very distressing."

"At first. Then it actually became funny," she said with a flash of that smile that brightened not just her eyes but something inside Sebastian. "My family was all here at the time, and we laughed and laughed."

Her smile fading had the effect of the sun going down. Despite the sparkling white lights on the tree that continued to be denuded by the demon cat, the room seemed to darken and chill a bit. "That was Dad's last Christmas. Now he's gone, and Mom's painting in Tahiti, while Shelby's working on a dig in Mexico."

"A dig?"

"She's an archeologist. They've found a Mayan village that she believes proves that earth was visited by beings from outer space around five hundred B.C."

In reality, it was closer to 750 B.C., but there was no way Sebastian could share that information without having to explain that the visit—which had brought the Mayans advanced knowledge and contributed to a building burst of monumental architecture—was common knowledge in the annals of intergalactic history.

"But your brother and one sister are still here," he said, wanting to bring back that smile.

"They are," she agreed. "And unless he gets caught up in work at the brain factory yet again, Nate and I will be having Christmas dinner at Emily's. Fortunately, except for people who come over for Winterfest, we don't get many tourists here on the island during winter, so she doesn't have to lose any customers."

Desperately wanting to know exactly what Nathaniel Pendleton was currently working on but deciding that those questions could wait until later, perhaps when he met her brother, Sebastian brought his mind back to something else Kirby had said.

"You said you dreamed about me. Or, more precisely, a man who looked like me."

"Yes. Well." She sighed. "I was hoping you'd forget that."

"That wouldn't be possible. Since my memory is both eidetic and semantic."

"I know the first is like photographic. What does the second mean?"

"A long-term memory that retains concepts and facts. It requires a similar encoding process as episodic memory, yet semantic memory mainly activates the frontal and temporal cortexes of the brain, while episodic memory activity concentrates in the hippocampus. At least initially, until they're consolidated and stored in the neocortex."

She surprised him by laughing at what he'd felt was a very simplistic answer to a complex process. "Yet more proof that you're an escapee from the brain factory."

He was about to assure her that he had not escaped

from any such place when she shook her head, breathed out a long breath, and continued her answer to his question.

"It's going to sound foolish, but I was sitting at my desk, watching the snow come down—as it has for too many days—and I was feeling a little sorry for myself, so I began fantasizing about being back on the beach, at Venice. The sun was bright and hot and the sand was warm and you—or at least some hottie who looked just like you—were rubbing coconut oil on me."

Sebastian's first thought was that this explained how he'd gotten his coordinates crossed. When he'd been scanning minds, searching through the myriad random thoughts for a link to Venice, California, he'd accidentally stumbled into this woman's romantic fantasy. As amazing as the mathematical odds must be against such an occurrence, Kirby had been daydreaming of a man who looked like him. That being the case, there had been no reason for his features to change.

His third and most intriguing thought was the idea of spreading oil all over Kirby Pendleton's curvaceous body. As Sebastian focused on the appealing mental image forming in his uncharacteristically unruly mind, he considered that perhaps his detractors were right about him being a throwback.

"That sounds like a very good fantasy," he said. He especially appreciated the definition his translator had finally come up with for *hottie*.

"I don't know why I'm telling you all this," she said. "It must be the solar flares. I'm really going to have to talk to Nate about how everyone, including me, has been behaving so out of character lately..."

"Do you believe in ESP?" she asked, seeming to change the subject.

"Of course," Sebastian answered promptly. Finally, he thought with a great deal of relief, a common ground.

"I never did," she admitted. "Except for the sometime twin thing I share with Nate. But I never accepted the idea of telepathy. Of course part of that probably stems from the fact that I was born and raised in Maine, and Lord knows we're a practical bunch. But how else do you explain the fact that I was thinking about you at the very same time you needed my help? It's almost as if we're connected, on some weird sort of mental level."

She risked a quick glance at him. "Boy, I really sound like I'm ready for the funny farm, don't I?"

The idiom had not been on Rosalyn's data disks, but before the translator could sense his unfamiliarity with the colloquialism and decode, Sebastian got the general idea.

"Not at all. There are a great many unsolved mysteries in the universe." But now, thanks to him, intergalactic travel without a spaceship would no longer be one of them.

"I suppose so," Kirby agreed.

She fell silent, immersed in her own thoughts, thoughts Sebastian could easily read but chose not to, deciding that after saving his life, Kirby Pendleton was entitled to privacy.

Under normal conditions, he would never have intruded on another's personal thoughts without first being invited. Such a breach of etiquette was highly un-Logosian. He had always struggled to keep his telepathic powers in check by his steely control. Sometimes too much control, his terran mother had worried. But despite Sebastian's best intentions, occasionally the reins slipped.

As they had with this woman. Writing such unpremeditated indiscretion off to his near-death experience, Sebastian vowed to maintain stricter control in the future.

The warmth from the fire caused her fragrance to bloom in the room like his mother's hothouse moonflowers.

Sebastian sipped the hot coffee, drank in her alluring scent, and decided that although it definitely wasn't California, Rum Runner Island, Maine, would do quite nicely after all.

9

A STRIDENT SOUND from somewhere in the woods shattered the morning silence.

"That'll be Nate," Kirby said.

She stood, walked over to the window, pushed aside the blue-and-white-checked curtains, and peered out into the falling snow. The cat, apparently having concluded his attack on the tree, used his huge furry paws to ruffle the red material beneath it into a pile, then curled up and promptly went to sleep.

The sound grew closer. A moment later, two figures, one in bright orange, the other in black, seated astride a black machine that reminded Sebastian of a jetcycle, came to an abrupt stop outside the door.

"Oh, beans."

"What's wrong?"

"He brought Whitney with him."

"You do not like this Whitney?" He didn't need to read her mind—lines bracketed her rosy lips, furrowed her brow.

"Not really," she admitted with obvious reluctance. "It's not really personal, but I just don't think she's the right woman for Nate."

"And you care a great deal for your brother," he said.

"I love him," Kirby responded. "More than anything. And I honestly want him to settle down with a loving wife who'll happily put up with his idiosyncrasies and have a houseful of little geniuses."

"But not with Whitney."

"No. Not with Whitney." Kirby sighed. "Personally, even allowing for scientific eccentricity, I get bad vibes whenever I'm around her."

"Vibes?"

"You know, vibrations," Kirby elaborated. "Feelings. Like intuition."

"I've found that intuition can be a valuable tool."

"Me, too. And I've always had a pretty good sense of people. I mean, sometimes back in California, my work, and even my life, depended on it, you know?"

Still having trouble imagining this woman as a law enforcement officer, Sebastian merely nodded.

"The problem is that, whenever Whitney's around, my needle just starts going off the Richter scale."

Even as Sebastian struggled to make logic of the statement, she said, "But it's probably that we've got a dual dislike thing going on. I don't like her because I don't believe she's right for my brother, so she doesn't like me back because she knows I think that." She sighed. "And Nate's love life really isn't any of my business, is it?"

As if on cue, the kitchen door opened, and the pair on the machine burst into the room, bringing with them a stiff gust of icy air.

Nathaniel Pendleton, clad in a bright orange jumpsuit resembling those worn by Logosian transport pilots, was a great deal taller than his sister, even allowing for the expected differences between male and female. His eyes were a deeper shade of blue.

When he pushed back his hood, his hair, Sebastian noticed, was not the bright copper silicate hue of his sister's, but rather a glistening black that resembled the obsidian mountains of the Logosian moon Gaoliana.

"Lord, it's cold enough out there to freeze the—"

When he caught sight of Sebastian, Nate stopped in midsentence.

"Well. Hello." His tone was polite, his intelligent eyes filled with both a curiosity—which Sebastian suspected was second nature—and surprise.

For the second time this morning, he experienced a very un-Logosian-like satisfaction to know that a man in Kirby Pendleton's house first thing in the morning was not a common sight.

Nate pulled off his gloves and thrust out a hand. "I'm Nate Pendleton, Kirby's brother."

Sebastian stood and shook hands. "Sebastian Black-thorne."

"And a dead ringer for Heathcliff," Nate's companion offered.

She pulled off her gloves, looking at him as if he were a specimen in some laboratory experiment. "I'm Whitney Reynolds."

Sebastian nodded. "I know."

She arched a delicate brow. "I hadn't realized my fame was such that my name would have garnered recognition."

"I wouldn't know about that," Sebastian said frankly. "I knew your name because when you arrived, Kirby informed me that her brother's companion's name was Whitney."

"Oh?" Thin lips, outlined in a pale shade that was nearly as white as the snow outside, twitched in something that resembled a smile as Whitney glanced over at Kirby. "And what else has Kirby told you about me?"

"You two must be absolutely freezing," Kirby said quickly. Too quickly. It was obvious to everyone in the room that she didn't want to continue this particular line of questioning. "Let me pour you both some coffee."

"Kirby makes excellent coffee," Sebastian offered.

"I'd prefer herbal tea," Whitney said. Then turned to Kirby. "If you have it."

"I think I've got some Red Zinger," Kirby offered with far less enthusiasm than Sebastian had witnessed from her thus far.

"Perfect." Whitney flashed a smile at Sebastian. "I don't believe in putting artificial stimulants into my body. And caffeine definitely affects my ability to concentrate. Which in my work could be disastrous."

"What is your work?" Sebastian asked politely.

"Genetics."

"Ah. A fascinating field."

Coming from a mixed marriage, Sebastian had always found genetics interesting. Especially since he had inherited a disturbing number of human traits. "You must work at the laboratory. With Nate." It seemed almost disrespectful, referring to such a renowned scientist with such familiarity.

"Why, yes. We work together." Whitney exchanged a glance with Kirby's brother that revealed Kirby was right about work not being the only thing the two had in common. "Well, not exactly together, of course. We're involved in different projects."

Sebastian was about to inquire as to the nature of those

projects when Nate said, "How do you know my sister?"

Kirby's brother's face, so open and friendly and curious earlier, hardened, and the energy radiating from him was in no way hospitable.

"I found Sebastian out on the road yesterday," Kirby divulged as she filled a copper kettle with water for Whitney's tea. "He was unconscious and suffering from hypothermia. Most of his clothes had been stolen, so I lent him some of yours."

"I thought that sweater looked familiar," Nate agreed. Although his tone was mild, his eyes, as they riveted on Sebastian's, were not. "What are you doing in our neck of the woods?"

"I'm not sure," Sebastian hedged.

That much was the truth. So far, nothing about this experimental travel had gone as planned, and he still had to work out how he was going to get back to Logosia to the proper time.

"He has amnesia," Kirby said.

"Amnesia." Nate chewed that over for a minute, appearing openly suspicious. "Interesting."

"It's also disturbing," Sebastian said. "And although I'm not sure how I ended up on the island, I do know that I'm not a headhunter. Although I won't deny that I have heard of you," he tacked on, struggling to maintain some balance between the white lie born of necessity and the Logosian dictates of honesty and reason.

"Really." Nate took the mug his sister offered. "Thanks," he murmured, slanting her a distant smile that didn't quite reach his eyes.

He took a sip, continuing to eye Sebastian thoughtfully over the rim of the mug. "If you have amnesia," he said slowly, "how would you know that you're not a headhunter?"

Good question, Sebastian acknowledged. And as highly logical as he would expect from a man with such a brilliant scientific mind. "I would know." His tone was strong and sure.

"Amnesia," Whitney said on a long, heartfelt sigh as she patted a hand over her heart. "This is so wonderfully romantic. A dark hero right out of a Brontë novel, stranded in the blizzard, is rescued by our innocently naive heroine, only to realize, after they've spent the night together, that he can't remember who he is."

She smiled suggestively at Kirby. "I know women who'd kill to be able to live out that particular fantasy. For just one night."

"We didn't spend the night together," Kirby said on a flare of heat. "At least not the way you mean," she said stiffly. "Besides, Sebastian remembers his name," she pointed out.

"Sounds like retrograde amnesia. Did you notice any head injuries?"

"No, but a concussion doesn't necessarily leave an outward sign."

"True. It could also be a fugue, which is, admittedly rarer."

"A fugue? Like a musical composition?" Kirby asked.

"Same pronunciation," Nate said. "Different meaning. I was referring to the psychiatric definition in which a dissociative amnesiac may leave home and start wandering around, ultimately beginning a new life."

"Do you think that's what happened in Sebastian's case?"

For the first time since he learned of her occupation, Sebastian could envision her as a law enforcement official. He could practically see the wheels turning inside her head. Indeed, as his mind slipped easily into hers, he realized that she was seriously considering emailing—whatever the hell that was—his photograph to other police departments in the area.

"Anything's possible," Nate said. "A violent psychological trauma, like from an attack, might bring it on."

"Isn't there something you can do?" Whitney asked. "Hypnosis? Or drugs?"

"Memory work is a big deal these days. They're working on drugs to help erase memories, such as for those suffering from PTSD. And, of course, it's like an arms race with everyone trying to find the magic bullet to help Alzheimer's and other dementia patients regain memory.

"But, in the case of both retrograde and organic amnesia, which is what a fugue is, eventually the memory returns. In time."

Although Sebastian did not want to be impolite, he was growing extremely annoyed by the way they were talking about him as if he weren't in the room.

"I'm certain that my amnesia will be short-lived," he said, his tone testier than he'd planned. "As you've pointed out, Dr. Pendleton, a blow to the head is undoubtedly the cause."

Nate's brows drew together into a worried frown. "How did you know I was a doctor?"

"I told him," Kirby said on an exasperated huff of breath. "I also accused him of having come here to track you down, but he assured me that's not the case. And I believe him."

Her tone implied that the subject was closed. But only for now, Sebastian determined, eyeing the still-interested glint in Nathaniel Pendleton's gaze. Possessing a decidedly un-Logosian amount of tenacity himself, Sebastian could recognize and appreciate that trait when he saw it in others.

"By the way, Nate," Kirby said, changing the topic, "next time you decide to have your computer in the brain factory start talking with the one here in the house, I wish you'd give me advance notice. That stunt you pulled last night cost me some much-needed sleep."

"What stunt?"

Her cheeks paled and Sebastian felt the icy fear that shimmied up her spine. Irrationally, he wanted to take her into his arms and comfort her. "You didn't log in to the computer from the brain factory?"

"I didn't need to. I had all the data I needed at the lab." His eyes narrowed. "What makes you think I did?"

"I thought I heard a noise. When I went to check, I could have sworn your monitor was warm. But all the windows and doors were locked, so I suppose I must have simply drifted off and dreamed I heard something."

She laughed with what was obviously forced casualness. "You know my overactive imagination. . .

"So, where are those muffins you promised me?"

"Right here." Nate reached into a backpack. "I also brought whole wheat bagels"—he pulled out a white container—"and cream cheese."

"Cream cheese," Kirby said on a pleased note that Sebastian would have expected from a woman who'd just received the deed to her own diamaziman mine. "You're officially off the hook for skipping out on dinner."

As he put his packages onto the counter, Nate glanced

over at the charred piece of meat at the bottom of the red pot. "Speaking of dinner, it looks as if I lucked out. That's not how I remember Grandmother Pendleton's pot roast."

"There was a slight accident," Kirby muttered.

"I can see that. When did the fire department leave?"

"In case you haven't noticed, Kirby is not the domestic type," Whitney informed Sebastian needlessly.

Sebastian noticed how Whitney's comment gave birth to a hot flash of irritation in Kirby's eyes. Strangely, and highly illogically, since Kirby had openly admitted her lack of cooking skills, Sebastian experienced a similar annoyance.

"It was my fault," he said. "Kirby was about to turn off the cooking pot when I became delirious and distracted her."

"Delirious?" Nate asked.

"Yes." Sebastian studiously avoided what he knew would be Kirby's surprised expression. "I vaguely recall her saying that she had to tend to her dinner and would return shortly, but then this feverlike state came over me, and I drifted into a strange, dreamlike world, and when I came out of it much, much later, she was still beside me, soothing me like the lovely angel of mercy she is."

Unable to resist, Sebastian looked at Kirby, whose flushed cheeks had nothing to do with the warmth of the kitchen fireplace.

A shared memory of the way they'd awakened in each other's arms shimmered between them, warm and seductive. That memory was immediately followed by mental images of her alleged earlier fantasy, of Sebastian spreading fragrant oil all over Kirby Pendleton's near-naked body. The fantasy that had brought him to Rum

Runner Island in the first place.

Sebastian didn't need Logosian telepathy to know that they were sharing the same fantasy. His chest tightened, making breathing difficult.

And finally, just when the air in the room seemed filled with heat and smoke, another more recent memory gripped him. When they'd seen each other through a pane of glass and their minds had, for one stunning moment, joined in perfect, sensual harmony.

A hunger, as dangerous as that once-wild animal whose picture she wore on her tunic, came alive inside Sebastian. He wanted Kirby Pendleton. With every atom of his terran-Logosian body.

"Gracious." Whitney began fanning herself. "Has it suddenly gotten extremely steamy in here? Or is it just me?"

Silence came crashing down like a steel gate. When her brother's intelligent gaze drilled into his once again, Sebastian knew that he was being thoroughly summed up.

He managed, with effort, to meet that challenging gaze with a bland look of his own, realizing, as he did so, that Nathaniel Pendleton's midnight-blue eyes never missed a thing.

"I think I'll go for a walk," Nate said finally, shattering the silence.

"It's freezing outside," Kirby protested. "Besides, you just got here."

"And now I'm going for a walk." He was talking to her, but as he pulled his gloves back on, his eyes didn't leave Sebastian's. "Would you care to join me, Sebastian? I believe I left an old ski parka in the closet you're welcome to wear."

Sebastian had never been one to turn away from a challenge. "I'd enjoy a short walk," he agreed. "Perhaps it will stimulate my memory."

"Exactly what I was thinking," Nate agreed.

10

THE SNOW HAD stopped falling, leaving the air crisp and clear and icy. Sebastian breathed shallowly, not wanting to draw too much freezing air into his lungs. After his near-death experience yesterday, he was not yet at ease in such frigid climes.

He was not surprised when Kirby's brother got right to the point.

"All right," Nate said, stopping in a grove of pine trees not far from the house. "What the hell are you up to?"

"I don't know what you mean," Sebastian said carefully. "If you're referring to my alleged interest in you or your work—"

"I don't give a damn about any interest you might have in me," Nate said on an explosion of frosty breath. "If you've come here to try and recruit me, you're wasting your time. If you're here to steal my work or try to sabotage it in any way, I'm capable of dealing with that. What I want to know is what are your intentions toward my sister?"

"Intentions?"

Nate's gloved hands curled into fists at his sides, giving Sebastian the impression that the man, if pushed, could be extremely dangerous. "If you're using her to get to me—"

"I'm not." The idea was so preposterous that Sebastian's shocked honesty was obvious.

"Have you slept with her?"

Before Sebastian could answer honestly in the affirmative, the calm voice of the ecumenical translator explained the idiom.

Grateful for the assistance, he said, "No." It was the truth, so far as it went.

"But you want to."

When Sebastian didn't immediately answer, Nate said, "I'm a man, dammit, and I know what's in a man's mind when he looks at my sister the way you were looking at Kirby."

"Your sister is a very attractive woman."

"She's also a very vulnerable one. I don't want her hurt."

"I have no intention of hurting Kirby." This time he was speaking the absolute truth.

"But you do intend to sleep with her."

Reminding himself that he would undoubtedly act the same way if some stranger had inappropriately lustful designs on Rosalyn, Sebastian understood Nathaniel Pendleton's need to protect his sister. But that didn't mean that the man had to be privy to every intimate detail of her life.

"I don't wish to be rude," he said mildly, "but I do not see where that's really any of your business."

Emotions—irritation, worry, frustration, regret—all ran quickly over Nate's face and were just as quickly controlled.

"I suppose it's not," he said. "Particularly since she's already been married once, but—"

"Kirby was married?"

"Yes. I take it she hasn't filled you in on that story yet."

"No, she hasn't." Even as he vowed to learn about Kirby's marriage at the first opportunity, Sebastian wondered why it suddenly seemed imperative that he know why she was no longer with her legal bondmate. "I don't suppose you would be willing to enlighten me further."

"No. I wouldn't." Above them, high in the treetops, a jay scolded and went ignored. "But I will tell you this," Nate advised. "If I ever get my hands on the son of a bitch who used to be her husband, he'll be walking funny for a very long time."

The warning was clear. "I will keep that in mind," Sebastian said.

Nate nodded. "I'd suggest you do that."

Matters temporarily understood to both men's satisfaction, they began walking back toward the house, following the deep tracks their boots had made.

"You really have no idea what you're doing here?" Nate asked with a casualness that Sebastian knew was feigned.

"Not really. Kirby thought perhaps I work at the laboratory."

"If you did, I'd know you."

"Yes. That was my thought, too. Especially since I am an astrophysicist."

Nate stopped. "Strange that you should remember that."

"Amnesia is an unpredictable thing."

"True." Obviously unconvinced, Nate began walking again. "Who do you work for?"

"I'm presently between official assignments," Sebastian said. "But I've done some work of my own on antimatter."

Sebastian knew that at this point in time, antimatter

existed on Earth solely as ephemeral particles created by giant accelerators. It was, in actual operation, more theory than fact. A theory that would ultimately prove true. When antimatter combined with ordinary matter, mutual annihilation occurred with a force far greater than that produced by thermonuclear fusion.

It had been the fuel of choice for interstellar travel for over a century. A chunk of it was currently stored in his pocket accelerator.

"Antimatter." Although Nate didn't slow his pace, Sebastian didn't have to read his mind to know that he was more than a little interested.

"There's been a lot of work done to create antihydrogen," Nate allowed. "But no one's been able to force an antielectron into orbit around the antiproton."

"It's difficult getting the electrons to fall into stable orbits around atomic nuclei," Sebastian agreed. "However, if one were to draw significant energy from the particles before they are combined—"

"The system would work." Nate continued striding through the snow, but now his steps were less deliberate, his pace definitely slowed as his mind clicked through the possibilities. "But it would still be difficult to store."

Sebastian had already decided that if he was to return to Logosia in the proper time, he would need help working out whatever glitch had sent him through the time warp. Such help would be beyond the understanding of most Earthlings.

Most. But not this man.

He was just human enough to appreciate fate. And fate, he believed, had brought him to this place. At this point in time.

"Not if it were stored in the form of antihydrogen."

That did it. Nate stopped and stared at him. "At what temperature would it remain stable?"

"Two degrees above absolute zero," Sebastian answered what was common knowledge to any second-level Logosian. "Held in a container made of ordinary matter at the same temperature, the ice would not explode."

The excitement of scientific discovery held Nate absolutely still. "And its atoms would annihilate at such a gradual rate that it could be safely stored to last for a very long time," Kirby's brother said softly, working out the problem with an alacrity of mind that even Sebastian had not fully expected. "It could even be used for interstellar travel."

He stood there, looking out into the distance, quietly thoughtful. "All those sightings," he murmured. "All those crazy, hysterical reports about little green men."

He turned toward Sebastian. "They were true."

As dangerous as it might turn out to be, Sebastian decided to trust this man. "Not exactly."

"No." A faint smile curved Nate's lips. "You are far from little. And not the slightest bit green from what I can tell. Of course, if you'd eaten Kirby's pot roast, things might be a little different in that regard." He shook his head. "I have so many questions."

"I thought you might."

"But I haven't the faintest idea where to begin." He rubbed a gloved hand over his cheek. "Where are you from?"

"Logosia. It's not in your galaxy," he elaborated at Nate's blank look. He went on to explain, as well as he could without a star chart, the location of his home planet.

"Logosia. Amazing. Where's your ship, or vehicle, or whatever you call it?"

"I don't have one."

Nate's shoulders sagged, his disappointment obvious. "I should have known," he muttered. "You're just another crackpot."

Sebastian decided not to take umbrage at the definition the translator supplied. He wasn't certain that, under the same circumstances, he wouldn't have come to the same conclusion.

"Actually, there are those on my planet who would agree wholeheartedly with you," he admitted. "Especially whenever I attempted to explain my theory of quantum jump physics being a superior means of intergalactic travel."

"Quantum physics?" Nate asked with studied casualness.

"I theorized that the component atoms that make up life could be taken apart, transported through space utilizing the theory of quantum electrodynamics, then be put back together when they'd reached their destination."

"Anyone who's watched *Star Trek*, which would be just about everyone on the planet, would know the concept."

"Not just your planet," Sebastian said. "Mr. Spock is quite revered on Logosia. Many consider his Vulcan character to be based on our own values, which prize intellect and an emotionally detached, logical perspective toward life."

"Good answer," Nate allowed. "But it doesn't prove anything. How do I know that you haven't gotten your hands on a copy of my work in progress?"

"But I have," Sebastian agreed cheerfully. "Your textbook on quantum jump time travel is where I got the idea in the first place."

"I haven't written a book on time travel."

"Not yet. But you will. In fact, it's required reading at the science institute. Along with your work on solar flares, of course."

"Solar flares? Never mind," Nate said quickly. "We can get to that later."

He rubbed his chin again with his gloved fingers. "Okay. Let's go through this one step at a time. You allege to be from the planet Logosia. Perhaps you ought to fill me in on the year."

"Years are calculated differently on Logosia," Sebastian said. "But from what Kirby told me, I seem to have gone back in time on my journey here."

"Kirby knows about this?"

"No," Sebastian assured him quickly. "She only knows that she found me, near freezing, on the road yesterday." He frowned. "Although I am extremely grateful, I am not certain it was very wise of her to take a stranger into her home."

"Kirby's always been too open for her own good," Nate said. "When she was a kid, she was always rescuing strays. The house was constantly overrun with animals. It used to drive my parents crazy, but I have to admit, she invariably managed to find homes for all those mangy dogs and cats she dragged home."

Sebastian, who wasn't exactly pleased to be compared to a stray dog or cat, remained silent.

"Like that damn anti-Christ of a feline she's got living with her now," Nate said. "I remember the day she found it when she was patrolling the waterfront. It was filthy and its fur was matted, but she took it home, gave it a bath, got it shots, and now you couldn't get the damn animal out of her house with a hand grenade."

"She said the *cat* owns *her.*"

"Yeah. That's why, if I weren't too busy to take care of one, I'd rather have a dog. And although she's smart as a whip, Kirby's too softhearted for her own good. She even went to law school, after graduating college, because she had this wide-eyed optimistic goal about helping the underprivileged," he divulged.

"Kirby was an attorney?" Sebastian tried to picture Kirby Pendleton wearing the stark black robes and grim expressions favored by the barristers on Logosia and couldn't.

"For a short time. Unfortunately, the system moved too slowly for her, so she decided she could help people more by putting the bad guys behind bars, where they couldn't hurt anyone. Even after all those years as a cop, dealing with all those criminals, she still manages to see good in almost everything. And everyone." He shook his head with a mixture of admiration and fraternal worry.

"She believes I have amnesia."

"Although my sister is twenty-nine years old, she still suffers from a romanticized view of life and people. I used to think she'd grow out of her naïveté, but I've come to the conclusion that she'll probably never entirely throw away her rose-colored glasses. For the record, while she might buy that excuse, I didn't believe you for a minute."

"I know. That is one more reason why I decided to trust you with the truth," Sebastian allowed. "Because I knew that you would discover it on your own, anyway."

"What are the other reasons?"

"I cannot pass up the opportunity to work with a man whose name is legendary in the scientific community."

"Legendary?"

Sebastian could tell Nathaniel Pendleton liked that idea. "The name Pendleton ranks right up there along with Galileo, Copernicus, Newton, Darwin, Einstein, and Pournelle."

"Pournelle?"

"He's still a few decades in the future."

"Oh." Nate considered that. "Speaking of which, you still haven't told me what kind of time lag we're talking about here."

"One hundred and eighty-three of your Earth years. Which is the most important reason I decided to tell you the truth. Even in my era, you have no peers when it comes to your knowledge of time travel. I need your help to build a terran-based transporter. And to work out the coordinates through subspace that will allow me to arrive home in my proper time."

"Now you're talking science fiction."

"Science, yes. But it is not fiction."

Nate took a long time to consider the request. "You've no idea how badly I want to believe you. And I honestly don't want to insult you, but you have to remember, I'm a scientist. I deal with facts and figures and theorems. I need proof. More than your word about all this," he said apologetically.

"I thought you might." Without so much as a blink of his eye, Sebastian disappeared. The only sign of his former presence was the footprints in the snow. Footprints that abruptly, mysteriously, stopped beside Nate's.

"Sebastian?" Nate looked around at the silent woods.

"Where the hell are you?"

"Right here."

Nate spun around on his heel and viewed Sebastian leaning against a tree. An instant later, he was beside him again.

"Well?"

Nate threw back his head and laughed, a bold, hearty laugh that caused the birds on the branches overhead to take flight with a flurry of wings.

"Hot damn," he said. "Beam us up, Scotty, we've got to get to work and figure out a way to send this man home!"

"Then you'll help?"

"I'd like to see you try and stop me." Nate's gaze immediately sobered. "There's one more thing you should probably know about me. Something you won't find in any book."

Engrossed in already planning his return to Logosia, Sebastian failed to hear the warning edge to Nate's tone. "What's that?" he asked absently.

"When Kirby was sixteen years old, she began dating the son of a local lobsterman."

Strange how all it took was the woman's name to garner his absolute attention, Sebastian mused. "You didn't approve."

"Not because of his family," Nate insisted. "For the record, I'm not an intellectual, or any other kind, of snob. What I objected to was the kid's reputation."

"Which was?"

"He was the hometown stud, infamous for scoring with a new girl every Friday night."

"And you didn't want your sister to be one more conquest?"

"Exactly. And I made certain that she wasn't."

"By threatening him?"

"It wasn't a threat. I merely told the horny kid that if he laid one grubby paw on my sister, I would personally saw him into little pieces and use him for bait in his own lobster traps."

"That sounds eminently reasonable," Sebastian agreed. "Under the circumstances."

Nate couldn't conceal his surprise. "This planet you come from, this Logosia—"

"Is perfectly peaceful," Sebastian assured him. "We haven't experienced armed conflict for centuries. But I, myself, have an unmarried sister who, coincidentally, is the same age as yours. One I care about very deeply. And if it eases your concerns, you should know that I was, until recently, betrothed to one of my own people."

"That's not entirely reassuring," Nate argued. "Having split up with your fiancée, you're an ideal candidate for a rebound romance."

"The rift is only temporary." Sebastian frowned as he recalled his former bondmate's cold, final-sounding words. "Zorana resented the undue attention my work had attracted, but once I return to Logosia with proof that my theories are valid, I know she will put aside her objections."

"Oh." Mollified, Nate's lips curved into a faint smile. "Then we understand one another?"

Against all reason, thoughts of Kirby flooded Sebastian's mind. Kirby of the soft, fragrant skin, enticing breasts, and sparkling eyes. He remembered the way she'd felt in his arms. The way her smile could send a glow of bright sunshine streaming through his veins.

Tightly garnering the reins of mental control once again, Sebastian reminded himself that he had been bonded to Zorana since childhood. Their marriage had always been a foregone conclusion, and Sebastian had not a single doubt that once he regained his lofty position in society, she would honor her betrothal promise.

And even if he weren't planning to marry Zorana, Kirby Pendleton was a terran. She was also the sister of a man who had become, in only a few minutes, not only his lifeline but also his friend.

Forcing down uncharacteristically ambivalent feelings toward Nathaniel Pendleton's twin, Sebastian answered, "Absolutely."

11

KIRBY SENSED THE difference in the two men the minute they returned to the kitchen. Her brother was as excited as she'd ever seen him. Sebastian was excited, too, she determined, but he was better at concealing it.

She greeted them with a smile and two mugs of steaming coffee. "I was about to send out the Saint Bernards."

"Thank you," Sebastian said as he cupped his hands around the warmth of the mug and took a drink. "Your police department was very fortunate to have you willing to make such excellent coffee for them."

"You made coffee for the police?" Nate asked.

"It's a long story." Kirby waved off his question. "I was getting concerned that Sebastian may have had a relapse."

"We were just talking," Nate said. "Sebastian remembered he's an astrophysicist."

"Really?" Kirby and Whitney asked in unison.

Kirby's eyes narrowed thoughtfully while the other woman smiled at Sebastian.

"That's quite a coincidence," Whitney said.

"It also might explain what you're doing here," Kirby said. "Perhaps you were looking for Nate, after all."

"He was. But Sebastian's not a recruiter," Nate said before Sebastian had a chance to respond. "It turns out that he's the new man I hired to join my project."

"Oh?" Kirby's gaze moved from her brother to Sebastian to Nate again. "I don't recall you saying anything about a new man."

Nate shrugged. "I probably forgot to mention it. You know how absentminded I get when I'm engrossed in work."

That much was true. She'd heard the same excuse countless times. But there was something else. Something neither man was prepared to tell her.

"I am much the same way," Sebastian jumped in. "Even without my amnesia."

"Yet another thing you remember," she said dryly. They were already working well as a tag team. "Funny how retrograde amnesia works, isn't it?"

Realizing that she was being stonewalled by two scientists whose individual IQs undoubtedly exceeded the combined numbers of most of the citizens of Rum Runner Island, she decided there was no point in pressing them any further.

But surrendering that hill didn't stop her from being annoyed at the way Whitney was looking at Sebastian the same way Darcy looked at a bowl of fresh cream. She was surprised the woman wasn't licking those red, red lips.

"Well, it's nice that the mystery of why you're here on the island is cleared up," she said briskly. "Or will be once Nate unearths your records. Now all we have to do is find out what happened to all your things and what you were doing out in the middle of the snowstorm."

"He undoubtedly got mugged," Whitney offered.

"That's probably it," Nate agreed.

"I agree that it's the most likely answer," Kirby said. "But it's also a rather disturbing thought. Since we never have muggings on Rum Runner Island."

"There's always a first time," Nate said cheerfully. Too cheerfully, Kirby considered.

"It's still strange," she said.

Sebastian watched Kirby's eyes narrow. Since arriving back from his talk with her brother in the woods, he could actually see her as a police detective. It was apparent she didn't take anything at face value.

Seeming to put her suspicions aside for now, she took a brown ring from the slots, spread it thickly with cream cheese, and handed it to Sebastian, who took a tentative bite.

This bagel was hot and chewy, the cheese smooth and cool. The textures and tastes exploded on his tongue. "It's delicious," he declared after he'd finished chewing. "Even better than the coffee."

"Unfortunately, it's also horribly fattening," Whitney said. She nibbled daintily at her own ungarnished bagel. "You know what they say," she said silkily, "a moment on the lips, a lifetime on the hips."

Her languid yet pointed gaze slid to Kirby, whose bagel, like Sebastian's, was spread thickly with cream cheese. "You've no idea how I envy you, Kirby. Not many women would permit themselves such a calorie-laden indulgence."

"If you think this is an indulgence, stick around," Kirby said. "I was planning to bring home a pepperoni pizza for dinner."

Whitney shook her head. "You really should take better care of yourself, dear. Even if you don't worry about your dress size, I shudder to think what all that fat and choles-terol is doing to your heart."

Sebastian watched the fire flare in Kirby's blue eyes, and when, strangely, he felt that same anger begin to flow through him, as well, he studied the other woman more closely.

She was severely dressed in black from her head to her feet. Her hair was black, as well, and hung over her shoulders in a shiny curtain. Her dark eyes were lined with a black pencil, a decided contrast to her complexion, which was as pale as the snow on the pine trees outside the window.

Whitney Reynolds could have been a genetically de-signed Logosian, he mused, as his gaze took in her ascetically slender frame clad in the black tunic and trousers. Her breasts were almost nonexistent, and her hips were as slender as a boy's. She could have been Zorana's twin.

"Well, speaking of my clothing," Kirby said with a sharp-edged briskness he imagined she might have used in her police work. "As much as I'd love to sit around and chat all day, I need to take a quick shower, change, and get to work so I can contact other New England agencies to see if anyone's reported a missing person."

"Good luck with that," Nate said.

"It can't be that hard," she said. "He didn't exactly beam down from outer space, like one of those green men everyone was talking about yesterday." She pulled out her phone, pointed it at Sebastian. He heard a click.

"What was that?"

"I need a picture to send around."

"Is it necessary?"

"Well, I could describe you, but since you're standing right here, and I assume you want to fill in more blanks in your life, a photo seemed to make more sense."

He was starting to realize when she was being sarcastic. She was also reminding him more and more of his sister. They'd be friends, he realized. If they'd ever meet, which was improbable. He was also uncomfortable about having any record of his visit end up in the planet's archives.

"I suppose that is logical," he said.

"Gee, thanks," she drawled. "I guess all my police training hasn't entirely gone to waste."

"You're speaking ironically."

"Bull's-eye. Give the man a stuffed moose."

"Well," Nathaniel said, obviously wanting to escape the argument that was brewing, "we'd better be getting back to the lab. Could you drop Sebastian by the lab on your way into town?"

"Are you certain that's wise?" Frowning, Kirby turned toward Sebastian. "After all you've been through, you should at least spend today in bed."

Sebastian found the suggestion vastly appealing. As long as Kirby joined him in that warm, wide bed. Unfortunately, for many reasons, including his understanding with her brother, that would not be possible.

"I'm feeling very well now, Kirby," Sebastian assured her. "Thanks to your good care."

"But still—"

"I'm a doctor, Kirby," Nate reminded her. "I promise to keep my eye on him all day, in case he starts feeling shaky."

"You won't notice. Not if you're in the throes of scientific creation." The spark of annoyance in her eyes had been replaced by seeds of worry.

"You needn't worry," Sebastian said. Not accustomed to such personal consideration for his well-being from someone who wasn't his immediate family, he was moved by her concern. "I promise not to overtax myself. But it's important that I join your brother at the lab, and I would be very appreciative if you would drive me there this morning."

"Scientists," she huffed with very real frustration. "You're all crazy." She shook her head, turned away, and marched into the bedroom, slamming the door behind her.

"Well, I take it that was a *yes*," Whitney drawled.

The obvious derision in her tone irritated Sebastian. "Her concern for others is commendable."

"Concern?" Whitney laughed at that. "Oh, I think it's a great deal more than concern that has Kirby forgetting her manners." She smiled up at Sebastian as she rose and began pulling on her gloves. "I'll see you later." Waggling her fingers, she left the kitchen.

Nate stood in the open doorway, letting cold air into the house as his gaze went from Sebastian to the closed bedroom door, then back to Sebastian.

"Your brotherly concern is unnecessary," Sebastian said quietly. "I have already promised not to hurt her."

"I believe you mean that." Nate's expression was grim. "But if you were to stick around Earth for a while, Sebastian, you'd realize that humans—especially the female of the species—are, by nature, subjective, emotional, and highly unpredictable. Which makes it difficult, if not impossible, to deal with them in an objective, quantitative fashion."

"My mother is a terran," Sebastian felt obliged to point

out. "From your planet."

"Seriously?" Observing the glint in Nate's eyes, Sebastian had the feeling that scientific curiosity had just temporarily overridden Nate's concern for his sister's emotional well-being.

"Most seriously," Sebastian assured him. "Although intermarriage is rare between the ruling classes on Logosia, my father broke tradition by bringing back a bride from one of his diplomatic missions to Earth. Both Rosalyn, my sister, and I are half-terran and half-Logosian."

"I can't wait to get you on an examining table." Outside, Whitney called to him, complaining about waiting in the cold. "I'm coming," Nate called out to her.

Then, just when Sebastian thought the conversation was over, Nate warned, "Don't hurt her."

And then he was gone, wading his way through the snow to the black machine.

12

THIS WAS RIDICULOUS, Kirby told herself as she stood in the shower that, up until this morning, had only been used by her brother and her. She didn't even know Sebastian. Not really. He was merely a man she'd rescued in the line of duty. There was nothing personal in their relationship, for heaven's sake.

Well, there had been that unsettling incident this morning, when she'd awakened in his arms. But that had merely been an anomaly, two people forced to share a bed, caught up in their own sensual dreams. It could have happened with anyone.

But it hadn't. It had happened with Sebastian Blackthorne, and although she'd sworn never to get involved with another impossibly good-looking man again, Kirby recognized her own vulnerability. Which was why she'd had to go outside when she'd heard the shower running. Just imagining him naked, with hot water streaming over his broad shoulders, his washboard torso, his flat stomach, strong, muscled thighs, and impossible-to-forget morning erection, had caused a spike of hormones that had her irrationally wanting to strip off her own clothes and join him beneath that water.

Which was when she'd changed into jeans, put on her boots, and gone out into the snow to feed the birds, who were noisily reminding her that she was late.

Now, as she rubbed the bar of soap into a lather, then ran the bubbles over her own body, her unruly mind imagined that same water flowing over Sebastian Blackthorne's naked body.

In her fantasy, her hands became his. Trailing down her throat, over her collarbone, her shoulders. Her breasts had become so sensitized from her erotic thoughts the pulsating massage spray was nothing like its usual invigorating morning wake-up. Instead, the water created a sensuality that bordered on pain as it hit wet skin that felt as if it were tightening beneath her fingertips.

Her stroking hands went lower over her quivering stomach, until she was inches from attaining bliss. Then, like a bolt from the blue, she remembered that she'd left the object of her sexual frustration in the other room.

"Damn." Reaching up, she changed the setting to a gentler rain flow, finished her shower in record speed, and rubbed away at her body with the towel in a less-than-effective attempt to scrub the naked hot man out of her mind.

✧   ✧   ✧

SHE'D JUST GOTTEN dressed when there was a knock on the bedroom door. "Kirby?" the all-too-familiar deep voice called. "Is everything all right?"

"Everything's just hunky-dory," she called back.

There was a moment's silence. "May I come in?"

She was pinning on the five-sided star that her father had proudly worn for thirty-two years. "I'll be right out."

Vulnerable she might be, but she wasn't a total idiot. Not so much that she'd be alone in her bedroom with a man who could, with a single glance, create such havoc to her senses.

Of course, he hadn't gone away. When she opened the door, he was standing there, observing her with his probing dark gaze that, as impossible as she knew it to be, seemed to be able to look inside her mind.

"Whitney upset you," he diagnosed.

"I'm not that easily upset." Which was true. Usually. But there'd been nothing usual about the past fourteen hours. "I told you, Sebastian, I just get bad vibes from the woman."

"So do I." Without waiting for an invitation, he crossed the room and stood in front of her.

"Do you?"

"Absolutely." Kirby heard the honesty in the single word, saw it in his eyes. "But I have a feeling that this is about more than bad vibrations," Sebastian suggested.

"No, really—"

When she would have turned away, he caught her chin in his hand. Closely, calmly, he examined her. "What's wrong, Kirby?" The warmth of his touch sent a new flood of emotions bubbling through her.

"It's just that she's so damn thin."

"Yes. She is."

He didn't have to agree so fast, she thought miserably. "And I'm not."

"That is also true." His gaze, as it moved from her face to take a slow, judicious tour of her body, set her nerves to ringing like bells inside her head. "I still do not understand."

She ran an agitated hand through her hair, frustrated with him, with herself, with this unsettling situation she seemed to have found herself in. "Forget it. It's not important." She didn't have any body issues, dammit. Except when she was around Whitney, who, if it weren't for her flat chest, could've been a body double for Angelina Jolie.

Freeing herself from his light hold, she backed away.

"What if I told you that I find your body very appealing?" Sebastian took a step toward her. "Just as it is."

Kirby took another backward step. "If that's supposed to make me feel more comfortable around you, it doesn't."

"I was afraid of that." When she continued to back away, Sebastian matched his steps to hers. "Your brother told me that you'd been married."

The backs of her knees were pressing against the bed where she'd awakened in his arms. Short of scrambling over the top of the mattress or using some of the martial arts skills she'd learned in Venice, she was effectively trapped.

"So?"

"He also informed me that your husband hurt you."

"Nate had no right to tell you that."

"I think he did." Sebastian argued. "As your older brother, it's only logical that he would want to protect you. And ensure that this didn't happen."

"That what didn't happen?" But she knew. Oh, yes, how she knew exactly what he was talking about.

"This." He lifted a hand to her cheek. "Me wanting you. You wanting me."

"Well." Kirby blew out a harsh breath. "You certainly don't beat around the bush, do you?"

Sebastian grasped the meaning an instant before the translator decoded it for him. His knowledge of English idioms, he considered with a burst of un-Logosian pride, was improving. "No. I don't."

In contrast to Whitney's ice, Kirby was heat. From the bright sunset color of her hair to her golden complexion, to her full rose-hued lips, to the intriguing color that rose periodically in her cheeks, as it was now.

Her scent, which was much like the soap he'd used in her shower but even more fragrant, was surrounding him like an enticing ether cloud, while her skin was soft against the palm of his hand. Sebastian's mind was in a disorderly, tangled turmoil. He'd never been so distracted. So on the edge of being out of control. Even when he was, technically, breaking the rules of scientific exploration, during those last minutes as Rosalyn had sat at his command console, programming in the codes he'd spent years developing, he was never, *ever* out of control.

Except for that moment when he'd been breaking apart, only to hear her warning him that he was destined for an entirely different place and time. Perhaps the leap through time and space had injured his brain.

And if that were the case, was such damage temporary? Because if it proved to be permanent, his situation would be much, much worse.

"What makes you think I want you?" Kirby asked, shaking him out of yet another distraction. His thoughts and emotions had become like unruly atoms, bouncing around without anything to bond them into a coherent structure.

Her voice was steady, but as his thumb brushed against the fragrant flesh of her throat, he had proof that her pulse was not. "Don't you?"

His feelings for her were highly illogical, atypical, and dangerous. Unable to resist the lure of her lips, he ran a fingertip over them. When they parted instinctively at his touch, Sebastian reminded himself that even an emotion-driven terran male would be cautious enough to take a pace back to consider his actions before stepping off the edge of a cliff.

"I'm sorry." His voice was too stiff. Too gruff. But rather than try to soothe the situation with an apology that could end up making things even worse, and to give himself some much-needed physical and emotional distance, he backed away and began to roam the room.

"For what, exactly?" Her voice sounded as unsteady as his heart.

"I had no right to ask that question. Just as I had no right to touch you in such a familiar manner."

Needing something, anything to do with his hands to keep them off her, needing to gather his scrambled thoughts back into order, he opened an opaque white jar. As he scooped a bit of the pink cream onto his thumb, Sebastian was struck with a sudden, almost uncontrollable urge to rub that fragrant cream into her smooth, round breasts.

"Then why does it feel as if you do?" Kirby asked with what he was beginning to understand was her unrelenting honesty.

Having acquired proof that he was not alone in these disorienting feelings had hunger hitting like the fiery jolt of a laser blast in the gut before sending flames downward to his groin. It took a Herculean effort, but Sebastian managed to ruthlessly control it.

"Nate will be waiting," he reminded them both.

"And I need to get to work." Her voice was calm and professional. The crackling energy emanating from her flower-scented body was not.

"To your police station."

"Yes." Her chin tilted up in a challenge, daring him to make one chauvinistic remark. "To my police station."

He swept a gaze over her again. Despite the ugly uniform, she was the most desirable female he'd ever met. Which made him wonder if this was how his father had felt when he'd first met his mother.

"I much prefer what you were wearing this morning." There were already too many lies between them. He intended to be as truthful as possible. "Those blue trousers and the tunic. Despite the wild animal."

"That wild animal just happens to be Bananas the Bear, the University of Maine mascot. And I really hate to disappoint you, but jeans and an old college sweatshirt don't exactly create an appearance of authority."

"I can appreciate that." He nodded. "But if you think that stiff and heavy uniform will make a man forget that you're a woman—a very, sensual, desirable woman—Kirby Pendleton, you're mistaken."

As if pulled forward by some yet undiscovered Newtonian force, Sebastian came to stand in front of her again. His hand cupped her neck, slid into the silk of her hair she'd not yet tied back from her face, as she'd worn it on her police job yesterday.

"On the contrary," he murmured, having to force the words from his strangely parched throat, "it makes a man want to strip it off, piece by stiff, ugly piece, and discover what soft, feminine secrets you are trying so hard to conceal."

She did not melt into his arms. Nor did she pull away. She simply stood there, looking up at him. Watching. Waiting.

Sebastian lowered his lips to within a whisper of hers, then hesitated.

Here there be danger, the ancient explorer's saying tried to make itself heard.

His logical mind, the part of him that knew this could be a fatal mistake, wanted to allow her to back away now. Before they found themselves in a situation that could not end well.

The emotional, often distressing human side to his nature, the part of him that had irrationally become linked to her from the moment he'd entered her fantasy and had been drawn into a place so different from his intended destination, knew she would not do the sensible, *logical* thing and move away.

The moment his lips brushed against hers, Sebastian realized exactly how badly he'd miscalculated. He'd intended to control the kiss like an experiment. After all, it was the not knowing how she'd taste that he'd found impossible to resist. Once he'd discovered the answer, he could move on. After observing her carefully, knowing that the ability to maintain control was important in a law enforcement professional, he'd assumed Kirby would be cool, collected, and sweet.

Sweet she most definitely was. But cool? Collected? There was nothing cool about the mouth that clung so hungrily to his. There was nothing collected about the hands that thrust into his hair. All his earlier hypotheses flew out the window as he felt the heat flare, the passion rise.

There was something mindless happening here. Something dark and dangerous. Something he couldn't analyze. Sense was seeping out of him. Logic disintegrated. Sebastian found himself lost in a smoky, turbulent world unlike anything he'd ever known.

It could have been a minute, an hour, an eternity. When he finally took his mouth from hers, Sebastian realized that his hands, which had taken hold of her shoulders sometime during that heated kiss, were far from steady.

He craved her now.

Immediately.

Desperately.

He wanted to drag her to the bed or the nearest chair or even the hard wooden plank floor and strip away that thick, dark uniform she wore like a suit of armor and bury himself deep inside her warmth.

When he realized that sometime during that shared kiss, desire had gone blazing over the line into need, this time it was he who backed away.

"Well," she said after a few seconds. She lifted a hand to her throat. "That was... um... certainly different."

So she'd felt it, too. He'd wondered but had been too rattled at the time to read her emotions. "Yes. It was."

They stared at each other.

Kirby swallowed. "It could also be a problem."

"Only if we let it."

He knew that his curt tone had hurt her when her exceptionally expressive face closed, folding like the petals of a moonflower as the pink light of dawn approached. She went over to the mirror, yanking her hair back into that low tail. When she next scooped a handful of coins from the top of the chest of drawers into her trouser pockets, Sebastian noted that her hands were shaking.

She was right, he admitted reluctantly. This could be one Herculean problem.

"I want to have sex with you, Kirby Pendleton," he told her with a stiff politeness that took every ounce of his self-control. *With truth came reason*, Sebastian reminded himself of the Logosian mantra. *With reason came truth.* Once Kirby understood his motivation, she would undoubtedly cease to be so upset. "Very much. But I promised your brother that we would not mate."

"What?" She spun around and shot him a sharp look. "*Mate?* What Neanderthal cave did you just crawl out of, Sebastian? And what the hell does Nate have to do with this?"

The anger was radiating off her in waves. Realizing that this was one more instance where he'd gravely miscalculated, he decided against pointing out that Neanderthals had died out thousands of years ago. Instead, Sebastian took a deep breath and tried again.

"I explained that he told me about your husband."

"Steven is my ex-husband," Kirby corrected sharply.

"Ex-husband," he allowed. "I also explained that Nate informed me that your husband, ex-husband," he amended at her blistering look, "did something that hurt you. And since your brother cares for you very much, he made me promise that I would not permit you to become emotionally involved with me."

"Not permit me?" Her voice rose high enough to crack the crystalline dome of his home city. "Are you saying that Nate made you promise not to permit me to become emotionally involved with you?"

"Yes." Relieved to have made his point, Sebastian nodded. "That is precisely what I'm saying."

She folded her arms beneath those lush breasts. "And I suppose you agreed." Her tone was as icy as the stream he'd crossed yesterday while stumbling through the whiteout.

"Of course."

Once again Sebastian found the human feminine mind to be a mystery. He'd explained their situation. So why did she appear to be so furious? She reminded him of one of the smoking, simmering volcanoes on the planet Pelethian, just prior to eruption.

Kirby nodded. "Of course," she murmured scathingly. "Lucky for you he wasn't prepared to marry me off. Lord knows how many camels he'd ask for."

"Camels?"

After explaining that she was referring to a two-humped ruminant quadruped of the genus *Camelus*, the translator, obviously as confused as Sebastian was by Kirby's reference, turned frustratingly silent.

"We did not discuss any camels," he protested.

"You've no idea what a relief that is," she shot back. Cursing under her breath, she marched from the room.

Sebastian followed, coming to an abrupt halt when he saw what she was buckling around her waist.

She followed his startled gaze to the leather holster at her hip. "Haven't you ever seen a pistol before?"

"Not at such close range."

The few antique weapons he had been privileged to see had always been locked away in glass cases in government archives that required the highest security clearances.

Logosia had emerged from the Resistance Wars determined to remain an unrelentingly peaceful planet.

"And not worn by a woman, either," she suggested with a sarcasm not unlike that which Rosalyn would occasionally direct his way.

"No."

"I can imagine that would prove discomfiting."

"In truth, it does."

In theory, and put in the larger context of history, Sebastian had always found the primitive weapons used by other, more violent societies undeniably fascinating. Now, forced to accept the danger such a weapon might represent to a woman he already cared for a great deal more than he should, he found it unreasonably terrifying.

"Why doesn't that surprise me?" She pulled her jacket down from a peg by the door, shrugged into it, and pulled on her tall black boots. "If you're coming, let's go."

Scooping up the jacket Nate had loaned him, Sebastian obediently followed.

13

THEY DROVE DOWN the snowy road in silence. Having grown up in a climatically controlled city, Sebastian found the Maine tree-studded countryside a revelation. Within five minutes he had caught sight of innumerable birds, a white snowshoe hare similar to the ones on the planet Polaris, several bushy-tailed squirrels, and a furry flat-tailed animal his memory banks told him was a beaver.

He would have been having a wonderful time were it not for Kirby's uncharacteristically stony silence. As the dashboard odometer clicked away the distance in tenths of miles, Sebastian grew more and more uncomfortable.

"I'm sorry I kissed you."

"Don't you dare apologize." Kirby didn't take her eyes from the road, slowing slightly when a red fox suddenly sprinted out of the trees and ran in front of the Jeep, its mahogany coat contrasting brightly with the sparkling white snow.

"All right."

As the fox disappeared behind the curtain of pine trees on the other side of the road, Sebastian decided that he was going to ask Nate for the secret to what went on inside an Earth woman's seemingly unfathomable mind. After all, given that he was about to reveal the practical application of antimatter to Kirby's brother, such exchange of information would only be fair.

"Would it make you even angrier if I told you that I was sorry for apologizing?"

"The reason you don't have to apologize is because I enjoyed it." She did not sound at all pleased.

"Oh. I thought, at the time, that you did," Sebastian allowed. "But if you enjoyed kissing me, why are you so angry?"

"Because I enjoyed it too much."

"Enjoyment is a bad thing?" Rosalyn's studies had indicated that, for the most part, humans sought enjoyment of all aspects of their lives. Mates, children, home life, work, and sex. The last one proved how different their species were. If merely kissing could cause such disorientation, he could not imagine what full-penetration physical sexual intercourse would be like.

"I'm referring to the chauvinistic way you and Nate talked about me as if I were some precious piece of porcelain that had to be handled properly for fear of breaking."

Sebastian considered that. "He was only trying to protect you, Kirby. I would do the same for my sister."

She slanted him a sideways glance. He thought, or hoped, that he felt a slight thaw in the chill. "You have a sister?"

"Yes."

"What does she do? For a living?"

"She's a xenoanthropologist."

"A what?"

Belatedly realizing that this society did not yet have a

need for people who studied alien cultures found on other planets and galaxies, he said, "It's a type of anthropologist."

"Oh." Kirby nodded. "Sounds as if she's pretty smart."

"Oh, yes. She's quite extraordinary."

"For a woman?" she asked.

"I didn't say that," he reminded her mildly. "Actually, Rosalyn is one of the most intelligent persons—male or female—that I've ever known."

"Maybe there's hope for you yet," Kirby decided. "Is she younger or older than you?"

"Younger. By two years. Coincidentally, she's the same age as you."

"So, although she's one of the most intelligent persons, male or female"—she threw his words back at him—"you've ever known, you still feel the need to protect her."

"Of course."

"Because she's a woman."

"That's right." He was becoming uncomfortable. The back of his neck was getting itchy, but unwilling to show weakness, he resisted scratching it. This conversation was more than a little familiar. It was one he'd had with Rosalyn on too many occasions.

"What if she were your younger brother?" Kirby asked.

"She's my only sibling," Sebastian said. "Since she's my sister, I could not have a brother," he pointed out with perfect logic.

Kirby's frustrated sigh ruffled the coppery fringe on her forehead. "Let's try a hypothetical," she suggested. "As a scientist, I'm sure you understand how hypothesis works."

He thought he detected sarcasm in her tone but decided not to mention it because she was so obviously irritated.

It would also be highly unwise to get her more emotional while she was operating the vehicle. "Of course."

"Fine." Kirby nodded. "So, let's say—hypothetically speaking—that Rosalyn is now Robert, your younger brother."

"All right. Hypothetically speaking."

"And Robert met a woman he found attractive. A woman who found him equally appealing. Are you with me so far?"

"Absolutely."

"Would you feel the need to go to this woman and warn her to stay away from Robert? In order to protect him?"

"Of course not."

"Because he's a man."

"Yes."

Kirby was undeniably charming. And, knowing she'd been an attorney, Sebastian allowed that she was also intelligent. So why couldn't she see the simple logic of his reasoning?

"I give up." Obviously frustrated, Kirby threw both hands in the air, causing the Jeep, which had just hit a patch of ice, to veer dangerously toward the edge of the road.

"Damn." Grabbing hold of the steering wheel, she deftly maneuvered the Jeep back into the middle of the packed snow with a skill that Sebastian couldn't help but admire.

"That was very good," he said, hoping to deflate her anger.

"I had excellent professional precision driver's training."

She turned a corner, and suddenly a building that had been hidden away in a grove of pine trees came into view. It crossed Sebastian's mind that if he hadn't known the laboratory was here, he never would have found it.

"Well, here we are," she said. "Safe and sound."

Sound, perhaps. But far from safe. Because he and Kirby Pendleton were rapidly approaching something that could prove inordinately perilous.

"Thank you. I appreciate your driving me here."

She shrugged. "There wasn't room for three on Nate's snowmobile. And although you make me want to throw things at your chauvinistic head, Sebastian, I'd rather put up with your frustrating, maddening company than Whitney's smug superiority."

"Is that a compliment?"

"I suppose it is." The smile he was rapidly becoming addicted to bloomed on her lips and in her eyes.

"In that case…"

Leaning toward her, he touched her face. Not seductively, not soothingly, but with a masculine possessiveness that he half expected to anger her all over again but, for some reason he couldn't comprehend, didn't.

"I enjoy your company, too, Kirby. Very much, as a matter of fact."

"Thank you."

Knowing he was playing with fire, he brushed the pad of his thumb against her mouth. "Your brother's going to wonder where I am."

"Nate's an intelligent man. He'll figure it out."

"That's what I'm afraid of."

Although it was the hardest thing he'd ever done, Sebastian backed away, literally and emotionally from what was quickly becoming a highly illogical, extremely volatile situation.

Her lips curved in a reassuring, seemingly amused smile. Her pique, Sebastian noted, was like a shooting star—a quick, hot flare before disintegrating.

"I'm twenty-nine years old, Sebastian," she told him. "And as much as Nate might dearly like to think otherwise, what I do or whom I do it with is none of my brother's business. Meanwhile, have a good day in the brain factory. I'll try to run down your stuff and discover what happened to you. See you later."

"Later," Sebastian agreed. If he found being alone with Kirby distracting, he was appalled at his reluctance to leave her. "Despite what I promised your brother, I still want you."

The Ancient Ones were wrong. Truth wasn't always synonymous with reason. At least not when it came to his feelings for Kirby Pendleton.

"I know."

"I've also discovered, against all logical reason, that I *need* you. And such need terrifies me."

Her gaze softened and she touched a hand to his cheek to soothe. "I know that, too."

"I rather thought you did," Sebastian agreed. "Since we inexplicably seem to share the same thoughts quite often." His eyes remained on hers as he resisted the urge to draw her close for another taste. "You were correct about it being a problem."

"I'm not about to try to deny that."

"But we will deal with it."

She nodded, her heart once again shining in her expressive eyes. "Yes."

It was only after he was walking toward the door of the laboratory that Sebastian realized that it was possible that, rather than assisting him in resisting their shared attraction, she'd just agreed to make love with him.

Which, after he'd specifically promised her brother not to, would not only be unethical and illogical, it would be insane. Yet more evidence that his brain had somehow been damaged between Logosia and Rum Runner Island, Maine.

Nathaniel Pendleton held the key to Sebastian's very survival. Without his assistance in correcting the time sequence, Sebastian could very well arrive home during the wrong time. Even before the Ancient Ones had arrived with their superior intellect and laws and reason, and civilized what had once been an inhospitable, primitive, warlike planet.

And that would be suicide.

So what was it about Kirby that had Sebastian willing to risk exactly that?

Like all scientists, he had always enjoyed solving problems. Even as a boy, he'd enjoyed puzzles, the more complicated the better. He enjoyed dissecting a problem, pulling it apart piece by piece, until finally, after meticulous study, he would have the answer.

He knew that, with due diligence and Kirby's brother's help, he would solve the puzzle of time and distance and return safely to his planet.

Unfortunately, the answer to his more personal dilemma, Sebastian suspected, could not be solved by logic or scientific method. As horrified as he was to realize that he was behaving more like a human than a proper Logosian, he couldn't remember when he'd enjoyed anything more than he'd enjoyed kissing Kirby.

A problem the Earthling female might be, Sebastian acknowledged honestly. But she was also the most delectable, enticing, delightful problem he'd ever encountered.

✧   ✧   ✧

THE LABORATORY WAS, unsurprisingly, tightly secured. Sebastian stood in front of the all-seeing eye of the video camera and was about to press the button to the intercom when the front door suddenly slid open.

"Well, hello," Whitney greeted him. "I was wondering when you'd show up." She glanced over Sebastian's shoulder. "I suppose Kirby's on her way to work."

"Yes." Once again Sebastian found himself uncomfortable with the polite small talk that seemed to be the custom on this planet. "To her police station."

"For the life of me, I can't imagine why any woman would want to be a police officer," Whitney said.

"Nor can I," Sebastian responded.

Whitney rewarded him with a slow, distinctly feminine smile that had Sebastian wondering if perhaps Nate hadn't claimed this woman, after all.

"I mean, it's such an unfeminine occupation," she said. "Don't you think?"

In all truth, he did. But there was a predatory glint in her dark eyes that had him feeling decidedly uncomfortable. That and the way this woman made Kirby feel inferior had Sebastian avoiding a direct answer.

"I think Kirby is the most feminine woman I've ever met." He'd never, in all his thirty-one years, uttered a more truthful statement.

"Well." Her smile turned chilly. Frost tinged her eyes. "You can't blame a girl for trying, now, can you?"

"No. You cannot."

She gave him a curious look tinged with renewed humor. "You're a strange one, Sebastian. But then again, aren't we all?"

She pulled on a pair of thick black gloves. "I'm going for a walk," she divulged. "A brisk stroll through the woods always clears my head when I'm stumped. Go on in," she said. "The receptionist at the front desk will page Nate for you and take care of getting you a proper ID."

That said, she left the building, walking away without a backward glance. Sebastian watched for a moment, wondering why the smooth movement of her hips did not affect him in the way Kirby's did.

Then, deciding to dwell on that question later, he entered the building and discovered that apparently everyone in this time brought trees indoors. Unlike Kirby's, this was made of metal, set on top of a table. An ancient motherboard served as a base to the tree decorated with spare computer parts, including letters cut from keyboards put together to spell out holiday words, and what he recognized from Logosia's famed technological museum as shiny DVDs and Game Boys.

Less than a minute after giving his name to the receptionist, Nate appeared and took him into a small room, where Sebastian once again had his photo taken, his eye and hand scanned.

"The palm's better for security," Nate said, which Sebastian already knew. "But we're still using the eye scanner just in case someone gets their hands cut off and bad guys try to use the disembodied hands to get in."

"That is an unnecessary precaution, given that the reflection method of illuminating the palm with an infrared ray captures the light given off by the region after diffusion through the palm," Sebastian argued. "The vein pattern is then used to authenticate the individual. However, the sensor can only recognize the pattern if the deoxidized hemoglobin is actively flowing within the veins. So, an amputated hand would not work."

"Good call," Nate said easily. "And yet more proof you belong working here. The actual fact is that we bought the iris scanner at a discount from Whitney's father's company and the contract has another year to run. She initially voted against earlier palm scanners as unhygienic due to having to put the hand on the scanner, but this one you only need to hold it near. Still, sometimes it's easier just to go along to get along.

"So, now we've ended up with a two-part system, which can be a pain, but then again, it is double security, which is never a bad thing in our business. Especially since some of the people working here have national security clearances. You can tell them because they never interact with anyone and look sort of like vampires."

"Vampires?"

"You know. Pale. Like they've never been outdoors during the daylight. Which, from what I can tell, they haven't. They have their own wing to themselves and aren't the least bit sociable, so we don't see them much, anyway."

After his credentials were taken care of, Nate opened yet another series of doors, leading into a long, wide hallway on which individual laboratories had been built on either side. Most of the doors were shut, but he paused at the open one just as the occupant looked up.

"Hey, Fred," Nate said. "Meet Sebastian Blackthorne. He's going to be one of us for a while. Sebastian, this is Fred Simpson."

"Hello," Sebastian said. Since the man did not stand up from behind his desk or invite him in, he did not hold out his hand.

"Is he working on your project?" the man said as he swept a gaze over Sebastian. His eyes were a pale blue, hidden behind the lenses of black horn-rimmed glasses. He was wearing red suspenders over a black T-shirt that read *Asteroids are nature's way of asking "How's that space program coming along?"*

Although Sebastian couldn't see behind the desk, he'd have bet he was wearing the high-water pants that were still a nerd staple nearly two hundred years in the future in another galaxy. He wondered if the nerds of his time had taken their fashion sense from the same old forbidden films he and his sister enjoyed.

"Yeah. He's the new guy I was talking about hiring."

"Oh." Apparently deciding there was nothing else to say, he returned his attention to the monitor and began tapping away.

"Is he considered one of those more sociable scientists you have here?" Sebastian asked as they continued walking down the hallway.

"No. He's nerdier than most. I don't think he's rude as much as shy," Nate said. "Though he's got a twelve-year-old's crush on Whitney."

"Who would eat him alive."

Nate laughed. "Called it in one. He's genius-level brilliant, though. He's working on the Chaos Theory."

The mystery, also known as the butterfly theory in this

time, concerned deterministic systems whose behavior could in principle be predicted. Chaotic systems might be predictable for a while and then appear to become random.

"That has been answered," Sebastian said as they came to a dead end at a set of curving stairs. "At least in part, concerning weather and traffic conditions."

"Really? Wow. I want to hear more, but no way am I going to share that with Fred. He's having too much fun—"

"That was difficult to tell."

"He's probably one of those guys who dances inside. Besides, if I tell him, then the question's now moot, and he'd lose his federal grant. With scientific funding being cut back every day, no way would I do that to him. Even if he isn't exactly Mr. Personality."

They were halfway up the stairs when Nate stopped. "Damn, I'm dense."

"Why?"

"Because it just sank in that you're here because you learned about my theory from reading my book."

"True."

"Which I wouldn't have written if you hadn't landed here on the island and Kirby hadn't taken you home."

"Possibly true." Sebastian suspected that Nate would have eventually achieved the theory on his own.

"Well, for the sake of argument, let's say it is. Which means that we've got ourselves an actual predestination paradox time loop going on here."

"That had occurred to me," Sebastian said. "But is it temporal or causal?" Causal being unchanging and self-orientating, while in a temporal time loop, there was a possibility for change.

"Good question. And one we might not really know

until you get back to Logosia."

"In which case, you may never know the answer," Sebastian pointed out. "Unless you come forward in time and space and meet up with me."

"And wouldn't that be wicked cool?" Nate said cheerfully as he held his palm up to a plate next to a thick metal door. "I could be like Indiana Jones in space."

Despite the antiquity of the tree's decorations, Nate's laboratory turned out to be far more advanced than any other of his time. The textbooks had claimed that Nathaniel Pendleton was extraordinary, and after spending a morning listening to him explain how he'd come up with his idea of quantum physics providing the key to time travel, Sebastian was more than a little inclined to agree.

It didn't take long for them to come to the conclusions that the magnetic electrical field caused by the solar flares had undoubtedly been the cause of him going off track as he'd slid around the folds and warps of subspace that had allowed him to cut across the light-years.

While Sebastian felt perfectly comfortable with that logical hypothesis, there was something else troubling him. Something he was not prepared to share with Nate.

Because the errant thought teasing at the far reaches of his mind was that perhaps solar flares were not the only answer. What if—and this was admittedly farfetched—he'd been drawn here by Kirby? By her sensual fantasy?

The idea was too unsettling and illogical to be taken seriously. But still, as hard as he tried, Sebastian found it impossible to completely dismiss.

14

NOT FULLY BELIEVING her brother's explanation about Sebastian's strange appearance on the island, as soon as she got to her office, Kirby contacted her former partner in Venice, who'd informed her that he couldn't find any record of a Sebastian Blackthorne ever living in the city. Nor had he ever had any warrants issued on him, been fingerprinted, gotten a driver's license, bought a home, served on a jury, or voted anywhere in the state of California.

Not as surprised as she might have been, she spent the next three hours doing an exhaustive search of all sixteen Maine counties. The only people who'd gone missing over the past three days were an elderly Bangor man with Alzheimer's who'd wandered away from home while his wife and grandchildren were busy decorating the Christmas tree and a family of five from Bethel who'd headed out to cut their own tree in the White Mountains in next-door New Hampshire.

Fortunately, the elderly man had been found eating a chocolate-frosted long john at the Dunkin' Donuts not far from his home. The owner had recognized him and called the police.

The family had spent a chilly night in their SUV, which had gotten stuck when it had slid off the road, but fortunately they'd been well prepared. According to the ranger who'd found them the next morning, the mother, who'd been openly displeased with her husband, had stated that in the future they were going to cut their damn tree at one of Maine's numerous Christmas tree farms.

Kirby also went to various businesses, showing the photo around, asking if anyone had seen him.

When that drew a blank, she returned to the office, more stumped than ever. None of his belongings had shown up anywhere on the island. No one could remember seeing him before she'd discovered him on the road. And since strangers were a rarity in this remote little corner of the world, especially in winter, she was forced to conclude that he'd been mugged on the mainland, taken to the island, and dumped.

During a blizzard? When the ferry wasn't running and taking a boat across the choppy, icy waters in near-whiteout conditions could be suicidal?

But, in the event that had actually happened, who'd even attempt to pull it off? And why?

Just as was the case in California, no New England police department from Maine to Massachusetts had any outstanding warrants for a man named Sebastian Black-thorne. It was almost as if he were a ghost. Or had dropped into her life from the blue.

Kirby sipped her coffee and was drumming her fingers on the scarred wooden arms of her father's old chair, trying to sort her professional feelings for the dark, mysterious stranger from her personal ones, when the door opened on a gust of frosty wind, and her sister blew in carrying a thermal bag.

"I heard about Grandmother Pendleton's pot roast," she said, placing the bag on the wooden counter between them. Snowflakes glistened in her sleek brunette hair. "I thought you might be hungry, having gone without dinner."

"I had half a lobster roll left over from lunch."

"Well, wasn't that handy? But this is lobster mac and cheese."

"It sounds terrific." Some people might find eating the readily available Maine lobster two days in a row excessive. Kirby was not one of them.

"It is," Emily said easily. Their parents had taught them the fine art of being proud of their accomplishments without sinking to braggadocio, which was definitely not approved New England behavior. "I also have plates, utensils, and napkins."

Of course she did. Which was why *she* was running a B and B and Kirby was keeping the peace. "What else did our brother tell you?"

"Oh, you know." Emily unzipped the bag, came around the counter, cleared a space on Kirby's desk, and placed a woven red, green, and gold Christmas plaid placemat on each side. "Just this and that."

The flatware was a good stainless steel Lexington pattern from Liberty Tabletop. A perfectionist, Emily had originally intended to use the Pendleton family sterling that had been passed down from generation to generation since the late 1800s, but Kirby had argued it would probably take about a month of guest pilfering for her to be down to plastic takeout forks and knives. The fact that the company was the last to make flatware in America had won her socially conscious sister over.

"We talked about the weather." Emily placed two white plates dead center on the mats.

"As one does."

"True. And, of course, about his work."

"Which he never talks about because it's always hush-hush." Kirby went over to the counter against the wall and poured two cups of coffee from the pot she'd made right before Emily had arrived.

"Again true." The office filled with the amazing scent of three types of cheese and buttery lobster as her sister scooped the mac and cheese onto the plates. "I made enough for you to take home and freeze."

"Super." One of these days she was going to have to learn to cook, Kirby decided. Especially since nearly every restaurant in town closed down for the winter. "Thanks a bunch."

She was just thinking Nate might have actually kept the news of Sebastian to himself when Emily said, as if an afterthought, "Oh, and the naked stranger you took home last night came up over the course of the conversation."

So much for thinking her brother would treat her life with the same secrecy he did his own. "He wasn't naked." At least he hadn't been when she'd first found him, but there was no point in getting into the details of her stripping those beach jams off. "But he *is* a stranger. I've taken his photo to every business in town, along with emailing it to various police departments around the tri-state area and came up with zilch."

"Maybe he was visiting friends," Emily suggested.

"Maybe. But if you had a friend who didn't come home the night of the worst blizzard in fifty years, wouldn't you call in a missing person report?"

"I would. Unless he'd worn out his welcome."

Kirby gave her a hard look. "Ha-ha." She took a bite of the hot lunch and nearly swooned. "This is the most amazing thing ever." Even better than sex. Not that Kirby could swear to that, since it had been so long since she'd actually had sex with a partner that her memory could have faded a bit.

"Isn't it?" Emily actually preened. As was her right, considering that if she were ever a contestant on *Chopped*, she'd win, hands down. "I'm planning to serve it for a wedding rehearsal dinner party I'm hosting in the parlor."

"Since when did you become a party planner? I thought the whole idea of a B and B meant people get a bed and a breakfast. And perhaps some local tourist tips."

"That's usually the case, although some offer dinner. But although I wasn't planning to be open this month, I got a call from Connie Bratton. You remember her, right?"

"Of course." The daughter of an old New England family who'd made their fortune in whaling, then later banking, she, her parents, and bratty brother had "summered" on the island. Despite having been the first person Kirby had ever heard to use the season's name as a verb, despite her wealth and obvious privilege, Connie had been a nice, unpretentious girl.

She'd invited Kirby and Emily to her home several times for sleepovers, although she'd seemed to prefer spending time at the Pendletons' house.

"Well, she's living in Boston now. She and her fiancé— whose family has lived on Beacon Hill forever—are both stockbrokers."

"How nice for them." Kirby didn't really care that

much about the pair, but since they were keeping Emily from probing more about Sebastian, she was more than willing to keep this conversation going. "You'd think they'd want a big shindig in some fancy venue. Not that the house isn't lovely the way you've fixed it up, but—"

"You're right. To keep his parents happy, they're having a do-over full-mode Gatsby reception in the Grand Lobby of the Opera House next June. But Connie's husband-to-be was pushing for them to tie the knot before the end of the year. Something about investments and taxes and other financial stuff I honestly zoned out on when she called in a panic last week.

"One of the reasons I brought it up is that they're bringing a bit of a crowd with them. Nothing like the two hundred besties they're inviting to the June blowout, but enough to fill my place and every other B and B and motel in town. The Whale Cove Inn, which you know closes down every year after the Labor Day weekend crush, even opened up especially for the occasion."

Emily paused as she took a bite. Chewed. Then took a long drink of coffee. Making Kirby wait for her to cut to the chase. "So, the point I'm making is that, if you don't find out where your naked stranger belongs, you're going to have problems finding him a place to stay. Unless you put him in a cell."

"Not doing that," Kirby said.

"Maybe he could stay at the lab? Since he's working there?"

"That's a possibility, I suppose." Kirby felt just like that time she'd brought home a stray beagle she'd named Buster when she was six. She'd insisted that he'd followed her home from school, leaving out the part about luring him with bits of the Oreos she'd bought at the market along the way. "Can I keep him?" she'd asked her parents, who'd given in as they always had.

Her mysterious houseguest might take logic seriously. Not being nearly as rigid, Kirby wasn't having all that much trouble with the illogical desire to keep *him*.

"The thing is," she said, "the sleeping rooms at the lab are like monks' cells. I'd hate to think of him spending the holidays alone out there."

Emily arched a brow and studied Kirby over the thick rim of the white stoneware mug. "Do you actually expect the man to be on the island that long?"

"I've no idea." Kirby shrugged. "But I can't exactly throw him back into the sea like a short." A short being, in Maine fishing law, a lobster too small to keep. And she knew firsthand that there was nothing small about her mysterious house guest.

Her sister frowned, proving what Kirby had suspected all along. The lunch had been merely a ruse. Not that different from the vending machine Coke and chips she used to use to bond with bad guys so they'd confess. At least Emily's mac and cheese was far tastier.

"You don't know anything about him. He could be dangerous."

"I'm a cop who has both a Taser and a Glock and knows how to use them." Not that she'd ever had that occasion on Rum Runner Island, and she hoped she never would.

"Now you can sleep with your eyes open?"

"No. But I have good instincts that were honed by years of law enforcement. He's a nice guy, Emily. Despite being a bit too analytical and formal for my taste." Which should have been true, were it not for the fact that having experienced that tear in the steely curtain of Sebastian's self-restraint, she was dying to test it further.

"I just don't want you to end up as a *Dateline* murder victim of the week."

"Not going to happen. And, speaking of strangers in houses, I don't see you running an FBI background check whenever you take a reservation."

"That's different since my guests tend to be couples."

"So were Bonnie and Clyde."

Emily frowned. "That's not funny."

Realizing that her sister was serious, Kirby was forced to consider how she'd feel if their situations were reversed. Hadn't she worried about Emily opening up her house to total strangers when she'd come up with the idea of the B and B after having worked her way up to being Director of Hospitality at the Boston Whitfield Palace Hotel?

She stood up, went around the desk, and hugged her sister. "But I do appreciate your concern."

"Thank you. And I want to meet him."

"Given up on Tinder, have you?" It was a joke, given that Emily was the least likely woman she'd ever met to enter into the hit-it-and-quit-it Tinder hookup lifestyle.

"I'd rather run stark naked down Old Town Road at the height of the summer tourist season than join that dating apocalypse," Emily claimed with a shudder. "And no, I'm not interested *that way* in your naked stranger. I just want to check him out."

"Nate's already vouched for him."

"Like our brother would even notice if a guy looked like Charles Manson or the Unabomber so long as he was an asset to his precious lab."

"He doesn't look anything like either one of them. And Nate's not as single-focused as you'd think. He warned Sebastian against having sex with me."

Her sister's hazel eyes widened. "He did that in front of you?"

"No. While they were outside supposedly talking about lab stuff. Sebastian told me later."

Kirby opted for not telling Emily that her stranger—and yes, she was now admittedly thinking of him as *hers*—was warned against "mating" with her. It would only give her sister another reason to worry. Even without the mystery of his background and sudden appearance on the island, there was definitely something off-kilter about Sebastian Blackthorne. Then again, that could be said for their own brother. Who was absolutely harmless.

"Well, I'm glad he's watching out for you," Emily said. "But I still want to meet him. The rehearsal dinner's tonight with the wedding tomorrow. Once everyone's out of the house, I want the two of you to come to dinner."

"He might be working."

"If Nate, who can be even more clueless about real life than most men, recognized the need to give the man a warning, obviously he spotted some vibes."

Kirby decided to give up the ruse. This was her sister she was talking with. The one who'd assured her she was better off without teen boy slut Branson Smith, who'd dumped her the day of the annual Winterfest and gone with Margot Keene, who everyone in school knew put out. Emily had always had her back. As had Shelby. But her other sister was currently digging up an ancient city with a trowel and unavailable for romantic consultation.

"Or felt the earthquake," Kirby admitted.

Emily lifted that brow again. "That strong?"

"I have never, ever felt that way in my life."

"Well." Her sister stood and began gathering up the dishes. "Now I definitely need to meet him. To make sure he's good enough for you. I'll expect you both the day after tomorrow for pot roast. Six o'clock."

"If he's not working," Kirby hedged. As much as she wanted her sister's take on Sebastian, she also, conversely, wanted to keep him to herself. Bad enough she had to share him with Nate.

"Six o'clock," Emily repeated, giving Kirby a very good idea how she must've sounded when ordering staff around at the five-star hotel whose trademark, known around the world, was *When Deluxe Will No Longer Do.* "No excuses. Now, I have to run to finish arranging the flowers for tonight's dinner."

With that, she was out the door, leaving Kirby behind with a mac and cheese casserole and those same unanswered questions.

✧   ✧   ✧

FIVE HOURS LATER, still as clueless as she'd been about Sebastian earlier, Kirby was getting ready to leave the office when her cell chimed.

"Hey, sis," Nate said. "Where are you?"

"At work. For the next thirty seconds."

"Would you mind picking Sebastian up?"

"Of course not." *Hello, huge understatement.* "But I assumed you guys would be working late."

"Yeah. That was the plan. But he seems to still be suffering some lingering effects from last night. He nearly passed out on me a few minutes ago. He wants to stay, but

I really think he needs a good night's sleep."

Damn. She'd known he should've stayed home. Not that her house was his home, but how many humans could nearly die, then a few hours later be headed off to work in a place as high-intensity as she suspected the brain factory was? She would have gloated but was too concerned.

"I'll be right there. Do you think he needs to go to a hospital?" Now that the snow had let up, Mac should be able to fly.

"Not necessary. His vitals check out okay. Like I said, he just needs some bedrest." He paused. Then said carefully, "And food."

"As it happens, Emily brought extra lobster mac and cheese."

"A comfort meal," her brother said approvingly. "Perfect."

"I'm ever so glad you approve. See you in a bit."

Unfortunately, there was nothing comforting about the way Kirby's unruly girly parts began getting all tingly in anticipation on the way to the lab. "Stop that!" she scolded them. "That's not the type of bedrest Nate is prescribing."

Not that she didn't want Sebastian in her bed. But neither did she want Nate to kill the first guy in a very long time she'd even contemplated having sex with.

Her brother wouldn't really commit murder, she assured herself. Still, although those who didn't know him well might consider him absent-minded and easygoing, she'd grown up with him.

She'd seen Nate's temper. Not at anything done toward him. Insults and other bullying had simply rolled off him like water off a pelican's back. But injustice or cruelty of any kind, toward people or animals, was enough to make him retaliate with surprising force.

She'd first witnessed the power of his fury when
George Perkins, a high school sophomore, had caught her
on the way home from middle school, knocked her down,
and washed her face in the snow. When she'd come home
with tears streaming down her gravel-scraped cheeks,
thirteen-year-old Nate had pulled on his jacket, then walked
out the door, marching the two blocks to the Perkins's
house.

When George had opened the front door, Nate had
demanded to know if he'd been the one to attack Kirby.
When the bully had dared to laugh and say he'd just been
having himself some fun, Kirby—who'd followed him to
watch events unfold—had heard him say, "Well, then, let's
have a little fun of our own."

It was as if some superhero inside him had made him
larger, more dangerous, like the Incredible Hulk losing his
temper. But without turning green. He'd dragged Kirby's
nemesis down the front steps, out into the front yard,
where he'd thrown him facedown onto the snowy
driveway, knelt, and, straddling his back, shoved his face
down so deep into a drift at the edge and held it so long
Kirby had been afraid he might accidentally kill him. No
way would she allow her twin to go to prison!

She'd run over and begun pulling the back of Nate's
jacket, but he shook her off. "It's okay, Kirby," he'd
assured her as he jerked a lobster-red-faced George out of
the snow, then stood him up just long enough to throw
him back down again, this time so he landed on his butt.
Hard.

As George had struggled to stand up again, Nate had
bent down and jabbed a finger into the front of the older

boy's hoodie.

"If you ever so much as even look at any one of my sisters again, I will get a rusty hacksaw, saw off your dick, and stuff it down your damn throat."

"Like you'd really do that," George had retorted, spitting out snow and gravel. Stunned by her brother's metamorphosis, Kirby had been amazed anyone would have had the nerve to attempt to stand up to such cool, controlled rage. Which just went to show that George was not only a bully. He was stupid, too.

Nate's eyes had blazed. "Just. Try. Me."

And then, as quickly as it had started, the confrontation was over. Nate was no longer looming over the driveway like a superhuman avenger, but back to her sweet, brilliant, absent-minded brother.

"Come on, kiddo," he'd said, holding out a hand to her. "Let's go home."

He'd always been her closest sibling. But that day he'd become her hero. And her protector. Which could have proven a problem during her first marriage if she'd let it. And although she was a grown woman and knew that Nate wouldn't really saw off Sebastian's dick, she didn't really want to put it to the test.

15

ONCE AGAIN, SEBASTIAN found himself conflicted. He hadn't wanted to leave the laboratory. He'd wanted, *needed* to stay and work with Nate on the accelerator. But, on the other hand, after several hours running through programs, bringing Kirby's brother up on nearly two centuries of scientific discovery he'd not yet experienced, his head felt as if it were being attacked by Janurian storm troopers, and he was feeling as weak as a newborn. The idea of collapsing into Kirby's cloud of a bed was all too appealing.

Unfortunately, that brought up images of her lying beside him. Beneath him. On top of him. By the time her machine pulled up in front of the building, his head wasn't the only body part aching.

He watched her jump out of the vehicle and come striding toward him, looking as if she had everything and everyone on the island under control. But before she'd opened the Jeep door, he'd caught her checking her hair in the rearview mirror and smoothing some color over lips that he could have told her needed no artificial enhancement.

"You do not have to say it," he greeted her as he left

the building to meet her halfway.

"Say what?"

"That you were correct. That I should have allowed my body time to rest."

"Why should I point out what you're smart enough to have already figured out for yourself? I will say that I'm glad you agreed to come home."

Home.

Kirby Pendleton's house was not Sebastian's home. Nor was this island. Or even the planet. But that single word, reverberating in his throbbing head, caused his heart to begin to tumble in a way that had him wondering if he could possibly be having what, in this time, was known as a heart attack. That particular medical problem had been cured eighty years ago, but perhaps something about entering the Earth's atmosphere had negated any genetic advances.

"It was not exactly a unilateral decision," he admitted. "Your brother can be very persuasive."

Whenever she laughed, he heard music. Every school child had listened to the sounds terran scientists had sent out—like a bottle in a cosmic ocean on the *Voyager* spacecraft in the year 1977.

There were spoken greetings in fifty-five ancient and modern terran languages, sounds of nature, such as waves, rain, and storms, and musical selections from different cultures and eras. Sebastian's favorite, to his sister's annoyance, had been a musician named Chuck Berry's "Johnny B. Goode." But if only they'd included Kirby Pendleton's laughter, every man in all the galaxies would be racing to purchase transport tickets to Earth.

"I have to warn you about something," she said as they

crossed a covered wooden bridge.

"What's that?"

"I have this tradition."

"Traditions are a good thing." One of Logosia's most enduring traditions was the annual celebration of Truthfest. Which caused Sebastian's head to throb even more painfully when he thought of how Rosalyn planned to disrupt this year's events.

Disrupt? How about blow them sky-high?

He shouldn't have come. The only reason he'd done so now was that this solar period was the only time that all the planets in both their solar systems would be in proper alignment. And his sister had promised not to do anything drastic until he'd returned. Which he now realized could have well been a lie. He'd never known her to tell a falsehood. But then again, how did anyone really know a person? Even one you'd shared a life with?

Although he knew Nate loved his sister, he was holding back truth from Kirby. For her own protection, he'd claimed. Sebastian knew Rosalyn loved him. So wouldn't it be logical for her to do the same thing for the same reason? She wouldn't want to be responsible for him abandoning years of work. Especially since it would be another century before the alignment would occur again.

"I've always thought so," Kirby agreed, bringing his mind back to its original track. "Which is why I watch a holiday movie every night of December."

"A Christmas tradition. Like your tree."

"Precisely." Her smile, in the slanted silvery moonlight, could have lit up the entire island. "And you're in luck, Sebastian. Because tonight, not only are you getting my sister's lobster mac and cheese, if you can stay awake, you're watching *It's a Wonderful Life*. Even though, like everyone else on the planet, you've probably already watched it a gazillion times."

After the translator informed him of the meaning of gazillion, although he didn't understand why anyone would use an indeterminate number when a specific one would be preferable, he decided against questioning her.

"I don't believe I have," he said instead.

She glanced over at him, her expressive face revealing surprise. "Never?"

"Not that I remember."

"It's got to be the amnesia," she said to herself as much as to him. "Well then, you're in for a treat."

TWO HOURS LATER, after a warm bath, which, in its own way, had felt as good as the shower, and two servings of lobster mac and cheese, which Sebastian could have happily eaten for every meal for the rest of his life, he was sitting in bed, a bowl of white corn she'd exploded in the microwave on his lap, watching a movie Rosalyn had apparently missed in her search for films depicting Earthlings.

"Why is it not in color?" he asked as the words rolled onto the television screen.

"Because it's old." She tossed some corn into her mouth. "But some stories never become outdated."

He took in the black-and-white starry sky. "Is that outer space?"

"No. It's heaven. Everyone's praying for George Bailey, who's gotten himself in a mess and lost his faith."

"Who is George Bailey?"

She blew out an exasperated breath. "This is like a prologue," she said. "If you just watch without trying to analyze every moment, you'll enjoy it a lot more."

Sebastian didn't need any principles of analytic reasoning to deduce that she wanted him to shut up. So he did, content to watch the story unfold as he drank in the scent of her hair and ate the salty, buttered treat.

"Why does he tell her he'll lasso the moon?" he asked after a time.

"Because he's feeling romantic."

"I can think of better ways to show a woman you want her than that." He regretted the words as soon as he'd heard them leave his mouth. That was the problem with being anywhere near this woman's force field. His brain deserted him.

She slanted him a gaze that was both scolding and amused at the same time. "And isn't that just like a typical male."

Not having entirely lost his mind, Sebastian didn't tell her precisely how atypical he was.

"If she believes it's possible to pull down the moon with a mere rope, she'll be disappointed," he did feel the need to point out. "How is that romantic?"

"She doesn't believe he can actually lasso the moon," she said on another exhaled breath. "George has just told her that he'll give her anything she wants. That shows her that he loves her."

"Wouldn't it be simpler and lead to less possible misunderstandings if he told her outright?"

She hit a button on the control, pausing the movie. "Have you ever been in love, Sebastian?"

He thought about that for a moment. "No," he decided. "I don't believe so."

What he had with Zorana was more companionship. Yet it was nothing like this simple act of eating exploded corn kernels and watching a movie about angels in a small town that reminded him a great deal of Rum Runner Island and sharing a bed with this woman. What he'd had with his former fiancée was more duty. Which, he thought, as Kirby's foot casually brushed against his and caused his pulse to spike, was surely more logical than ephemeral, and often painful, human love.

"Neither have I," she said.

Which was a surprise, considering what Nate had told him about her having been married. Granted, he wasn't an expert on terran behavior, as Rosalyn was, yet he'd have thought this human would not have entered into a marriage if her heart hadn't been fully engaged.

"I thought I was," she continued, answering his unspoken question. "But I later realized I'd just had stardust in my eyes."

Earthlings, he was coming to realize, were very fond of metaphors, which had disappeared from his language because, when words were precise, there was no need to elaborate or explain.

"Anyway," she said, shaking off memories he wasn't about to intrude upon, no matter how curious he might be, "I'm guessing that if you'd fallen in love, you would've known it. Which, thinking about it, makes us a pitiful pair, Sebastian. You thirty-one, me twenty-nine, and neither of us have fallen in love."

"Or perhaps we're not as much pitiful as choosy," he suggested. A bright strand of hair had escaped the elastic band she'd wrapped around that ponytail. He curled it around his finger and drew her face closer to his.

She tasted exactly the way a woman should taste. And her lips felt exactly the way a woman's lips should feel—soft and warm and generous. Sebastian decided that he could drink from them forever.

When her right hand gripped the front of the flannel pajamas she'd given him to wear, he decided that once again they were sharing the same thought.

He ran kisses over her upturned face as emotion stronger than anything he'd ever felt before swelled in him.

Sebastian's first thought was that he *was* falling in love.

Which should be impossible. Every Logosian knew that the term was an outdated euphemism for something a great deal more basically biological. But even knowing that fact couldn't quite diminish the feeling that he'd come all the way through time and space specifically to meet this one very special woman.

Outside the house, the snow, illuminated by the moon, had begun to fall again, soft white flakes that drifted to earth like floating petals.

Inside, the air began to thicken and heat.

Her breast, even covered by another of those bear-faced tunics, fit so perfectly in his hand that his head, feeling as if it were filled with helium, began floating, as it had in the lab right before he'd nearly passed out and Nate had insisted he go home.

She smelled of flowers and tasted of the heaven the people of Bedford Falls had been praying to. This was every bit as good as this morning's dream. No, Sebastian thought, as she lifted her arms to fork her fingers through his hair, which pressed her warm, soft body against him, it was better.

He needed more. He wanted everything.

"This is a bad idea."

He hadn't realized he'd spoken out loud until she responded in a throaty voice that vibrated through every atom in his body. "Sometimes the best ideas are the bad ones. At least the naughty ones," she suggested.

The smile she bestowed on him was even warmer and a great deal more seductive than the one Mary had welcomed George Bailey with after she'd fixed up that ramshackle old house for their wedding night.

Both Sebastian's head and heart told him that it wasn't fair to encourage a relationship when he couldn't offer her any future. His body, as it had been doing since he'd first awakened with her in his arms, was offering up a heated argument.

"You don't know me," he said. And wasn't that the understatement of several centuries?

"And you don't know me. But you do think I'm a bad idea." The mood had changed. The undercurrent in the room was now tense and edgy. And the hurt in her eyes pained him in a way he had no words for.

"No." Panic and shame tangled his gut. All this woman had done was to show him kindness and affection, even to the point of offering herself to him, and what had he done but appeared to have rejected her. "You're wonderful. Perfect." Again, the truth.

"You said you wanted me."

As moisture glistened in her remarkable blue eyes, Sebastian was tempted to pray to that same black-and-white heaven to fix this mess he'd gotten himself into. To bring the smile back to Kirby Pendleton's eyes and lips, which, in turn, would bring the sunshine back to him.

"I did. I do." As he began to run his hands up and down her arms in a clumsy attempt to soothe, she jerked away and jumped out of bed, spilling popcorn onto the bedding, which woke the cat, who began vacuuming it up.

"Dammit, Darcy!" As if he'd turned invisible, she ignored him as she scooped up the cat, who growled in response. "You're not supposed to eat that!"

Wanting to do something, anything, to attempt to redeem himself, Sebastian gathered the scattered kernels up and put them into his own bowl. As the cat—whose hair was now standing on end as if electrified—began caterwauling in a way that threatened his eardrums, Sebastian wondered how an evening that had been going so well could have gone downhill so rapidly.

None of this emotional and noisy chaos would ever happen on Logosia.

Then again, neither would he ever have been lying in bed next to a woman who made him feel things too complex to sort out, watching what appeared to be a simplistic old-fashioned story about love and hope and family. Yet Sebastian realized the story of George and Mary and Clarence, a most unlikely angel, represented a dream life to Kirby.

A life he could never, ever give her. It would, he considered grimly, be easier to give her the moon.

"I'm sorry," he said.

She put the squirming mass of orange fur down on the floor and folded her arms. "About what?"

"That I started something I couldn't continue."

"You didn't exactly start it on your own," she pointed out. "It was totally mutual. You're just the one who blew the whistle on the play."

Sebastian had always prided himself on being a quick study. He was getting better at grasping metaphors. "Would it help to know that I didn't want to blow any whistle?"

"Then why?" Her brow furrowed and he heard her thought an instant before she spoke. "Oh. You didn't have any of your things when I found you. So you couldn't have a condom."

"No." Desperate to soothe things over, he grasped on to a possibly acceptable explanation before the translator could explain. When it did kick out the definition, he was relieved that his answer had been appropriate to the topic. "I don't."

"Neither do I. At least I don't think so. It's been a while, and even if I did find one tucked away in a purse or drawer somewhere, it'd probably be too old. I don't know what the expiration time is on them, do you?"

"No." Another honest answer. Both pregnancy planning and sexually transmitted diseases were far more easily handled with injectable implants in his time.

"Of course you don't. Any man who looks like you probably never has to worry about expiration dates…"

"Well, in case we do decide to go the full Monty, we have a problem, since by now probably everyone in town knows that I have a strange man sleeping in my house. So, if I just sauntered into the market and bought a box, I'd undoubtedly keep the gossip grist mill going until the spring thaw." She sighed heavily as she began to pace. "And we can't ask Nate."

"That would be unwise," he agreed.

"So, that leaves Emily."

"Your sister. The Martha Stewart of Maine. Who made

our very delicious dinner."

"That would be her. She was dating a lawyer from off island a few months ago. I'll ask her to share."

She appeared so pleased with herself Sebastian felt as if the snarling bear on her shirt had come to life and begun ripping away at his gut.

"There is another problem."

"And that would be?"

"I don't expect my work at the laboratory to last that long. I can't offer you the future you deserve."

She surprised him by giving him that smile he knew he'd still be remembering when he took his last breath. "Don't worry, Sebastian. I'm not asking for the moon. Or forever after. But, hey, the nights are long and dark and cold up here in this neck of the woods. I'm attracted to you, you're attracted to me, and we set off enough sparks that if we do have sex, we'll probably throw off enough heat to warm the island until after the New Year. So, the way I see it, it pays to be prepared."

"I promised your brother—"

"Who doesn't have to know. It's not as if I'm going to march into the lab and announce that you and I are screwing our brains out."

Since he knew that was physically impossible, even with the energy he felt whenever he was around her, Sebastian accepted it as another very descriptive metaphor. Still...

"I don't want to hurt you."

"Don't worry." She climbed back into bed next to him. "I'm not looking for a husband. Just some orgasms that don't involve a slippery bar of soap or batteries."

That stated, she picked up the television remote again. "Now, since I don't trust either one of us to be able to fool around without ending up going all the way, we might as well watch the rest of the movie."

Snuggling up against him, she laid her head on his shoulder. "Oh, this is where poor George is about to jump off the bridge and things really pick up."

As he watched the movie's mistaken but well-meaning concept of alternate reality, Sebastian decided that, at this moment in time, there was no other place he'd rather be.

16

THREE DAYS LATER, the policewoman in Kirby was irritated that she hadn't solved what had to have been a simple assault-and-battery case. The woman in her couldn't stop thinking of the way Sebastian's eyes darkened with sensual intent whenever he looked at her. The police chief had decided to extend her queries to New York, while the woman wondered what it would be like to lie with him in front of a roaring fire while a blizzard raged outside. Just like in that first night's dream.

Not that it appeared she would find out any time soon. Because, despite having scored half a box of condoms from Emily, despite her assurance she wasn't seeking a serious, ever-after affair, the man seemed determined to honor that damn promise to Nate.

Ever since she'd practically thrown herself at him, Sebastian had spent nearly every waking hour at the laboratory. At night, he slept on the couch, arriving home long after she had finally given up waiting for him and allowed herself to fall asleep.

Each morning, he would be dressed—in more of the clothing Nate had given him—and gone by the time she got up. And on those rare occasions they found themselves alone together, he conveniently thought of something, somewhere else, that urgently needed doing.

That he was avoiding her was more than a little obvious.

What was so distressing was exactly how badly that hurt.

"Just ask him what the hell's going on," Emily advised.

"I put my cards on the table." Along with, she belatedly realized, her heart. "I can't exactly throw an anchor rope around him and tie him to my bed."

"Kinky."

"You know I didn't mean it *that* way."

"I do. More's the pity, since you're in serious need of some hot sex."

"Like you're not?"

"It's hard to find a guy when you've grown up with every man your age on the island. Not only do you know all their flaws, you know everyone they've already slept with," her sister pointed out. "But you were lucky enough to have a likely candidate land in your lap. Or bed, to be more specific."

"If we're being specific, he landed on my road." Before she'd dragged him into her bed. "And, not only might he have suffered a head injury, he was dizzy when Nate sent him home from the lab. Maybe he wasn't thinking straight."

"Or maybe he was. The question on the table is, do you want him?"

"Yes. I really, really do."

"Then ask him. Or since you haven't brought him over for dinner yet, I'll come over to your place, wait for him to arrive home, then ask him myself."

"Spoken like a bossy big sister."

"Rank has its privileges," Emily returned. "If you—who are, may I point out, trained in the art of interrogation—aren't going to grill him, I'll just have to do it myself. In fact, the more I think about it, the more I like the idea. I could go to the lab and play bad cop, while our brother plays good cop."

"Don't you dare tell Nate!"

"I won't have to bring him into this if you just ask Sebastian what his plans are concerning your relationship."

"That's extortion. Or blackmail. Or something." Heaven help her, the man had her brain so scrambled she couldn't even remember her penal codes.

"No. It's merely a big sister watching out for her sibling."

"You and Nate do realize I'm an adult, correct?"

"Of course. But that doesn't mean that we don't all have each other's back. Let's not forget you're the one who didn't like Jerry."

"Jerry the ambulance chaser," Kirby muttered. She had disliked Emily's last boyfriend on sight. And not just because he was a lawyer, which wasn't her favorite profession. "Who turned out to be married."

A terrible, horrible, very bad thought just occurred to her. "You don't think Sebastian could have a wife back home, do you?"

"Ask him," Emily repeated. "Gotta run. I have a meeting with a contractor from the mainland who's going to turn the attic into a bridal suite."

"Good luck with that." The last time Kirby had seen the home's attic, it had been crammed with family stuff going back to her high chair and Nate's Junior Scientist

Lab Kit.

"Oh, ye of little faith," her sister shot back. "It's going to be amazing. I'm also putting in a private entrance with its own stairway. And windows that look out over the bay."

"Okay. That does sound pretty cool," Kirby allowed.

"Doesn't it? And, even better, not only did Connie's wedding inspire the idea, it's pretty much paying for the entire job."

"Even better. Have fun. And let me know if the off-island contractor turns out to be hot." Kirby would love to have their conversations revolve around her sister's love life for a change.

She'd no sooner hung up when the 911 line rang.

"Police department."

Just what she needed, Kirby thought with an inner groan as the caller reported a fight at a local tavern. A waterfront brawl.

Her deputy, Danny Mayfair, had gone to lunch, claiming a sudden hankering for Nicolette Dupree's Wednesday afternoon chowder at the Gray Gull cafe. From the way the fifty-five-year-old man blushed whenever Nicolette's name was mentioned, Kirby had the feeling that he was interested in a lot more than clam chowder.

Hating to disturb him, Kirby dialed his cell. When she didn't get an answer, she figured he must have left his phone on the front seat of the truck. Again.

That left her two choices. Since the Gray Gull was in the opposite direction of the harbor, she could waste much-needed time driving by the cafe to pick up her deputy. Or she could handle things herself.

"The day you can't handle a few drunks is the day you should hang up Dad's badge."

Making her decision, Kirby left the warmth of the police station, climbed into the Jeep, and headed toward the waterfront.

✧   ✧   ✧

SEBASTIAN AND NATE had finished running a program when Nate said, "We've worked past lunch. You must be starving."

Sebastian was surprised at how much time had flown. "I am hungry."

Nate stood up and stretched. "There's some leftover pizza in the lunchroom fridge. We can heat it up in the microwave. Unless you'd like something else."

"Pizza is fine," Sebastian said, not having any idea what he had just agreed to, but since, so far, everything on Earth—most especially some magical mixture called peanut butter—tasted wonderful, he was eager to try something new.

This was even better than wonderful, Sebastian decided ten minutes later. Although the too-hot cheese had burned the roof of his mouth, he found the combination of textures and taste to be a gastronomical delight. Sebastian was considering the logistics of taking a lifetime supply of frozen pizzas back to Logosia with him when Whitney appeared in the doorway.

"Would you gentlemen mind if I joined you?"

"Of course not," Nate said.

"I didn't want to interrupt your work." Her husky voice reminded Sebastian of the purr of a polar cat. And as she entered the room on that loose-limbed glide, he decided the feline analogy definitely fit.

"All you'd be interrupting is a discussion of the wonders of pepperoni," Nate informed her.

She glanced down at the cheese-stained cardboard box with obvious disdain. "You and your sister have the most horrendous eating habits."

Nate grinned. "I'd rather live to be eighty eating pizza than one hundred eating the Styrofoam disks you live on."

"Rice cakes are very nutritious." As Sebastian watched, she took a package down from a shelf. "Would you care for one?"

"Thank you. That would be very nice," Sebastian answered politely. How bad could it be?

A moment later, he found out exactly how bad. "It's very good," he said, chasing the dry, hard chips with a swallow of the effervescent cola Nate had introduced him to.

"And you're a liar," Whitney responded, her tone as dry as the rice cake Sebastian was having difficulty swallowing. "But a handsome one." She smiled over at Nate. "How are things going?"

"About as good as can be expected," Nate answered obliquely. "How's the Emily project coming along?"

"I was hoping for a cell split this morning, but something went wrong. Again. But I took a little walk to clear my head, and I think I've got this latest bug worked out."

"Well, good luck," Nate said.

"Thanks. At this stage in the cloning process, I'm going to need all the luck I can get." Glancing down at her watch, she sighed and said, "But since luck alone won't do it, I'd better get back to work."

She paused in the doorway. "Will you two be working late?"

From the obvious invitation in her tone, Sebastian

knew that it was not scientific curiosity that had her asking the question. He'd observed over the past three days that Whitney Reynolds and Nate Pendleton were a great deal more than mere platonic friends.

"Probably." Nate exchanged a look with Sebastian. "We have a lot to do."

"I feel like cooking tonight. And it's no fun to cook for one." Her voice had deepened once again to its throaty polar cat purr.

"Sorry, but I think I'd better take a rain check." Nate offered Whitney a conciliatory smile.

Small white tension lines appeared around her pale lips. Her eyes hardened. "Of course. Far be it from me to interfere with genius."

The word was flung at him like an epithet. Then she stalked from the room.

Nate sighed. "Women."

"She seems to care for you," Sebastian observed, even as it crossed his mind that he hadn't seen that same light of desire in Whitney's eyes that burned so brightly in Kirby's whenever she looked at him. At least when he'd been around for her to look at. He knew he was being a coward, but he felt trapped between doing what he knew was the right thing and giving into temptation.

"I thought she did, too, in the beginning," Nate agreed with a shrug. "But lately I've come to the conclusion that Whitney uses sex in the same way she climbs her stair-stepper for an hour every morning. As an exercise designed to burn off dreaded calories.

"Not that sex for sex's sake is necessarily a bad thing," he said. "But a lot of the time I get the feeling that while her body may be in bed with me, her mind's back in the nineteenth century."

"She said she was working on genetics?"

"Yeah. She's trying to clone Emily Brontë."

"Emily Brontë?" The name rang a distant bell.

"Yeah, you know, the novelist. Actually, thinking about it, you probably don't know. The woman wrote *Wuthering Heights* back in the 1800s. Whitney bought a locket at a flea market in London a few years back that turns out to have been owned by Branwell Brontë, the brother. There was a curl of dark hair in the locket that Whitney believes is Emily's. So she's determined to clone herself a new romance novelist."

"I thought, when Whitney called me Heathcliff, that the name was vaguely familiar," Sebastian said. "My mother has a copy of that novel."

"An actual copy? Bound and everything?"

"The book is a family heirloom," Sebastian said. "Although it is rather the worse for wear. My father cringed every time she read it because, although it's kept in a hermitically sealed library, such frequent use has caused more pages to fall out."

"I can imagine." Nate shook his head. "Sounds as if your mother's a romantic."

"I suppose that would describe her," Sebastian agreed.

"What about your sister? Is she a romantic, too?"

"Oh, Rosalyn is definitely nothing like our mother," Sebastian said quickly. "She inherited far more of our father's traits than I did, although she is, unfortunately, mindblind."

"Mindblind?"

"Most Logosians possess telepathy," Sebastian explained. "Especially those descended from the Ancient

Ones, as my father's house is. Unfortunately, Rosalyn did not receive that gift."

"Did you?"

"Yes, although I've been finding it increasingly difficult since I arrived here on Earth. For example, I have received what Kirby referred to as vibes from Whitney, yet I cannot determine what, exactly, she's thinking."

"That's probably just as well," Nate decided. "How about me? Can you read my mind?"

"I don't know. Logosians are taught at an early age that it is not polite to enter one's thoughts unless invited."

"So now you're invited." Nate leaned back, crossed his legs at the ankles and waited. "Give it your best shot."

Something was definitely blocking Nate's brain waves. Sebastian looked at him, baffled. "I can't." He tried again, then ran his hand through his hair, frustrated. "I don't understand."

"Perhaps it's the difference in atmosphere."

"Perhaps," Sebastian agreed, unconvinced. "This inability is decidedly unwelcome. If I were Rosalyn, I would become very frustrated to live this way."

"And she doesn't? Become frustrated?"

"Oh, no. Rosalyn would never experience frustration. She's unfailingly cool and calm along with being logical to a fault. Logical for a woman, that is," he felt obliged to add. "She does have distressingly strong feelings concerning feminine equality."

Nate laughed at that as he gathered up the paper napkins, the pizza box, and the two red-and-white cans, putting them into the proper recycling bins.

"Sounds like Kirby. It seems we've got a lot more than our work in common, Sebastian."

"More than you think," Sebastian muttered. "Both our sisters insist on pursuing work that is potentially dangerous."

"Your sister's work is dangerous?"

Sebastian sighed as he thought about his sister's secret quest. "During a recent research excursion, Rosalyn discovered a packet of documents defaming the Ancient Ones."

"Your ancestors were among the Ancient Ones," Nate recalled.

"That's true. And our history reveres them for bringing peace and reason to a savage, uncivilized planet. But Rosalyn insists that she's found a diary alleging that a vibrant, matriarchal society existed on Logosia long before the arrival of our ancestors. It also claims the Ancient Ones came not in peace but at the bequest of the husband of the Elder Mother—the planet's ruler."

"Yours certainly wouldn't be the first society to fudge when writing its history books."

"True. But if Rosalyn's documents prove legitimate, our entire system of belief and laws is based on a falsehood. The diary claims women ruled Logosia in peace and prosperity for several centuries with a vision of equality for all."

"That is a bit different from what you've told me about Logosia's past," Nate allowed.

"It gets worse. Rosalyn also has letters alleging that the Elder Mother's husband—with assistance from our ancestors—initiated a bloody purge to gain absolute control. And when it was over, to ensure that the females would not be allowed to reestablish their claim, any members of the original ruling families who weren't brutally killed were banished to the moon Gaoliana, which eventually became a penal colony for those individuals who could not adapt to the strict rules of Logosian law. A law based on logic and reason. And the unequivocal biological superiority of males."

"Wow." Nate whistled softly. "If those papers really are legitimate, your sister is sitting on a virtual powder keg."

Sebastian cursed and dragged his hand through his hair. "If anyone at the institute discovers what she is working on, she could be arrested for heresy. Or treason."

There was a long, drawn-out silence as both men considered that unpalatable possibility.

"Well," Nate said finally, "I suppose that's all the more reason to figure out how to send you home in the proper time. In case you have to break your sister out of prison."

The intended joke fell decidedly flat.

Their spirits lowered by the peril Rosalyn Vardanyian insisted on courting, Sebastian and Nate returned to the lab, where they worked for the next two hours. Sebastian was plotting new data into the computer when he stood up so quickly the chair overturned.

"What's the matter?" Nate asked, glancing up from his perusal of the lettuce-green printout.

"It's Kirby. She's in trouble."

Nate's brow furrowed. "I thought you couldn't read minds here on earth."

"I can read hers. And she needs a backup." He frowned as the ecumenical translator remained distressingly mute. "What's a *backup*?"

"Help." Nate hit a few vital keys on the computer keyboard, saving the information while locking it safely from probing eyes. Then he was on his feet, as well. "Can you see where she is?"

Sebastian closed his eyes and concentrated. The image was vague, as if he were looking through a thick cloud of fog. "There are a great many trees."

"Terrific," Nate muttered. "That could be anyplace on the island."

"And a rocky shore with a sand beach."

"At least that narrows it down a bit," Nate said. "Keep trying."

"There is an old building. It has writing on the side."

Sebastian was finding it difficult to concentrate when his heart was pounding so hard. Since he'd never experienced absolute fear, not even his first day on the island when he'd thought he was going to die out in that blinding-white blizzard, it took him a moment to recognize it.

"It reads Willow Fish Hatchery."

"Bingo." Nate grabbed his coat and headed toward the door.

"Wait," Sebastian called after him. "She is not there."

"What?"

"She passed it on the way to her destination."

"Which is?" Aggravation roughened Nate Pendleton's tone.

"There is a lighthouse. And boats. And many bright buoys bobbing in a cove."

"Those mark the lobster traps. So she's at the wharf."

"It appears so." Sebastian nodded. "There's another building. The sign says The Stewed Clam. That's where she is."

"Oh, hell," Nate muttered. "That's a harbor bar—no telling what kind of mess she's gotten herself into this time."

Sebastian remembered seeing a bunch of Janurian warriors get into an argument over an attractive Alean barmaid after imbibing too much Enos Dew. The ensuing fight had practically brought the place down.

"I will meet you there," he said, not wanting to waste the time it would take for Nate's machine to maneuver over the snow-packed roads.

He crossed his arms, focused every atom of his being on his target, and vanished from the laboratory.

17

KIRBY WAS DETERMINED not to let what had begun as a reasonably harmless fistfight escalate into a brawl. Experience had taught her that a calm word, a quiet attitude, and a low but authoritative voice could settle a situation with more efficiency than physical strength.

Even in a situation as potentially dangerous as this one. Two lobstermen were accusing another pair of raiding traps, which in this part of the country was on a par with horse stealing in the days of the Old West. The fact that all the parties involved had been drinking did not make matters any easier.

Kirby was still trying to determine the facts of the case when the door opened and an all-too-familiar face appeared in a sudden flash of light.

SEBASTIAN FELT LITERALLY drained. The brief astro-projection had left him physically exhausted, which wasn't encouraging. But he had more important things on his mind at the moment. Garnering much-needed strength, he glanced around, taking in the situation.

The waterfront tavern was much the same as the

skyport taverns in his own galaxy. The air was thick with the smell of smoke, fish, sweat, and a moldy odor that was a distinct contrast to the crisp salt air outside. The bar shelves held only the basics—whiskey, vodka, tequila, rum, and gin, from the labels. The gin bottle was dusty, suggesting that it wasn't used all that often. Peanut shells and empty beer bottles littered the tops of tables.

Neon beer lights flickered, valiantly trying to cut through the clouds of smoke pouring from an ancient wood stove in the corner. Although three bare light bulbs dangled from long cords, and a tree that was dripping its needles onto the floor was lit with colored lights, the tavern was still dim.

The silver on the back of the mirror behind the bar had worn away, cracking the faces that looked back from it. Sections of brass bar rail were worn through. Above the bar was a painting of a well-formed woman clad in thigh-high rubber boots and a yellow hat, tilted at a rakish angle atop her sleek blond head.

Four men, wearing mackinaws and watch caps, stood in the center of the room, hands curled into fists, faces twisted in anger. One man had a cut and bleeding lip, while his companion squinted through an eye surrounded by skin that was rapidly turning a bright blue. Realizing that Kirby had interrupted a brawl hit like a punch to Sebastian's gut.

He strode over to where she stood between the two pairs of men, looking very small and very vulnerable.

"What is the problem?"

"Nothing I can't handle," she said.

"None of your damn business," the man with the cut lip spat out at the same time.

"Well, whatever the problem, I'm sure we can settle it

without bloodshed," Sebastian offered, ignoring the blistering glares directed his way.

"Sebastian—" Kirby warned quietly.

"Logic can be a very useful tool," he said helpfully, ignoring her warning as he ignored the men's glares.

"Who the hell is this guy?" the lobsterman with the darkening bruise slurred.

"My name is Sebastian Blackthorne." Sebastian held out his hand. "And you are—?"

"Fed up." The taller of the two alleged poachers turned to leave, brushing Kirby aside.

The sight of that man's beefy red hand touching her shoulder made something snap inside Sebastian. Although he'd never engaged in any sort of physical violence, something dark and primal, something decidedly un-Logosian, surged hotly through his veins.

He struck out with a speed barely perceptible to the human eye. The only proof he'd moved at all was the sight of the four men crumpling to the floor unconscious, one after the other, like falling timber.

As he stood over his vanquished opponents, Sebastian tried to remember a time when he'd felt so vividly, wonderfully alive and came up blank. He flexed his fingers with decided satisfaction.

He had studied Tal-shoyna for years, appreciating the way it stressed mental, rather than physical, control over an adversary. But there was a seldom discussed darker side to the ancient martial arts method, as well—a movement that, if not carefully controlled, could break an opponent's neck quickly and cleanly.

Although there had been an instant when Sebastian had felt entirely capable of murder, he'd managed, at the last possible moment, to restrain the power surging through his fingertips.

"What the hell did you do?" Kirby turned on him, her fists on her hips.

"They'll come to in time," Sebastian assured her. She seemed angry at him. Which was, of course, impossible. She should be grateful that he'd managed to rescue her with a minimum of violence. "Although their necks will be stiff for several days."

"You had no right."

"You called for a backup."

"I did not!"

"Yes." He nodded. "You did."

There had been one moment when she'd wished that she could simply call for a backup in case things got a little sticky, the way she would have in California. But it had only been an instantaneous, fleeting mental wish.

She had no more time to think about it, because at that moment, the men awoke with ragged groans, appearing a great deal more docile than they had earlier.

Kirby was deciding what to do with them when the tavern door opened again, revealing Nate. Behind him was Danny Mayfield, looking decidedly sheepish.

"I figured you might need a little help," Nate greeted her. He glanced down at the men lying peacefully on the floor. "But I guess you and Sebastian have everything under control."

"*I* had things under control," Kirby snapped. "Before Sebastian interfered."

"*Interfered?*" His earlier satisfaction fading away like morning mist over her planet's rocky seacoast, Sebastian stared at Kirby in disbelief. He would have been no more surprised if she'd grown another head, like the aliens from planet Duality.

"Yes. Interfered." She shot him a hot, angry glare. "You're just lucky I'm not going to arrest you for obstruction of justice."

She turned to Danny. "Let's get these guys locked up so they can sleep it off. And then you and I"—she pointed at Sebastian—"are going to have a little talk. So stay the hell put until I get back."

Although he always enjoyed listening to Kirby Pendleton's musical cadence whenever she spoke, Sebastian realized that the promised conversation would be anything but pleasant.

"Well," Nate decided with false cheer, "now that everything's under control, I think I'll get back to work."

"You're afraid of your sister," Sebastian diagnosed.

"You bet your sweet ass," Nate agreed. "I've always made it a point to avoid pissed-off women packing pistols."

He patted Sebastian on the back and handed him some folded green bills. "Buy yourself some Dutch courage while you're waiting," he suggested. "And good luck. If you're still alive later this evening, I'll see you back at the lab."

With those ominous words ringing in Sebastian's ears, Nate left.

Sebastian glanced around and realized that he was still the subject of a great deal of interest. Telling himself that he didn't really need a drink to fortify his courage, that he was merely thirsty, he went over to the bar.

"What'll it be?" the bartender asked.

He nearly asked for a flagon of Sirocco ale, then, remembering where he was, just in time, he said, "I'll have what he's having." He gestured toward the fisherman sitting on the stool beside him. The amber liquid resembled ale.

"One draft beer, comin' right up," the bartender agreed. He took down a glass and pulled a lever that dispensed the brew. Foam billowed over the top of the glass, ran down the side, and went ignored. "That'll be a buck."

Having no idea of the denomination of the bills Nate had handed him, Sebastian pulled one loose from the small stack and put it on the bar, hoping it would be sufficient. The bartender scooped up the money and returned more green bills to Sebastian.

"You'd be new around these parts."

"Yes. I am." Sebastian took a tentative sip of the sparkling gold drink, felt the foam tickle his lips, then swallowed. The beer was smoother than the ale he was accustomed to drinking, more like water than a proper brew, and carried less of a kick.

"Since you know Nate Pendleton, you must be workin' out at that brain factory."

"Yes," Sebastian said noncommittally. "I am working at the laboratory." He took another drink of beer, finding that the taste was improving.

"What on?"

"Excuse me?"

"What ya workin' on? Or is it classified?"

"Yes. It is classified."

"Ayuh, I figured as much," the bartender agreed without rancor. He began wiping the bar with a damp rag. "Most of the stuff they're doin' out there is pretty hush-hush. Which is why them space alien reports didn't much surprise me."

"Space aliens?"

"Little green men," the man next to Sebastian supplied. "A whole spaceship load of them landed in the town square and hightailed it into the woods."

"The ship was this shimmering blue light," the man on the other side of Sebastian divulged. "I was drivin' home and it damned near blinded me."

"'Tweren't blue at all," the first man argued. "It was white. And shaped like a cigar."

"I heard it was silver and shaped like a flying saucer," the bartender said. He took Sebastian's empty glass without asking, filled it to overflowing again, and plucked a bill from the stack still lying on the bar.

"It was blue," the man to Sebastian's left insisted. "Filled with three-foot-tall green men with a single flashing red eye in the middle of their foreheads."

"You can't get anything right," the other man insisted. "They were seven feet tall and were wearing Reynolds Wrap."

"Now where the hell is a spaceman gonna get his hands on Reynolds Wrap?" yet another man called out from a nearby table.

For the next twenty minutes, everyone in the bar was heatedly arguing about whether the aliens were here on a peace mission to warn of impending global destruction, planning to take over Earth and enslave its population, or merely looking for brides to take home to their womanless planet.

Sebastian sat quietly, sipping his beer, waiting for Kirby, and wondering what these men would do if they knew the alien they were so enthusiastically arguing about was sitting in their midst.

"So what do you think?" the bartender asked him suddenly.

"About the aliens?"

"Ain't that what the hell we've been talking about? What do you think they're doing here?"

Sebastian shrugged. "I hadn't realized that it had been proven that such aliens even existed."

"Oh, they exist, all right," the man beside him said. "I went to one of them UFO conferences in Bangor last month and saw the proof firsthand."

"Proof?"

"Photographs. Tons of them. Why, there was this one saucer landed at this farm in New York, and after it left, the milk yield of each of the farmer's cows went from two and a half cans to only one. That was the bad news.

"But the farmer's wife had always had arthritis so bad she couldn't even hardly get out of bed. After that spaceship landed, the woman's arthritis disappeared, and she took up clogging."

"Clogging?"

"It's like square dancing."

"I see," Sebastian said politely, even though he was no more informed. "That's very interesting."

The man's bearded jaw shot up. "It's the truth."

"Well," Sebastian said, "if there *are* aliens here on Rum Runner Island, I'm sure they've come in peace."

"That's probably what the Poles said about the Germans just before World War One," one of the men muttered.

Sebastian was saved from any further discussion by Kirby's arrival. One look at her tightly set face and flashing blue eyes made him decide that perhaps *saved* was not the correct term after all.

✧   ✧   ✧

"IF YOU SAY so much as one single word to me before we get to the house, I'll toss you back out into the snow," Kirby warned him as they left the bar and headed for the Jeep.

From the barely reined fury in her tone, Sebastian decided it was not an idle threat. Not wanting to upset her further, he held his tongue and watched the dazzling scenery flash by outside the window while trying to determine what had her so obviously angry.

He understood the need for law-enforcement officials although the average Logosian was too passionless to even think about breaking the law. It would be illogical.

There were, of course, those who, like the men in the tavern, might over-imbibe in ale or other mind-altering substances. Which was when the guards would stop in. Occasionally biomental systems went awry, causing people to act in ways considered a threat to the group. But they were quickly taken away from society, and if the psychological mind-altering drugs did not solve the problem, they were deported to the moon Gaoliana, where they, and others like them, were doomed to spend the rest of their lives in exile.

Sebastian remembered when Rosalyn visited Gaoliana to study the lifestyle of its inhabitants. After returning, she'd shocked Sebastian by professing to admire the way each of the former Logosians had, on his own initiative, taken on a task suited to his individual abilities and talents.

They were, she'd claimed, surprisingly happy after

having been banished from civilization. She even considered what she'd referred to as freedom as a positive and, in many ways, more conducive to society than their own, more logically regulated one. At the time, Sebastian had not given a great deal of thought to Rosalyn's remarks. Now he was forced to wonder if perhaps his outwardly reserved sister had, at times, felt the same constraints of Logosian society as he often did.

That idea, like so many of the thoughts he'd been having lately, was a revelation.

He was given no more time to dwell on the possibility that he'd misjudged Rosalyn when they reached Kirby's cozy house.

Still surrounded by an icy aura, she left the Jeep, slamming the driver's door behind her. Sebastian followed.

They entered the house by the kitchen door. The wood stove was no longer burning, but the electric furnace kept the temperature at a comfortable seventy-four degrees. Sebastian watched as Kirby hung her jacket on the peg by the door, then crossed the room into the kitchen and filled the teakettle.

"No coffee?" he asked with a casualness designed to mask his disappointment. He'd grown quite fond of the dark, vaguely bitter brew.

"The way I'm feeling, if I have any caffeine, I'd probably start throwing those knives at your head."

He followed her gesture to the black-handled knives thrust into a piece of wood beside the stove. "By all means, have the herbal tea."

She tossed him a glare, looking as if she wished it were one of those knives. "Don't you dare patronize me."

"I wasn't patronizing you."

"Weren't you?"

The cat rose from the rug, stretched, then began noisily demanding dinner in a tone designed to shatter glass. Muttering an oath, Kirby opened a can of salmon and obliged.

"No," Sebastian said as the furry beast growled and gobbled. "I was in no way patronizing you."

She looked at him for a long time, finally deciding to take his words at face value. "Good. Because I hate being patronized."

"May I ask why you are so angry?"

"You honestly don't know?"

"If I knew, I wouldn't ask," he said with mild logic. When she didn't immediately answer, he asked, "Are you in your cycle?"

"Why is it," she muttered fiercely, "that when a woman gets angry with a man—for very good reason, mind you—he tends to blame her behavior on PMS? No, I am not *in my cycle*. Not that it's any of your damn business," she tacked on.

"Under normal conditions, that would be true," he agreed. "But it is obvious that you are angry at me. So it is only logical that I would attempt to understand your uncharacteristically foul mood by eliminating all the possible reasons."

"There you go with that damn logic again," she flared furiously. "Was it logical for you to interfere with my work?"

Sebastian was momentarily distracted by the temper blazing in her eyes. She was, he decided, the most passionate individual he'd ever met. "You were in danger."

"I was *not* in danger. I had things under control, damn

it!"

She stomped over to him, standing with her toes meeting his, and jabbed her finger into his chest. "I've already told you, Sebastian, before I came back home to the island, I'd arrested drug dealers, murderers, and rapists who were a lot meaner and a great deal deadlier than those four drunken jerks.

"I had everything and everyone under control," she repeated hotly. "So why the hell did you feel the damn need to interfere?"

Sebastian felt himself losing his own temper, a temper he'd never known he possessed. "Would you stop calling me rescuing you, *at your request*, may I point out, *interfering?*"

"I didn't ask you for anything."

"You did, in your mind. And we both know it. You needed me, Kirby Pendleton. And I came to you."

"I don't need anyone," she flared.

"That's where you're wrong. You may be a police officer, but you can't change biology."

"Now we're back to me being a woman."

"Yes. Which is not an insult. But despite all your impressive training and experience, you can't deny that you're physically the weaker gender. That being the case, it is the responsibility of the stronger sex—males—to protect you. And given that you are without a father or husband and your brother was detained at the laboratory, such duty fell to me."

"I am not anyone's effing duty!" His blatant male arrogance was infuriating to the point that Kirby's head was on the verge of exploding. "You had no right to do what you did."

"On the contrary. I had every right."

"That's what you think."

"That is what I know," he shot back heatedly. "Because against all reason, I believe I am falling in love with you, Kirby Pendleton."

18

"T HAT'S IMPOSSIBLE." THE teakettle began to whistle, its strident demand shattering the sudden quiet. Kirby dragged it off the burner.

"Would you like some tea?" she asked in a voice that was not nearly as steady as her usual one.

"I think you know what I'd like, Kirby," Sebastian said softly.

Her back was to him, but he could see her taking a deep breath and garnering strength. "I thought you said it was a bad idea."

"It is," he said. "And entirely unlike me. I am known for taking things slowly, for working out every possible consequence before I act."

"A typical scientist."

"Yes. But you are a far-from-typical woman, Kirby. Which, I believe, is why I have been responding so uncharacteristically to you these past days. Not to mention the nights. Dreams of you have invaded my mind, causing my body to ache and making sleep impossible."

"You could have fooled me." She poured the water into a mug, then dipped a tea bag into it, seeming to find vast interest in watching the liquid turn a light amber brown. "You've been ignoring me ever since I brought up the idea of having a holiday fling."

The translator had been cutting out on him more and more, but he got the gist. And knew she was wrong. Whatever was happening between them, whatever might happen, it would be nothing as simple and careless as a mere fling.

"I was trying to do the right thing. In my own way, I was attempting to keep from hurting you."

"I thought you'd changed your mind. That you didn't find me attractive anymore."

How ironic was it that by maintaining such steely restraint, as hard as it had been to stay away from her, he'd ended up making her feel unattractive? Which was the furthest thing from the truth. "It's because I found you so appealing that I forced myself to back away from a potentially harmful situation."

"Oh." Kirby appeared to consider that. "I haven't exactly been myself, either," she admitted. "I've never been one to throw myself at a man I don't even know."

"I'd hoped that was the case."

"Ah, the male ego," she murmured. "How men can continue to insist that they're the stronger sex when they possess such fragile egos is beyond me."

The reluctant smile had warmed her eyes in a way that made Sebastian decide that fighting was the last thing he wanted to do with Kirby.

As if she'd read his mind, she gave up on the tea and came to stand in front of him again. This time, instead of jabbing her finger against the front of his shirt, she pressed her palm against his chest.

"I want you," she admitted in a husky voice that curled

around him like smoke. "And although it doesn't make a lick of sense, I think I wanted you before I even met you."

He could feel the warmth of her hand against his skin beneath his shirt. Which had him wanting to feel it everywhere. "When you were fantasizing about us together on Venice Beach."

"Yes. But I've spent a lot of time these past days thinking about it, Sebastian, and I've come to the reluctant conclusion that you're right."

"About what?" There were so many threads of this conversation going on he was finding it hard to keep focused on them all while both his body and his brain were being bombarded with pheromones.

"That you probably will hurt me." She lifted her hand to his cheek. "I believe that you won't mean to," she said quickly, as if expecting him to argue. Which, in all honesty, he couldn't. "But you will."

Even if Nate hadn't explained about her generous heart, Sebastian would have realized that this was not the type of woman capable of having a brief, meaningless affair. Kirby Pendleton was a warm and caring woman. She deserved a family, with a husband who loved her as deeply as she loved him, and children they could both love.

And if he did give in to the impulses that seemed to be ruling his behavior whenever she was near and took her to bed, as she had already admitted that she, too, wanted, what future could he offer her?

None, Sebastian considered bleakly. None at all.

Even as he felt himself wavering in his commitment to return, even as he considered the logistics of remaining on Earth with Kirby Pendleton, Sebastian reminded himself of how much he had to teach his scientific community back on Logosia. What would have happened if Copernicus and all the others who followed him had kept their discoveries to themselves?

"You're right." He backed slowly away. "It is obvious that you are a forever-after kind of woman."

Regret struck him like a fist. All his life he had been brought up to be totally honest. Never had the truth hurt so much.

"As much as I would like to offer you a future, I cannot give you what you need, Kirby. What you deserve."

"Well." She bit her lip and turned away again. "A woman certainly can't accuse you of not being totally honest, Sebastian."

"It is the only way I know how to be."

As she glanced up at the bird clock, it crossed Sebastian's mind that it could be a metaphor for many of the terrans he'd met during his brief stay: strange, funny, totally illogical, and oddly appealing.

"What time do you have to be back at the brain factory?"

"Within the hour." Sebastian damned his new enemy—time. Although he knew he should be spending every waking hour in the laboratory, he wanted to savor whatever little bit of time he had left on Earth with this woman.

"So soon." She did not even try to conceal her disappointment.

"There is a great deal of work to be done, Kirby," Sebastian said quietly. "And much of it must be done before the end of the solar flares."

"Solar flares? Are you and Nate studying their effects on emotions?"

"That's one of the things we are examining."

"It would be comforting to discover they're what's making everyone, including me, behave like a road company cast of *A Midsummer Night's Dream*."

Since his mother had the play on holodisc, Sebastian was familiar with the Shakespearean sexual comedy of errors. He decided that her description was fairly accurate except for one important difference. His feelings for Kirby had not been stimulated by any magical juice from a flower. They were, unnervingly, all too real.

"The flares may prove to be responsible for many things that have happened," he agreed. "But not my feelings for you."

"Then why... Wait." She held up a hand. "Are you married?"

"Married?"

Sebastian was shocked that she'd even consider such a thing. If he were the type of self-indulgent man who could commit adultery, he definitely would have already experienced the pleasure of Kirby in bed.

"No. Of course I'm not married."

"Are you certain? After all, you still have amnesia, and it's possible—"

"I'm not married," he repeated firmly.

"Engaged?"

He'd already discovered his ability to hedge, or even to prevaricate, when necessary. But the plea in her soft blue eyes made Sebastian tell the truth when a lie would have sufficed.

"I had an agreement with a woman."

"Oh." Kirby's shoulders sagged. "Well, far be it from me to poach on another woman's territory."

"But she broke it off."

"Oh." It could have been his imagination, but Sebastian thought he saw a faint smile teasing at the corners of her lips.

He could have left it at that. Perhaps he even *should* have left it at that. But in all fairness, he couldn't. "I had hoped to change her mind."

The slight smile faded as a shadow moved across her lovely eyes. "Well. I'm sure you will. I can't imagine you not succeeding in anything you choose to do," she said flatly.

He wanted to tell Kirby that meeting her had made him question everything about his life, including Zorana. He was aching to take her in his arms and experience what he suspected would be a mindblinding experience. He wished he could stay here, with her, forever.

"My grandmother Pendleton had a saying," Kirby said quietly. "'If wishes were horses, beggars would ride.'"

How could she know he'd made a wish? Had his control slipped again, making him speak out loud? Or had she read his mind?

"It is as if we were bonded in some essential way," he said slowly. "You called for me—"

"I did not."

He waved away her protest with his hand. "You called for me," he repeated stubbornly. "And I came. And now, although everyone knows that it's impossible, you are in my mind, reading my thoughts."

"I wasn't reading your mind."

"Then how do you explain knowing what I was thinking? What I was wishing?"

"I was reading your face," Kirby said. "You have a very expressive face, Sebastian."

"I do?"

That came as a surprise. It was something he would have to work on when he returned to Logosia. Experiencing emotions was bad enough. Letting others know he was feeling them would further diminish his credibility in the scientific community.

Kirby laughed as she watched the surprise in Sebastian's eyes be replaced by first alarm, then resolve. He was so honest, this man she feared she was falling in love with. And so very different from Steven. For her former husband, lying and cheating had been much the same as breathing. He did it regularly and without any conscious thought.

"Now it is you who has the expressive face," Sebastian murmured. He traced her frowning lips with his thumb. "I hope I am not the one who caused that scowl."

His light touch was leaving sparks on her skin. Why was it that, although they both knew there was no future in this relationship, although they both continued to swear not to continue it, they couldn't seem to stop touching each other?

"No. I was thinking of someone else."

"The man who hurt you."

"I don't want to talk about Steven," she insisted. "I don't want to even think about him."

She'd let her heart rule her head once in her life. After she'd survived that debacle, she had sworn never to give her heart to another man. And here she was about to make the same mistake.

Sebastian nodded. "I can understand how such a subject could be painful to you."

"Not painful," Kirby flared. "It just makes me angrier

than hell."

The damn cuckoo clock struck the hour, the strident bird coming out of its wooden house to shatter an expectant silence that was growing more and more dangerous by the moment.

"You'd better be getting back to the brain factory."

"Yes." Sebastian's own tone was as reluctant as hers.

"Why don't you take the Jeep? I won't be going out." Since she still hadn't been able to locate any of his belongings, Nate had loaned him one of the lab snowmobiles. But the forecast was for more snow and she still worried about him.

"Thank you." He nodded. "You're very generous."

"I've been told that's my problem."

He gave her another of his long, thoughtful looks. "Perhaps," he agreed finally. "But it's also one of your more endearing charms."

He caught her chin in his fingers and kissed her, a quick, nonthreatening brush of lips that still possessed the power to weaken her knees. Appearing equally shaken, Sebastian dropped his hands to his sides and stepped back.

"Static electricity," Kirby managed to suggest through lips that burned from his touch. "The rug has a nylon backing."

"That's undoubtedly it," Sebastian agreed. "Nate will be wondering what happened to me."

"If my brother is working, an earthquake could happen right beneath his desk and unless his beloved computer fell into it, he wouldn't even notice," Kirby said dryly.

Sebastian smiled. "Rosalyn has been known to say much the same thing about me."

"Rosalyn's your sister," Kirby remembered. "The

something-anthropologist."

"Xenoanthropologist."

"That's right. I'd like to meet her. It sounds as if we have a lot in common."

"And have the two of you discussing me like a frozen slide under a microscope? I know you, Kirby Pendleton. Within five minutes of meeting Rosalyn, you would have her revealing all my secrets."

"Do you have all that many secrets, Sebastian?" Kirby asked. It was not a casual question.

Sebastian Blackthorne was not an easy man to know.

He would definitely not be an easy man to love.

"Enough," Sebastian said. "But there's no time to discuss them because I must leave."

"Sure." Damn. The walls between them had gone up again. Kirby shrugged with feigned nonchalance as she handed him the Jeep keys. "I wouldn't want to keep you and my brother from earning the Nobel Prize... Drive carefully."

"I will do my best not to crash your Jeep."

"The Rum Runner Island Council that paid for it would appreciate that," Kirby said. "Perhaps, if you finish up at a reasonable hour," she suggested, "we could have a late supper."

"I'd like that. But I don't want you to go to the trouble of cooking on my account."

She laughed. "I have no intention of putting your life at risk. I thought I might heat up a frozen pizza. And maybe I'll wait to watch tonight's movie. *Christmas in Connecticut* is a fun 1940s movie about this writer who pretends to have this perfect life and gets herself in trouble when her boss insists she cook a perfect holiday meal at the farm she doesn't really have, for him and a returning war hero. Needless to say, chaos ensues, but eventually love wins out in the end."

"Love seems to be a running theme," he observed. "As if holiday films exist as much to present an affirmation of courtship as they celebrate the season."

Despite being less than pleased that his work was taking him away again, Kirby couldn't resist smiling at the way the man always had to find a reason for everything. Including Christmas movies. In many ways, Sebastian was a great deal like her brother—startlingly brilliant, impossibly driven, yet, at the same time, possessing a warm and caring heart.

"Can't have one without a happily-ever-after," she agreed.

He bent his head and brushed his lips lightly, briefly against her smiling ones again.

Then left the house.

As she watched the Jeep disappear in the snow, as she reminded herself that not only had he not promised her a future—on the contrary, he'd been quite specific about his inability to offer her any type of long-term commitment— her unruly heart seemed determined to overrule her cautious head.

Her feelings for him had become hopelessly tangled, frustratingly complicated.

But whenever she'd try to sort them out, the bottom line was always the same. Despite every vestige of Yankee common sense she possessed, she was falling deeper in love with Sebastian Blackthorne with each passing day.

❖   ❖   ❖

"WHAT ARE YOU doing tonight?" Kirby asked the next morning as they drank their coffee and read the weekly *Rum Runner Island Yankee Observer* at the kitchen table. Although it was available online, Sebastian found sharing the old-fashioned print copy pleasantly domestic. Almost as if they were an actual couple. This week's edition was mostly local gossip, along with high school and New England Patriots' sports scores. It also had reported on the UFO sightings.

"I'm running a new program." He refrained from telling her that he and Nate had come up with a hypothesis regarding his trip home. A trip, that, if Nate's projections were correct, would be three short days away. "Why?"

"I don't know if you've heard about it, locked away for all those hours in the brain factory, but Winterfest is tonight."

"To celebrate the solstice. I believe Whitney mentioned something about that," Sebastian murmured obliquely as he got up to refill his mug. He opted against mentioning that the geneticist had invited him to accompany her to the annual festivities.

"I'll just bet she did."

Sebastian put the mug down and framed her frowning face between his palms. Her hair, backlit by the fire, resembled a coppery halo. "I should have asked you to attend the festival with me."

She looked out the window at the chattering birds who were noisily demanding their breakfast. "Don't do me any favors."

"It is you who will be doing me a favor, Kirby. I've never experienced a Winterfest." Until he'd arrived on Rum Runner Island, he'd never experienced snow or ice. "I can't think of anything I'd rather do than attend with you."

"You don't have to work late?"

"Work can wait." Sebastian could not believe he had actually said that. "I'd rather be with you."

Kirby smiled. "If we leave here by six, we'll be at the square in time for dinner. You haven't tasted anything until you've tasted a genuine Maine lobster. And not one already cooked into macaroni, but on a table with butcher paper and a hammer."

"A hammer?"

"Trust me. You'll love it."

He'd trust her with his life. Which, indeed, he already had. "Six it is."

19

I T APPEARED THAT everyone on the island had turned out for Winterfest.

Mother Nature had cooperated by bestowing a cold, clear night for the festivities. The black-velvet sky was spangled with glittering stars. The trees on Old Town Road had been sprayed with water that had frozen to a crystalline brilliance. In addition, fairy lights had been strung through the bare branches, while a towering white ice castle claiming the town square had, like the trees, been draped in tiny white lights.

"Oh!" Kirby stood, transfixed as she looked up at the tall turrets. "The guys the island council hired from Augusta to build this have had the entire square hidden behind a high fence. Even my badge wouldn't get me in to see it. But the wait was worth it. It's just like the Emerald City."

"Emeralds are green. This castle is white."

"Don't be so literal." She slapped his arm with a mittened hand. "The Emerald City is from the *Wizard of Oz*. Which I'm guessing is another movie you don't remember seeing."

"No. I don't."

"Well, we'll just have to download it. For the New Year."

Sebastian's heart froze as cold as the icy trees. He hadn't told her he wouldn't be here by the New Year. But by keeping silent, he'd committed a lie of omission. During his short time on Earth, he'd grown less and less able to remain true to the code of conduct that had been drilled into him all his life.

"Emily!" Distracted by someone across the square, Kirby didn't appear to notice his lack of response. "Come over here!"

The woman, whose dark hair skimmed the shoulders of her snowy-white coat, waved back and headed toward them. The man who'd been standing next to her came with her.

The two sisters hugged, then the other woman stood back and treated Sebastian to a long, deep look. "You'd be the mysterious Sebastian Blackthorne," she said.

"I don't know about being mysterious, but you're correct about the name. And you'd be Emily Pendleton. The Martha Stewart of Maine."

Her lips quirked at that. And her hazel eyes that were an intriguing swirl of gold, green, and brown warmed. "I wouldn't go that far."

"Your lobster mac and cheese was the best thing I've ever tasted," he said with absolute sincerity.

Apparently those were the magic words that seemed to win her over. "I like this one," she told Kirby.

"I like him, too," Kirby said, dimpling prettily as she slipped her arm through his. Then she turned her attention toward the man standing next to Emily. "Hello."

"Hi." He held out a hand toward Kirby, which was yet

more proof that Sebastian's sister knew her cultures. "I'm Noah Brewster. From Bangor. I was here inspecting the inn's attic, and Emily talked me into checking out your festival." After he'd shaken both their hands, he looked down at Kirby's pretty brunette sister. "Not that it took all that much convincing."

The vibes that Sebastian had found missing between Nate and Whitney were sparking like a downed electrical wire between the couple. He exchanged a glance with Kirby and saw that she'd noticed it, too.

"It's good to meet you," she said. "Emily was telling me all about her plans to turn the chaos of our family home's attic into a romantic bridal suite."

"She has a very strong vision in mind," he said.

Kirby laughed. "I'll just bet she does." She pulled her phone from her pocket and held it out to her sister. "Would you take a picture of us together? For my scrapbook?"

"I've never been able to get you into scrapping," her sister pointed out.

"Maybe that's because I've never had any photos that I wanted to keep," Kirby countered. When she smiled up at him, Sebastian waited for the bolt of lightning to come from the sky and turn him to cinders.

What he was about to do was unconscionable.

He'd realized, while driving through the snowy woods tonight, that he no longer cared about proving his theory right to a bunch of stuffy, closed-minded scientists. When compared to what he felt for Kirby, vindication and fame were no more than one of those lacey snowflakes that landed on his sleeve and instantly melted.

But neither could he leave his sister when she could be

in the most danger of her life. Her continual bucking of the system that had kept their planet peaceful so long, and had allowed it to prosper so well, would undoubtedly get her in serious trouble. Even deported.

And she wouldn't be the only one. If Rosalyn acted as she'd told him she planned to, with their father no longer alive to protect their mother, the two of them could be arrested as co-conspirators.

Which meant that he had no choice but to return home.

He strongly doubted Kirby would want to remember him after he'd deserted her, especially during what was obviously her favorite season of the year. But because it would have been rude and caused questions if he'd refused, he posed with her in front of the ice castle, his arm around her shoulder, while she cuddled close, as if they were any happy, carefree, *ordinary* couple on a holiday Winterfest date.

He smiled on command, but he knew it had been as stiff as he'd felt when Emily looked down at the screen, frowned, and said, "Let's try that one more time."

"I probably blinked," Kirby said. "I've never been very photogenic."

Because that idea was so ridiculous, given the images of her that he knew would be forever emblazoned in his mind, Sebastian actually laughed.

"Perfect!" Emily declared.

"Thank heavens," Kirby said beneath her breath. "She would've have kept us here all night until we managed perfection."

Knowing he was making the ultimate situation even worse, he couldn't resist bending down and brushing a kiss against her cheek. "You're perfect just as you are."

She turned her head so their lips were a whisper apart. Color that he knew had nothing to do with the icy air had turned her cheeks a deep rose. "You're prejudiced."

"Perhaps. But that doesn't stop it from being true." And then, because he couldn't resist, could *never* resist, he touched his lips to hers. And heard the click of the phone's shutter.

"Whew. You two had better come with us and get some lobstah," Emily said, exaggeratedly dropping the r as less and less islanders seemed to be doing since the days Kirby and her brother and sisters were growing up. "Before you melt the castle the council spent half the island's holiday budget on."

"It was worth it," Kirby said, slipping her mittened hand into his.

"Absolutely," he agreed. As delicious as he'd already discovered Maine's famous lobster to be, Sebastian knew the taste would never surpass the flavor of her lips.

"Would you stop looking at me like that?" she complained lightly. "We're becoming the center of attention. In another minute, everyone in town will have us headed down the aisle."

As dangerous as it was to even let his mind go there, Sebastian found that idea eminently appealing.

"Lobstah it is," he called out to Emily, echoing her local accent. "Lead the way."

They'd nearly reached the tent when Sebastian saw Nate and Whitney approaching. They were not alone.

"I'm surprised Fred Simpson is with them," he murmured.

"He seems to be dressed for an expedition to the

North Pole," she commented, taking in the layering of a
knit cap, blue furry earmuffs, and hoodie. His black down
parka looked as if he'd stuffed a pillow beneath it, and his
jeans, which came to the top of his logger boots, were so
bulky they had to be fleece-lined. "I don't remember ever
meeting him."

"Nate told me he's not very sociable," Sebastian responded as he waved back to Nate. "From the little I've
seen of him, I'd say that's an understatement. But apparently he's attracted to Whitney."

"Of course he is."

"Well, hello," the woman in question greeted them.
"Isn't this just the quaintest little festival? It's like going
back in time."

"Maybe you'll run into Emily Brontë." Kirby's tone
was tinged with snark. Sebastian had been on the receiving
end of the newly learned colloquialism from his sister
enough times to recognize it.

"And wouldn't that be fun?" Whitney said with a blindly bright, obviously fake smile. Once again her eyes
glittered like frost.

"I'm surprised to see you here," Sebastian said to Nate.
After insisting Sebastian take Kirby to the festival, her
brother had opted to stay behind to double-check some
algorithms.

"I finished up early, and since Whitney and Fred were
just leaving, I decided to come along. A lot of people get
tired of lobster, being that it's so available here, but I never
pass up a chance."

"I don't understand the appeal they have for you New
Englanders," Whitney said, wrinkling her nose in distaste.
"They always remind me of giant insects. Not to mention

the fact that they're basically a butter delivery system. I'll be able to hear your arteries clogging while you eat."

"Maybe Fred will loan you his earmuffs," Nate said cheerfully.

"I'd be happy to," Fred, who'd remained silent until now, spoke up. His words came out on little ghosts of breath that steamed up his horn-rimmed glasses.

"Thank you, Fred. That's very sweet of you." She patted his chapped cheek. "But I'm fine."

"You're better than fine," he said on what appeared to be a rush of pent-up emotion. "You remind me of Veronica. In the Archie comics," he supplied when her brow furrowed.

"Oh, of course. What fun," she repeated, then aimed a look at Kirby. "And Kirby can be Betty."

Sebastian had no idea what or who they were talking about, but he could recognize an insult when he heard one. He put his arm around Kirby's waist and smiled down at her. "Betty has always been my favorite," he said.

Whitney gave him another of those searching looks he'd grown used to receiving from her. "Well, you two have fun." She took hold of Nate's arm and began practically dragging him away. "I want to look at the castle."

"Thank you," Kirby said, as the threesome walked off.

"Thanks are not necessary. I know you can protect yourself, but I enjoy standing up for you. Who is Betty?"

"A character in a comic book series. She and Veronica both love Archie. She's the good girl and Veronica is the bad girl."

"Well, then," he said, "it seems Fred's description fit."

Apparently he'd said exactly the wrong thing, because

Kirby's jaw shot up. "I can be bad."

Totally at sea at how to get out of this conversation, Sebastian quickly backtracked. "I have no doubt you can be anything you want to be."

She laughed, diffusing the tension that had surrounded them like a force field ever since the other woman's arrival. "And isn't that exactly what you're supposed to say?"

Long tables had been set up beneath two large tents with tall heaters providing warmth. The red crustaceans, served with bowls of hot, dripping butter, more than lived up to their promise. As he cracked his apart with the supplied tools, Sebastian, who had quickly discovered the reason for the red bib Kirby had insisted he wear, wondered if Earthlings knew how fortunate they were to have such an abundance of rich and delicious foods.

The rest of the meal was a potluck with a dessert auction designed to raise much-needed funds for the local food bank that had been depleted by holiday demands. Many of the women in the town appeared to be determined to outdo each other, arriving with dishes designed to tempt the palate.

Kirby, not trusting her culinary skills, had purchased a chocolate cake from a local bakery. When she informed Sebastian that the rich concoction had been named *Better Than Sex*, he decided that such a comparison would depend upon the woman in question. From the way his body kept reacting to her kisses, he knew that no dessert could equal sex with Kirby Pendleton.

As they toured the display of ice sculptures created by citizens turned annual artists—a towering Statue of Liberty, a delicately carved fox, the ice moose, which caused Sebastian to wonder if they could possibly be that large in real life—he was treated to cups of hot spiced apple cider, crisp maple sugar cookies, and roasted chestnuts.

"I may never eat again," he said after sampling a paper bag of popcorn, which, unlike that which he'd eaten during the George Bailey movie, had been dipped in chocolate and salted caramel. While his home planet might be more advanced in some ways, this planet most definitely surpassed it not only in its variety of food but also in the way Earthlings used food to create personal connections and friendship. And, he'd come to realize, as Kirby had held out a creamy piece of rich, dark fudge for him to eat from her hand, as a way to demonstrate love.

"That's what you say now," Kirby said cheerfully. "But Emily's expecting Nate and us for Christmas dinner. She's also invited a few people who don't have anyone to celebrate with. And believe me, no one, not even Martha Stewart, puts on a Christmas feast like she does."

Christmas. Although he knew it was scientifically impossible, it felt as if the Earth's rotation had accelerated. Time had taken on wings, and every time she mentioned the future, he wished that he knew some way, *any* way, of slowing it down.

"Oh, and by the way," she added, unknowingly contributing to his guilt, "you'll be expected to wear a holiday sweater, but don't worry, Nate's got lots from previous Christmases. What do you think about a pair of stormtroopers wearing flashing red reindeer ears and noses?"

"I think that would be exceedingly ugly."

"Exactly!" Her eyes lit up like the mentioned noses. "Everyone has to wear an ugly sweater. Even perfect Emily. It's a Pendleton family tradition."

"If that's the case, stormtroopers with flashing red reindeer ears and noses sound eminently suitable."

"Then it's settled. I bought two online and am still wavering between the one with a lit-up leg lamp from *A Christmas Story* on the front and another with a smiling gingerbread cookie that reads *Let's Get Baked*. So, I guess I'll just surprise you."

Taking in Kirby's excitement about the upcoming holiday he wouldn't be here to celebrate with her, an expression Nate had muttered after Fred had blathered on about the supposed superiority of *Star Wars* over *Star Trek* during today's lunch break came to mind: Kill me now.

As she took him around, introducing him to more of the residents, it was obvious that all the members of one of the founding families were well liked. But as he, too, was welcomed to the festival, Sebastian felt a bonding, a sense of community that he had never experienced on Logosia.

A white horse clopped by, pulling behind it an old-fashioned red sleigh that reminded him of the one from last night's *Christmas in Connecticut*, where a beautiful woman had lied every bit as badly as he was lying to Kirby and still ended up with the man she loved and a perfect life. *Were it only that simple.*

"Come for a ride with me?" Kirby invited.

"Anywhere," Sebastian answered promptly.

Soon they were bundled up in the back of the sleigh, blankets wrapped tightly around them. The night was icy cold, the sky crystal clear. As the sleigh's runners clicked against the crunchy snow and the bells on the horse's harness jingled merrily, Sebastian drew her close. Kirby rested her head on his shoulder and sighed, that soft, pleased breath more eloquent than any words.

Her scent teased as they rode through the night. The ride was over all too soon. Sebastian was just about to suggest they take another when what people of this time laughingly referred to as a smartphone chimed.

This time her sigh was one of resignation. "I'd better answer it," she apologized.

Suddenly understanding how she must feel whenever he left for the lab, Sebastian bit back his frustration and forced a smile. "Of course you must."

The call was, as he'd feared, not good news. "Damn. I'll be right there."

"Another disturbance at the Stewed Clam?" Sebastian asked when she ended the call.

"Worse. Pete Olson got drunk and began arguing with his wife," she said with a deep frown. "From what I could tell, things were getting a little out of hand when the Olsons' teenage son came home and discovered that Pete had hit Eileen. According to their neighbor, who just called to report the fight, the kid pulled out a shotgun and is threatening to shoot his dad."

A hormone-driven teenage boy, even on Logosia, was capable of turbulent, unmanageable emotions. A terran teenager with a loaded weapon could be deadly.

"Let Danny take this call."

"Why?"

"Because it's dangerous."

"It's also my work. It's who I am."

"It's what you *do*," Sebastian argued. "Not who you *are*."

She gave him a long, unfathomable look. "You're wrong. Because it's both." Then she turned and headed toward the Jeep.

Sebastian followed on her heels. "I'm coming with you."

"I don't want you to."

"Too bad." Sebastian could practically feel his teeth grinding to dust. "You can try to stop me, but I have to warn you, officer, you'll have to use your weapon to do it."

She looked up at him, her gaze sweeping over his rigidly set features. "I don't have time to argue."

"Then don't."

"You have to promise not to interfere."

"Damn it, Kirby—"

"Promise."

Silently he raved his way through every Logosian curse he knew. And then he started in on a few of the more pungent outlander oaths. But, knowing that she was correct about the dangers in wasting time, he surrendered. "All right."

She gave him one more quick study, then shook her head. "Fine. Let's go."

They drove in silence through the dark, the Jeep's headlights cutting a yellow swathe through the night. There had been times when their silences had been companionable. This one was not.

In contrast to that first night, when the raging blizzard had forced her to drive him to her home with extreme caution, Kirby kept her foot on the gas pedal all the way out of town. Twice she nearly skidded on a patch of ice; twice she deftly corrected. Once again, Sebastian admired her driving skill. Which was far better than his beginner's effort. There'd been more than one occasion when he'd borrowed her Jeep, that he'd nearly crashed into a tree like poor George Bailey.

Less than five minutes later, she pulled off the main road and headed down a washboard-rough frozen dirt trail.

"I want you to stay in the Jeep," she said as she pulled up in front of a weather-beaten building.

"I only agreed not to interfere," Sebastian reminded her. "I never said I'd stay in the vehicle."

"Are you always this stubborn?" she flared.

"Always."

Muttering an oath, she flung open the driver's door, jumped down from the front seat, and began stomping through the snow. After countering with another string of archaic Logosian curses, Sebastian followed.

The scene in the modest but tidy living room was definitely not one of family harmony. A woman Sebastian judged to be in her late thirties or early forties stood beside a saggy sofa. Her sable hair was streaked with threads of gray, her thin lips, caught between her teeth, were unadorned with any flattering color. A bruise the shape of a human hand stained her cheek, darkening purple against a stark-white complexion. She looked worn and tired and scared.

In contrast, her husband's dark eyes flashed with malevolence when Kirby and Sebastian entered the house.

"Damn it, this isn't any of your business, Kirby Pendleton," Pete Olson growled.

"Sorry, Pete, but actually, it is. Being that I'm chief of police." She turned calmly to the boy, whose face—as snow white as his mother's—was blotchy with scarlet anger. "Eric, this is a very bad idea."

"The bastard hit Mom." Eric Olson was trembling so badly that the barrel of the shotgun began to shake. But he kept it pointed directly at his father. "And not for the first time."

"Damn it, it was an accident," Pete Olson insisted hotly. Not a single person in the room believed him.

"I'm going to make damn sure there aren't any more accidents." Eric's young voice, still in the process of changing, cracked.

"I understand you're upset, Eric." Kirby's voice was as calm as a tranquil sea, as smooth as glass. "I also know any mother would be proud to have such a protective son."

She paused a heartbeat of a second as the barrel of the gun lowered infinitesimally. "But think how your mother would feel if she had to spend the next twenty-five years visiting you in prison."

"I just want things to be the way they used to be," Eric complained.

"I know." Kirby started toward him. "Times have been rough on a lot of people. Especially with the additional stress of the holidays. Which is why families have to stand together now, more than ever."

"He shouldn't have fucking hit her!"

"It was an accident," Pete Olson insisted. The red flush rising from his collar proved otherwise.

"An accident," Eileen seconded her husband's assertion. Tears streaked down her cheeks, leaving black tracks.

Eric looked with disbelief at his mother. "How the hell can you stick up for him?" His shoulders sagged, his arms lowered. The barrel was now pointing at the floor. But the danger, Sebastian knew, was far from over.

"One thing I've discovered about life, Eric," Kirby advised carefully, "is that it tends to get sticky from time to time." Sebastian blew out a relieved sigh and felt his heart start to beat again as she took the shotgun from the boy.

"And sometimes it's unfair. But violence is never the answer."

"Try telling that to him," Eric blazed with a renewed flare of anger.

"That's exactly what I intend to do." Kirby turned to Sebastian. "Would you mind taking Eric for a walk to help him work off some of his excess energy while I talk with Pete and Eileen?"

"Of course." Not knowing what the hell he was supposed to say but trusting that Kirby had the matter with the parents well in hand, Sebastian threw his arm around the boy's shoulder.

"Come on, Eric," he invited. "Let's let Police Chief Pendleton do her job."

"She better damn arrest him," the teen said. If looks could kill, the one he'd shot at his father would've had Pete Olson six feet under.

As soon as they were gone, Kirby turned her not inconsiderable persuasion skills on his parents. By the time Sebastian and Eric had returned to the house twenty minutes later, Kirby's deputy, Danny, had arrived to book a subdued Pete into the island's single jail cell for the night, and both adults had agreed to begin family counseling.

Knowing their tenuous financial situation, Kirby had promised to help them with the red tape necessary to enter a program for low-income families.

"I'll check back with you and Eric tomorrow," she said to Eileen. She gave Pete a stern look as Danny led him out the door. "If the judge does let you bail out, and I'm guessing he will, I want you to stay at your brother's until after the New Year."

"I want to spend Christmas with my family."

"You gave that right up when you decided to assault your wife," Kirby said. "If I can locate a counselor willing to work on Christmas, I'll recommend a supervised visit. But if you return to this house before January and without obtaining proof of having received at least one anger-management session, I'll strongly encourage Eileen to get an order of protection. And believe me, Pete, that's just going to make things worse for all of you."

"I'm impressed," Sebastian said as they headed back down the rutted road. Kirby had stayed awhile after the husband's departure, to make certain Eileen not only had a list of emergency contact numbers but was willing to utilize them if necessary. She'd also removed both the shotgun and a deer rifle from the premises.

His quiet compliment should not have given her so much pleasure. But it did. "Thanks.

"When we arrived, I took one look at that boy's face and felt certain that there would be violence. But you managed to forestall it without even drawing your own weapon."

Her casual shrug belied the pleasure his words instilled. "That would have only created a worse problem. Contrary to what you see on television, the majority of cops would rather use their mouths than their guns. Hopefully, spending a night behind bars will be a wake-up call for Pete."

"And if it isn't?"

She squared her shoulders in a way that had become familiar. And, again, reminded Sebastian of his sister. "Then I'll handle it. I'm not allowing women to be beaten on my island."

Sebastian had not a single doubt she'd make certain of

that.

"I wanted to take you ice skating tonight," she said, changing the subject as they turned onto the main road. "But if you don't mind, I'd rather just go home."

"That sounds like a very good idea to me," he agreed. As impressed as he was with her poise during that difficult and dangerous event, she'd have to be a replicant or a cyborg not to be emotionally shaken.

"Thanks."

They drove in silence for a time as the snow began to fall again, dancing like flitterflies in the beam of the Jeep's headlights. It wasn't until she'd pulled up in front of her small house and turned the key, cutting off the engine, that she spoke again.

"When I first graduated from the police academy, I honestly believed that my job was to solve all society's problems."

"A Herculean, and highly improbable, task."

"I couldn't have put it better myself," Kirby agreed. "Anyway, eventually, I realized that life wasn't neatly black-and-white. That mostly it was varying shades of muddy gray. And that my job would be coming up with a tempo-rary solution for a long-term problem."

"I'm not certain I understand."

"Most of the problems cops encounter are started by someone or something else. And ultimately, they'll be finished by someone else. Hopefully, in the Olsons' case, a good counselor coupled with an upturn in the economy will ease some of the tension the family's been under. Meanwhile, we get the parts in between."

"The Olsons were fortunate to have you taking care of the in-between. I think you are a superior police officer,

Kirby Pendleton."

"High praise, indeed, from a professed male chauvin-
ist." Kirby rewarded him with a smile. "Perhaps there's
hope for you, after all, Sebastian."

Their eyes met. "Kirby—" Sebastian ran the back of
his hand down her cheek and felt her tremble.

"Yes."

She closed her eyes and allowed emotions too long
denied to surge through her. When she opened her eyes
again, her gaze was frank and open. "I'm tired of being
sensible. I don't want to wait any longer to make love with
you, Sebastian," she said in a voice that was as thick as
honey and as warm as a late-summer sun.

It was what he'd been wanting from the beginning.
Torn between honor and need, Sebastian hesitated. During
that fleeting vacillation, the cell rang again, shattering the
moment.

Slanting him an apologetic glance, Kirby scooped it up.
"Police department. Oh, Nate." Her tone was anything but
welcoming. "Yes, he's right here." She handed the phone
to Sebastian. "It's for you."

Frowning, Sebastian listened to Nate's excited voice.
And knew that fate had just intervened.

"He believes he's made a breakthrough," Sebastian
answered Kirby's questioning look.

That much was true. He refrained from mentioning
that someone had attempted to hack into the computer
files.

"So you need to go to the lab."

Stay. Go. He'd never been more torn.

Apparently taking pity on him, Kirby pressed her fingers against his tightly set lips. "Go to the brain factory,"

she advised. "There'll be another time."

Had there ever been a woman like this one? Sebastian wondered. "I won't be long," he promised.

"I'll be waiting."

20

THE FOLLOWING DAY dawned crisp and clear and cold. Kirby was sitting at the kitchen table, after having drunk too many cups of coffee, waiting for Sebastian to return.

He'd been gone all night. Again.

She'd called the Olson house and determined that Pete's brother had come to pick up his things after he'd, indeed, been released on bail first thing this morning. Danny had driven him to the farmhouse on the far side of the island. She was encouraged when Eileen related that her husband had sent along a letter and, according to the brother, was showing the proper amount of shame and embarrassment. Even Eric, proving the resiliency of youth, sounded back to normal.

So, that problem wasn't solved. But she had managed to put a Band-Aid on it. Hopefully until the New Year.

Frustrated by Sebastian's absence, lonely, and needing to walk off her irritation, she pulled on her hooded parka and left the house. Perhaps some exercise in the fresh air before going into the station to finish writing up her report of last night's incidence would clear her head. It was, she mused as she trod through the now-crunchy frozen snow, as if Sebastian possessed the ability to fog her mind.

She couldn't figure him out. It was obvious that he cared for her. Just as it was obvious that he'd tried very hard not to care. Kirby knew that the man she'd fallen in love with was hiding something. Although he appeared incapable of telling a lie, there was something he wasn't saying. Something important.

Determined to drive to the lab and settle matters once and for all, she called Danny at the station and told him she was taking some personal time, but to make sure he called if an emergency came up.

Then she headed back toward the house. Caught up in her tumultuous thoughts, she failed to see the figure emerge from behind a towering pine tree. Neither did she see the tree limb come crashing down on her head.

SEBASTIAN FOUND HER like that, crumpled like a dead robin in the snow. As he gathered her into his arms, for the first time in his life, he understood the sheer force of a fury that could drive a man to murder.

"Kirby."

His gloved hands moved over her face, brushing off the snow. "Please, wake up."

Her lashes were a tawny fringe against those cold-chapped cheeks. Her lips were softly parted. It was only the slow, steady breath he felt slipping between those lips that kept Sebastian from giving in to the panic he was feeling.

She wasn't dead. No thanks to him. Because although the thought was untenable, Sebastian suspected that whoever had attacked Kirby had been after his work.

"Kirby, please, you have to wake up."

Her lids fluttered open. "Sebastian?" Smiling vaguely, she lifted a hand to his face. "You came back."

"I told you I would."

Last night, damn it. He'd promised to return hours ago, but like a Haldon-headed idiot, he'd allowed himself to get immersed in Nate's mystery and had let the time slip away from him. His anger at himself for leaving Kirby alone for those long hours was steamrollered by an icy fear that if he'd lingered at the lab for only a few more minutes...

No. The thought was unpalatable. Shaking off the mental image of a lifeless Kirby, he gathered her into his arms and began carrying her back to the house.

But although the cut on her head was readily apparent, Kirby proved that her quick and agile mind had not been affected. "How did you get here?" she asked.

"How do you think? When I returned to the house and found you missing, I walked out here, looking for you." It was one of the few out-and-out lies he'd told her. In truth, when he'd seen her, in his mind's eye, lying in the snow, he'd transported himself to her side by telekinesis.

"But the only tracks in the snow are mine. Except for those," she said, pointing out another pair that disappeared into the trees. After apparently first coming up behind her. Since they were too small to belong to Sebastian, they could have only been left by her assailant.

Kirby stared around at the undisturbed snow, then up at Sebastian. He watched the confusion move over her expressive but still-too-pale face.

"I think," she said, "that it's time we had a long talk."

As he carried her back to the house, Sebastian attempted to come up with a plausible explanation and knew he'd have to tell her the truth: that he was a half-terran, half-

A PLACE IN TIME   213

Logosian space traveler who'd accidentally gotten a little off course while crossing subspace due to solar flares and landed on the wrong edge of the continent two hundred years before schedule.

Would she believe him? The chances were undoubtedly the same as her believing in those little green men who'd been reported.

"I'll put on a fresh pot of coffee," he said when they entered the house, stamping snow off his feet. "Or perhaps you should have tea, as you made for me."

"You can put me down now," she said. "And I have a feeling this is probably going to call for something stronger than coffee."

"I suspect it isn't wise to have alcohol with a head injury."

"That's what Mac, the emergency evac guy, said when I found you in the road. But I'm tempted to risk it this one time."

There was some logical, rational reason for all this, Kirby knew. All she had to do was figure it out. Perhaps, her desperate mind considered, she was merely dreaming of him. As she had every night since his mysterious arrival on the island. Eager to try anything, Kirby pinched herself. Hard.

"Why did you do that?" he asked as he set her onto her feet in the small combination entry/mudroom.

"I was hoping that I was dreaming."

"I'm afraid this is not a dream, Kirby." His deep voice was more solemn than she'd ever heard it. That, along with the regret in his eyes, frightened her.

"Yeah. I'd already come to that conclusion all by myself." Kirby went into the adjoining living room. Sebastian followed, running into her when she came to an abrupt halt.

"What's wrong?"

"It's Nate's computer. Someone's been using it." She ran her fingers over the keyboard. "You know, I thought I heard someone in here that first night you were here."

A memory flooded into his mind. He remembered knowing that Kirby was in danger and thinking that he must save her, but his rebellious, weakened body had refused to cooperate.

"You searched the room and found nothing."

"That's right." She was not as surprised as she might have once been that he knew what she'd been doing while he was supposed to be unconscious. "But finally I decided that it must have been my imagination playing tricks on me."

"Because of all the alleged spaceship sightings."

"I suppose they had something to do with it," she admitted reluctantly.

"Surely you don't think that little green men have been infiltrating themselves into Nate's top-secret study?"

"No. Of course I don't. But Nate's been real hush-hush about this project. It wouldn't surprise me to learn that someone was after it."

"That is a logical conclusion. Especially since the actual reason for Nate having called me to the lab last night was his discovery that someone had attempted to crack the security code at the lab."

"And you didn't feel the need to tell me that?"

"After the night you'd had, diffusing that problem at the Olson house, I didn't want to bring you into it," he said. "Especially since we were more likely to be able to find the potential hackers than you. Not that I mean to insult your intelligence, but—"

"No, I get it. I can manage email, the police department and website, and Facebook, but that's about the depth of my computer skills. I also understand that officially involving me in any hacking crimes might risk whatever you and Nate are doing out there becoming public record. Since I am a public servant."

"It appears whoever it was, when unable to get by the lab security system, came here in the hopes Nate's computer might be more accessible."

"Good luck with that," Kirby said. "I doubt Homeland Security's server is as secure as Nate's."

"Still, whoever was using his computer is likely the same person who hit you on the head."

"It would seem so," Kirby agreed. "And I'd call the police, but unfortunately, I *am* the police." She rubbed the back of her head where a headache was beginning to throb and was surprised when she took her hand away and saw the red stain on her fingers.

"You're bleeding!"

"It's just a flesh wound."

"You've already proven your bravery to me. There's no shame in admitting you're in pain," Sebastian said. "But we should clean it so it does not become infected."

"Good try, but I'm not going to let a little knock on the head and a break-in distract me. We need to talk."

"We will talk later. After we tend to your injury. Where is your disinfectant?"

"In the bathroom... Men," she huffed. "You're all so damn bossy."

"And women are all so frustratingly stubborn." Before

she could discern his plan, he'd scooped her up in his arms again and was marching toward the fragrant room with the flowered walls.

"Sebastian," Kirby protested, "I'm perfectly capable of walking a few feet by myself."

"You're pale. I don't want you to faint."

"That's ridiculous. I never faint." She combed frustrated hands through her hair, surprised when they came away with even more blood.

He closed the lid, then sat her down on the commode. Was it her imagination, or had the purple flowers on the wall begun to dance?

"Why, my rookie year I was on patrol with this veteran cop. He had nineteen years under his belt and was six months away from retirement when we got a call about a woman in labor stuck in traffic on the San Diego Freeway."

Kirby blinked. It wasn't her imagination, she decided. The flowers were dancing. And spinning like snowflakes in a Nor'easter. She closed her eyes.

"My partner told me to let him handle everything. But as soon as he saw the baby's head coming out, this big, strong, two-hundred-pound male passed out."

The floor beneath the commode tilted. "I ended up delivering the baby all by myself. It was a girl. Eight pounds, three ounces. They named her…"

Kirby slumped forward, and were it not for Sebastian catching her, she would have slid onto the fluffy white rug.

❖   ❖   ❖

IT WAS SUMMER. The sun was the color of rich, freshly churned butter. It warmed her face as she lay on her back in a field of purple and pink wildflowers. Her eyes were closed, and Kirby was luxuriating in the heady pleasure of a day spent doing nothing.

She heard the footfalls approaching and knew instinctively who it was.

"I've been looking for you." The deep voice was wonderfully familiar.

Because she felt so blissfully languid, it took an effort to open her eyes. And there he was, silhouetted by bright yellow rays of sunshine.

"And I've been waiting for you." She couldn't see his face, but she knew that his hair was as black as a raven's wing. And his eyes were like obsidian, only so much softer. Particularly when they looked at her.

He knelt beside her and she saw that she was right. Not questioning how or why he'd come, she lifted a hand to his beard-roughened cheek.

"I've been waiting," she repeated on a soft, breathless voice. "All of my life."

"And isn't that a wonderful coincidence?" he murmured. Taking hold of her hand, he pressed a kiss against her palm and made her flesh burn. "Since I've been searching for you all of my life."

Destiny had brought them together. And now there was no need for preliminaries. His clever hands undressed her, long, dark fingers maneuvering the buttons running down the front of her sundress with an ease she would have expected from a man who'd played the starring role in her romantic fantasies for years.

The flowered cotton dress disappeared as if by magic, leaving her clad in a peach camisole trimmed in ivory lace. "You are so lovely." He ran a slow, tantalizing finger along the lace at the bodice of the camisole, his touch burning her so she wondered why the silk and lace hadn't gone up in flames.

For some insane reason, she felt obliged to tell the truth. "I need to lose ten pounds." Fifteen, but who was counting? She was, dammit. *And hey, why don't you point out all your other flaws while you're at it?*

"You're my ideal woman." His hands skimmed over her. "Just as you are." He cupped her breast, caressing it with a tender touch that left her aching. When he brushed his thumb over her silk-clad nipple, Kirby felt a delicious tug of expectation between her thighs.

"Everywhere you have a curve, my sweet Kirby Pendleton"—his mouth dampened first the silken bodice, then the skin beneath it—"I have a hollow." Stretching out beside her, he brought her close. "See?" His lips nuzzled at her ear, her neck. "We are a perfect fit."

It was true. Her body fit against his as if it were one of two perfect parts of a puzzle.

"A perfect fit," she agreed, lifting her arms around his neck. Her body seemed gloriously light. Free. A sweet pleasure flowed through her like summer sunshine.

A soft breeze shimmied across the meadow, causing the blossoms to bob their purple heads. Hummingbirds, slender throats gleaming like emeralds, flittered here and there, gathering up fragrant nectar with their long beaks.

Just as the birds drank from the flowers, his lips were drinking from hers as if he would never get enough of her taste.

The sun seemed trapped in her skin, warming her all the way to the bone. The air swirled with the sweet scents of flowers and the salt tang of the sea. And the unmistakable scent of desire.

His arms tightened around her, fitting her to his body so tightly that even that zephyr of a sea breeze couldn't come between them. Their clothes were gone, as if seared away by the rising heat from their bodies, and as her hands explored the rippling muscles of his back, Kirby was rewarded with a low, masculine moan.

She heard her name vibrating against her breast, tasted it when he returned his mouth to hers. His chest was covered with an arrowing of crisp dark hair that rubbed against her taut, ultrasensitive nipples and made them ache.

Kirby had never felt so much a prisoner of her emotions. Never had she felt so free. Laughing softly, she pulled away from his embrace. Kneeling beside him in the bed of flowers, she moved her hands over his sun-dappled body, skimming, caressing, kneading, arousing.

She plucked a purple blossom and trailed it over his shoulders, down his chest, over his stomach. She drew it down first one hair-roughened thigh and then the other, fascinated by the way his muscles clenched beneath his dark flesh.

So much man, she considered headily. And he was hers. All hers.

They could have been the only two people in the universe. The first man and woman. Or the last.

Like Eve, she tempted.

Like Adam, he succumbed.

In that bright light of a summer day, dark secrets as old as time were revealed. There was no need to hurry. Anticipation only added to the pleasure.

And time, for this suspended moment, stood gloriously still.

Through the golden mists, she heard him say her name.

Kirby. All his feelings for her, all the love, vibrated in that single word. It sounded like a poem. Or a prayer. It sounded glorious.

"Kirby." Sebastian was running a cool cloth over her forehead, down her cheeks, across her closed lids. "Please wake up. You're frightening me."

No. Please. The dream was fading, back into the mists of her mind. Poised on the edge of fulfillment, Kirby struggled against the rising consciousness.

"Kirby." There was a low, inarticulate oath. "I'm going to call Nate."

"Why?"

"Because he's a doctor."

"No." Her fantasy disintegrated like fog over the tops of the trees, leaving her frustrated and unsatisfied. "I'm all right."

She reluctantly opened her eyes and found herself looking into Sebastian's dark gaze. She was no longer in the bathroom. Instead, she was lying on top of her grandmother Pendleton's poinsettia-pattern Christmas quilt. He was seated on the edge of the bed, concern etching lines around his eyes and carving furrows in his handsome face.

"I was dreaming about you."

Sebastian ran the back of his hand down her still-pale cheek. "I hope that explains the smile."

"It was a very good dream," she admitted. "It was summer and we were lying—"

"In a field of wildflowers. And you told me that you've been waiting for me all your life. And I told you that I'd been looking for you all my life."

"Yes."

His words should have surprised her. Only days ago,

she wouldn't have believed it possible for two people to be so in tune with each other. But that was before she'd met Sebastian.

"You were reading my mind, weren't you?"

"Yes. And I owe you an apology for that, but I find that I can't sincerely express regret. Since that was the moment when I realized it was true."

His gaze moved lovingly over her face, lingering on her lips. "I *have* been searching for you all my life. You've been the driving force behind all my years of work. It wasn't the solar flares that brought me here. It was destiny. And you."

He combed his fingers through her hair, avoiding her head wound as he sifted strands between his fingers. "Because *you* are my destiny, Kirby Pendleton."

And he was hers. It sounded so perfect. So wonderfully, magically perfect. But experience had taught Kirby that magic, while appealing, was merely cleverly staged illusion.

"If that's true, why do you look as if there's something terribly wrong? Is it that other woman? The one you were engaged to?"

"No. Yes." Frustrated by the circumstances, Sebastian stood up and began to pace. "Zorana's part of it," he admitted. "But not the way you think. It's just that, in a very real way, she represents where I've come from. Who I am."

"I think it's time you tell me the whole story," Kirby suggested with a great deal more calm than she was feeling.

"You're right. I owe you the truth. All of it." Being an honorable man didn't stop him from looking less than eager to get into the nitty gritty of his story. "But we still have to wash that cut," he said. "Also, I should telephone Nate and warn him that he's in possible danger. And then,

I'll tell you the truth about who I am. And what brought me here."

He looked as if he'd rather be used as lobster bait. Not encouraging. "Is it that bad?" she asked.

"I suppose that depends on your point of view."

He returned to the bathroom long enough to retrieve a damp cloth, a packet of sterile gauze, tape, and alcohol wipes.

"You're right about it only being a flesh wound," he agreed as he used the rag to wash around the cut. "The blood has already begun to congeal, and I don't see any splinters from the tree limb in the cut."

"I told you. I'm a professional. I've seen a lot worse injuries than this," she said distractedly, worried yet again about what secrets Sebastian was hiding.

"I'm trying not to think what you might have experienced as a detective third class," he muttered as he swiped an alcohol wipe over the area he'd washed. "Not because I don't believe you capable, but calling me sexist until the end of time will not stop me from being sanguine about the dangers you must have faced. Nor being concerned that someone tried to kill you."

"I've got a hard head," she said absently as she wondered what a man who was seemingly so rigidly honest could be hiding.

Kirby remembered feeling like this before. When she was six years old and the summer carnival had come to the island and Nate had talked her into going to the fun house, which hadn't been any fun at all. Her nerves battering away inside her, she'd gingerly made her way through the dark and narrow hallways, waiting for some unknown monster to pop out of the shadows.

That was when she'd discovered that the monsters you can't see are more frightening than any monster you might have to face.

"I've already discovered the hardness of your head myself." His dry tone suggested he was not talking about her skull. "There. All done."

"You have a very gentle touch." And didn't she want those hands on her? Everywhere.

"Your mind was so far away I doubt if you would have felt me attacking you with a hammer and chainsaw," he said mildly.

He left the room again. She heard brief snatches of a conversation she assumed was with her brother. He returned a moment later.

"Nate is concerned about you," he related. "I assured him that you were as well as can be expected, under the circumstances. I promised that I would not leave you alone. He's going to contact your deputy and tell him that you're taking medical leave for the next two days."

"That's ridiculous. I'll be fine."

"I seem to recall telling you the same thing. Before your brother had to send me home from the lab because I hadn't heeded your advice to stay in bed after a head wound."

"I hate having my own words thrown back at me," she complained.

"Which is only logical…" Sebastian took a deep breath before adding, "I also informed Nate that I was going to tell you the truth about my mission."

"Nate knows?"

"Everything. He cautioned me against telling you, then, when he realized I could not be dissuaded, wished me luck." After reclaiming his spot beside her on the bed, he sat for a long, silent time, as if seeking the words to explain the unexplainable.

"I don't really know how to start," he confessed.

"Why not at the beginning?"

He laughed at that, but the sound held little humor. "The beginning," he mused. "All right...

"It all began," Sebastian started slowly, carefully, "in a galaxy, far, far away."

21

"I DON'T BELIEVE it." Kirby stared up at Sebastian, her eyes wide, her headache forgotten during the telling of his outrageous tale.

"I can understand how it might be difficult to believe such a story," Sebastian allowed. "But it is true."

"You actually expect me to believe that you're an alien, come here from another planet."

"Logosia," he agreed. "But since my mother is an Earthling, I suppose that only makes me half-alien. And although genetically Earthlings and Logosians are nearly identical, terran physical genes usually prove dominant, so my body is human."

"You've no idea what a relief that is," Kirby said dryly.

She rubbed her arms with her hands to ward off the sudden chill caused by his calm words, his honest gaze. If she didn't know better, she'd think he was actually telling the truth.

The problem was that Sebastian truly seemed to believe he was some kind of intergalactic space traveler.

"Let's go."

When she would have left the bed, Sebastian stopped her by putting a broad hand on each shoulder. "Go?

Where?"

"To the mainland."

"I thought the ferry wasn't operating."

"That was during the blizzard. It might be back in service now." Though, she considered, with only one round trip a day in winter, they already would have missed it. "But I'm the police. I'll commandeer Wiley Palmer's lobster boat."

"Why would you wish to go to the mainland?"

"We need to get you to the hospital. You obviously suffered a more serious head injury than we thought that day I found you lying on the road."

"My head is fine, Kirby."

"Sebastian, listen to me." Her eyes widened, imploring him to reason. "What you're suggesting simply isn't possible."

"Not in this century," he agreed. "But it will be. At least on Logosia."

"Logosia." She combed a trembling hand through her hair, ruffling the strands in a way that made Sebastian long to reach out and smooth them back again. "I've never heard of a planet called Logosia."

"I explained that," he said patiently. "It's in another galaxy."

"Far, far away. I know. And you're a member of the ruling family, descended down from the Ancient Ones, who wrote a book of laws based on the ideals of truth and reason."

"That is true."

"Right. And your sister's a xenoanthropologist, while you're an astrophysicist, and you've been experimenting with ways to travel without a spaceship using antimatter, astro-projection, and some kind of quantum physics you discovered in a book Nate still hasn't written."

"That is also correct."

"And somehow, you managed to lock on to my thoughts and beam down, just like *Star Trek*. But the solar flares warped time, so you ended up nearly two hundred years before you'd planned to arrive."

"Exactly." He'd known she was intelligent, but he hadn't expected her to grasp the logistics so quickly.

"That does it. We are definitely taking you to the hospital."

"And risk them putting me in the psycho wing?"

"You were reading my mind again."

"I'm sorry. But it was a very strong thought."

"And a very serious problem. Because you're obviously hallucinating."

"I swear to you I'm not."

"If you're hallucinating, you wouldn't necessarily know it. You've must have suffered a serious head injury, Sebastian. You don't know what you're saying."

"I assure you, Kirby, my mind is crystal clear."

"If you really are from Logosia, two hundred years in the future, how do you explain knowing about *Star Trek*?"

"Those films are classics," Sebastian argued. "Rosalyn has all eighty-six of the movies on holodisc in her library."

"There are actually eighty-six *Star Trek* movies?"

"They were making number eighty-seven when I left Logosia," Sebastian divulged. "The plot was carefully guarded, but there are rumors that the crew is getting a new ship."

"Which wouldn't be necessary if they didn't keep destroying it," Kirby muttered.

"We agree yet again. The Logosian Council of Arts declared the films illogical, with flawed science wrapped in a dangerous diversity social message, and banned their distribution on my planet more than fifty years ago. However, a hard-core group of fans, such as my sister, remains. So Federation traders smuggle them past customs to supply a very efficient black market."

"Eighty-six," Kirby repeated softly. "Nate would be in seventh heaven. The week before *Star Trek Beyond* came out, he went to a Star Trek film festival in Portland that showed all the previous eleven movies in a row. People camped out for days for the best seats."

She waved that idea off and shook her head. Then flinched at what he knew to be pain. "This is ridiculous. You almost had me believing you."

"I have not lied to you, Kirby."

"Prove it."

He had never met a stubborner woman. Except, perhaps, Sebastian considered, his sister. For all Rosalyn's quiet poise, she could prove frustratingly intransigent at the most inconvenient times. Such as her discomfiting search for those ancient, heretical diaries. And of course there had been that time when Zoltar Flavius, ambassador to Galactia and a man twice Rosalyn's age, asked their father for her hand in marriage.

At the coaxing of his terran wife, Xanthus Vardanyian had agreed to permit Rosalyn to select her own life-mate. Which proved a disastrous political mistake when his sister refused to even consider a marriage contract with the powerful, wealthy ambassador, who, like Xanthus himself, was descended from the Ancient Ones.

News of Rosalyn's refusal had spread throughout Logosia, as well as the rest of the galaxy, like flashfire. Since women were not empowered to choose their own destiny, such freedom was considered abhorrent by old-line conservatives and vastly encouraging by proponents of female rights.

Unfortunately, Rosalyn's freedom of choice had proven to be Zoltar Flavius's public humiliation. A powerful man with a temper that was decidedly un-Logosian, he'd effectively gotten Xanthus Vardanyian removed from the governing body of city-states. Sebastian had suspected that his father's forced retirement had been the cause of his fatal heart failure.

Once he'd finished with her father, Zoltar had directed his fury toward Rosalyn. But before he could succeed in getting her dismissed from the institute, on the way back to Galactia, his space pod had been hit by a meteor shower, effectively putting an end to both the ambassador's life and his plan for vengeance.

"I'm waiting," Kirby's voice broke into his thoughts.

"Oh. Yes." Deciding to use the same method of proof that had won Nate over, Sebastian concentrated on sending his atoms across the room.

Something was definitely wrong. Try as he might, he couldn't generate sufficient energy.

"Oh, my God!" Kirby stared at the sparkling pieces of matter hovering above the very spot where Sebastian had been standing only a moment before. "I don't believe it!"

"Neither do I." Sebastian ceased trying and pulled himself together. Sweat glistened on his brow, above his upper lip. His shirt was drenched. "Even a fourth-level Logosian should be able to project himself across such a small space. But I find it impossible." He rubbed his temples, where his blood was pounding. "This is most disturbing."

"Is that how you reached me out in the forest without leaving footprints?"

"Yes. But at the time I did not have so much trouble." He crossed his arms and pondered that for a moment. "I don't understand."

Since he often thought better while moving, he began to pace. "Perhaps it was the adrenaline when we were in the forest," he mused. "I was aware that someone was trying to hurt you. I also knew that I had to move quickly."

"Adrenaline can give people an amazing rush," Kirby agreed. "I've read of cases where one-hundred-pound mothers have lifted cars off their children."

"I believe that must be the answer," Sebastian decided absently.

A terrible thought was teasing at the back of his mind. If he couldn't manage to project himself across the room, how was he ever going to return home? Even with the assistance of the accelerator and the transporter he and Nate had finally completed last night, he needed his skills operating at top speed.

"You really are from another planet, aren't you?"

"As I told you I was."

"You took your sweet time telling me," she complained. "All this time, I'd written all those UFO sightings off as hysteria, perhaps caused by the solar flares. But the proof was right here, in my home, in my *bed*."

"Yes. But I am not three feet tall or green-complected. Nor am I dressed in Reynolds Wrap." He paused to ask the question he'd been considering since that tavern incident. "What *is* Reynolds Wrap?"

"It's tin foil. You know, shiny and silver. We use it to wrap leftovers in."

"Ah. Tinanium sheets." Sebastian nodded. "My mother's cook does the same. But she often forgets to label them, making what's inside the packages a mystery."

"That happens on earth, too."

A significant little silence settled over them.

"Sebastian?"

"Yes?"

She was looking up at him, helpless fascination mingled with longing. "I can see that you're not green, or silver, and you don't have a face like a vacuum cleaner hose, but you said you were only half-Logosian, and your body, like your mother's, is completely human. Does that mean…"

Color flooded her face as her voice tailed off. "Never mind." Suffused with embarrassment, she turned away.

He didn't need to read her mind to know what she was thinking. The feminine invitation had been gleaming in her soft blue eyes.

Slowly, deliberately, Sebastian crossed the room on foot and reclaimed his place on the edge of the bed. "Are you asking if I make love like the men you're accustomed to mating with?"

"Yes. Though that isn't the word we tend to use on earth. You might want to try sleeping."

"Sleeping is not what I have in mind at the moment."

"It's an idiom."

"Ah. Well, then, yes. We are, once again, on the same thought plane."

"Well?" She looked up at him, silent, questioning.

"I don't know what kind of man you're accustomed to," he reminded her. "So, I suppose there's only one way to find out."

Her lips curved into a soft smile. "I was rather hoping that you'd come to that conclusion."

He was being unfair to her. Sebastian wanted her, with every fiber of his being. And even more remarkable was the knowledge that he loved Kirby Pendleton even more than he wanted her.

But he couldn't stay. And he couldn't take her with him. So where did that leave them?

Nowhere, Sebastian acknowledged grimly. Nowhere at all.

"Kirby." His voice was a rasp of agony. "I don't want to lie to you. Even if we share our bodies, this cannot go anywhere."

"Too late," she answered on a short, shaky laugh that was every bit as unsteady as her pulse. "It already has."

Wrapping her arms around his neck, she pulled him down to her and pressed her mouth against his. Hard.

22

SEBASTIAN WANTED TO take things slowly. Carefully. And not just for her but for himself, as well. He wanted to savor the moment, to create a memory that would unite them through the light-years that would soon separate them.

Her lips were soft and trembling but avid and mobile beneath his. And so, so sweet.

Scents. Remarkably, love had scents. They rose from her warming flesh, surrounding him in a dense, fragrant cloud. He breathed in the intoxicating scent of her hair and knew that he'd never see flowers again without thinking of this woman.

Tastes. Amazingly, love had tastes. The honey taste of her lips, the sweet, moist, sunshine taste of her warming flesh. These and countless other seductive flavors lingered on his tongue, spun in his head.

Feelings bombarded him. Emotions too numerous to catalogue rushed over him, until he felt as if he were drowning in them.

"I've been dreaming of this," she whispered as she slipped her hands beneath his sweater and ran them over his back. "I've been dreaming of you." She pressed her lips against his neck. "Wonderful, fanciful, lovely dreams."

Her breathless admission excited him. Tangling his hands in her hair, he kissed her hard and long. Need poured out of him and into her. Love flowed out of her and into him.

Beneath him, Kirby's body was soft and pliant, but he could feel the strength there, as well. Kirby Pendleton was forged steel wrapped in shimmering folds of silk. Sebastian found the combination impossible to resist.

For fifteen of his thirty-one years, Sebastian had always regarded the taking off of one's clothes as little more than a prelude to Logosian style intercourse. But now, as he pulled her blue uniform shirt loose and began to unfasten it, one button at a time, he realized that undressing Kirby was every bit as sensual an experience as the heady taste of her kisses.

With fingers he wished were steadier, he maneuvered each button through the hole, then folded back the material slowly, tenderly. He smiled when he saw she was wearing the peach confection she'd worn in her erotic dream.

"You can't tell me this is regulation for members of the Rum Runner Island police force." As he'd done in the dream, he ran his finger over the lace trimming the bodice.

"No." Kirby sucked in a deep breath as the light touch left a shimmering trail of heat. "It's not."

"Good." He lowered his head and pressed his open mouth against her breast, dampening the silk in a slow, sensual way that caused a corresponding dampness between her legs. "I like knowing that there's a sexy, feminine part of you that you keep hidden away." When his teeth closed, taking a nip of silk and nipple, Kirby moaned and moved against him. "I enjoy being the man to discover your private secrets."

The fire was building. Utilizing every atom of his hard-learned self-control, Sebastian banked it. For now.

He released the buttons on the cuffs of her shirt. Her body arched as he drew it away. And then his hands moved to her belt. A man's belt, Sebastian thought, smiling at her thinking she could possibly ever conceal so much vibrant femininity with these stiff masculine trappings.

The belt gone, he unfastened the wool pants and drew them slowly over her stomach, her hips, down her legs, inch by maddening inch, following the path with his mouth.

Her wool socks followed. When he lifted her legs, one at a time, placing a sizzling kiss against the arch of each slender foot, she gasped.

He whisked the peach top away.

"I knew it," he murmured against her mouth as his hands fondled her breasts. Just as he'd done in their shared dream that first night together.

"Knew what?" she said on a ragged moan.

"That your skin would be even softer than that silk."

And then his mouth was everywhere, creating heat and flames wherever it lingered. On her breasts, her thighs, the back of her knee, the beauty mark at the base of her spine, her shoulders. And even as Kirby waited for Sebastian to take, he continued to give.

She had dreamed of this. For years. But never, in all her fantasies, could she have imagined such raw hunger. Such burning need.

The heat was unbearable. She writhed on the flowered sheets. Her body became slick with sweat. She begged

Sebastian over and over again, in word and in desperate action, to end this torment, but still he continued, driving her higher with only his mouth and his clever, wicked hands.

Dreams became reality, secret fantasies fulfilled.

Her hands clawed at the sheets as she tossed her head back and forth, aching for him.

"Sebastian." His name came out on a ragged plea when his teeth nipped the delicate skin at the insides of her thighs, but there was no pain. Only more need.

"Not yet." His tongue soothed the flesh his teeth had marked. "I want you to remember this." His breath was a hot sirocco, wafting over what had become the wet, warm center of her world. Universe. Galaxy. "I want you to remember me."

"How could I ever forget you?" she gasped as his mouth moved to that nub of exquisitely sensitive flesh. "Or this?"

She arched against him, bowstring taut, offering, begging, challenging as, with only his mouth, he took her to the very edge of reason. Then beyond.

Shards of light and heat arced from that sensitive core, shooting outward like a comet, throughout her body in a surge of shimmering golden release.

He held her, waiting for her trembling to cease. And when it finally did, he stood up and stripped off his jeans, briefs, and sweater.

Kirby gazed up at him, taking in the breadth of his wide shoulders, the muscular torso covered by a dark arrowing of hair, his strong, dark legs, and realized that while he might be half-Logosian, he certainly looked all human male. And a very aroused one at that.

"Do you know how long I've waited for this?" he asked as he returned to the bed and drew her against him. "How long I've been waiting to lie with you like this?"

"All of a week?"

He heard the faint edge of regret creep into her tone and did his best to kiss it away. "All of my life," he corrected after they'd come up for air.

After reaching into her bedside table drawer, she pulled out one of the condoms Emily had given her. But before she put it on him, she pressed a kiss against the knobby tip, gathering in the moisture that had collected there with her tongue. When she would have done more, taken him deeper, he forked his hands through her hair and pulled her back.

"Not yet," he managed on a mouth that had gone as dry as the Saltakam plains. "I would never last."

"Next round," she suggested with a slow, dangerously erotic smile. He'd had to grit his teeth to keep from exploding as her clever hands rolled the latex deftly over his length.

Then he dragged her down onto the bed, his fingers digging into her waist as he pulled her on top of him. Hot skin against hot skin.

Slipping his hand between them, he stroked her still-ultrasensitive flesh. Kirby had never enjoyed being touched so shortly after climaxing, but his wicked clever fingers were teaching her that there was a razor-thin line between pain and pleasure. *More.*

He slipped one finger into her. "You're so warm." Another. "And wet." The wonder in his voice made her feel like the sexiest, most desirable woman on the planet. On both their planets, she thought, with a wonder of her own.

"For you," she said. He was the only man who'd ever made her feel this way. The only man she'd ever feel this way with.

Kirby splayed her fingers against his chest and met his smoldering gaze as she began to move slowly, gliding up and down, loving the feel of him inside her. Loving him.

Excitement began to rise, even higher and hotter than before. She tilted her head back, closed her eyes, and pressed her knees against his hips as she began to move in a rhythm as old as the forces that had formed both their universes.

The hunger, the *need* for her was in his blood like a drug, and Sebastian realized, with a sudden, blinding clarity, he could search all the galaxies through several lifetimes and never meet another woman so perfectly matched, both mentally and physically, to him as Kirby Pendleton.

To Sebastian, making love to Kirby was like being given a glimpse into a forbidden secret world. The idea of living the remainder of his days without her was unfathomable. But what choice did he have?

Before he could come up with a solution, logic disintegrated, reason dissolved, and there was only now. Only this mind-shattering feeling of absolute, amazing abandon.

Sebastian's first thought was that he was dying. The second and more powerful thought was that he had found the mythical heaven so many Earthlings believed in.

His last coherent thought was that he never would have imagined it possible to experience triumph and defeat at the same time.

✧   ✧   ✧

KIRBY LAY STEEPED in sensation, the blood pounding in her veins, her limbs as limp as wet spaghetti, as a series of aftershocks quaked through her body. She'd never been so attuned with anyone as she'd been when she'd felt his blood pounding inside of her with the same strength and rhythm of her own. They had, mind, body, and soul, *completely*, been one.

"I never knew," she murmured, as Sebastian returned from the bathroom after taking care of the condom. And didn't she need to write her sister a thank you note for her condom generosity?

"I know."

She feigned a pout at his blatant masculine pride. "Once again I'm fascinated at how the male ego manages to transcend normal realms of time and space."

"This has nothing to do with ego," Sebastian argued. "Male or otherwise." Joining her on the bed again, he ran his palm up the back of her leg, over her rounded butt, to the base of her spine. "I knew what you were thinking, my love, because I happened to be thinking exactly the same thing."

"Oh." She rather liked the idea that what they'd just shared was as important to him as it had been to her.

"I experienced my first sexual encounter on my name day," Sebastian explained, "when I turned sixteen. But lovemaking on Logosia is not the same as it is here on Earth."

She had to ask. "Is it better?"

She could feel his deep, rich chuckle against her breasts. "I always considered it quite satisfying," he allowed. "For a purely mental experience. I have recently discovered that there is much to be said for human physicality."

"You've never made physical love before?"

"No. At least not with a partner," he clarified, needing to be totally truthful after she'd been so honest in sharing her body with him. "Logosians are taught that they're too superior to mate as the populations of lesser groups continue to do. Adolescents are taught at an early age that it is selfish, unseemly, and fails to contribute to the group."

"Yet your population continues."

"Those the elders choose to reproduce use much the same method of artificial insemination as you do. Then the fertilized cells are implanted in surrogates or replicants."

"Replicants? Like in *Blade Runner*?" Nate had made her watch it with him back when she'd been in middle school, and she'd found the humanoids in the movie even scarier than any of the *Halloween* franchise films.

"In a way. Yet their life span is much longer than that of thirty years in the movie, and they're allowed, in rare instances, to form pair bonds of their own."

"That all sounds very depressing." Kirby felt a bit of the postcoital glow fading.

"I never gave it a great deal of thought, because that's how life was. *Is*," he said, as if to remind them both that this was not his home and he'd be returning once he and Nate were finished with their work.

"If you don't have physical sex, then how do you…"

She looked away, unreasonably embarrassed at the question, which was ridiculous, Kirby told herself, since she and Sebastian had been as intimate as two people could be.

"Know what to do?"

"Yes."

He ran his hand lazily down her body, from her shoulder to her thigh. "I merely followed my instincts."

"Your instincts are very good." Better than good. They were mind-shattering.

"Ah, but you provided all the inspiration."

His deep voice, rough with emotion, curled around her like a warm woolen blanket. She looked up at him, her heart in her eyes. "I love you, Sebastian."

"And I love you, Kirby Pendleton." He looked down at her, his gaze as sober as she'd ever seen it. "With my entire human body. And every atom of my Logosian mind."

She heard the regret in his voice, read it in his eyes. "But it doesn't change anything, does it? Not really."

"No."

He'd tried to warn her. Tried to warn himself. But the chemistry between them, as well as the never-before-experienced emotional bond, had been too strong from the beginning.

He framed her sweet, heartbreakingly sad face with his hands. "I wish I could say it did. But it doesn't."

Then he took her hand and lifted it to his lips, his eyes on hers as he kissed her fingers, one at a time. "I have to return home, Kirby. I have my work, my family, my life—"

"I know." She pressed her free hand against his lips, unwilling to listen to any more logical reasons why they could not spend the rest of their lives together. On the island. In her house and in her bed.

"Don't talk," she said desperately, pulling him onto her, drawing him into her again. "Not now. For now, I just want you to make love to me again."

Truth might be reason, but there was one truth Sebastian wasn't prepared to share with Kirby. He wasn't precisely the celibate a man of his level was expected to be. He'd started experiencing sexual release during his adolescence, and, as he'd gotten older, had, although he'd known it made him more human, less Logosian, continued masturbation into adulthood. Which, he'd assured himself over the years, was less of an infraction than other males he knew who'd frequent Janurian brothels while off planet.

But congress with his own hand, as stress-relieving as it might be, didn't begin to come close to equaling the mind-blinding lovemaking he'd shared with Kirby. Having once tasted the ripe, sweet, forbidden fruit of sexual pleasure, Sebastian was ravenous. His own desires no less fevered than hers, he willingly complied.

Again and again, all night long.

✧   ✧   ✧

SEBASTIAN WAS RELIEVED when Kirby agreed to spend the next day at home. Mostly in bed, which had become his favorite place to be.

When they weren't making love, they talked. Kirby wanted to know everything about Logosia, and Sebastian tried, as best he could, to explain his home planet, skimming over the part about it being a tightly held patriarchal society. He was feeling too good to get into yet another argument concerning female equality. Besides, his time with Kirby Pendleton had made him realize that his sister was correct. Their system was not merely sexist, but misogynistic.

And wouldn't Rosalyn laugh to know that it was a woman who'd made him see the light?

"What about Earth in your time?" Kirby asked. She sat up in bed, pulled her knees to her chest, and wrapped her arms around them. "Obviously it's still spinning."

"It is, indeed."

"That's good news in itself," she decided. "That we haven't managed to blow it up or pollute it out of existence. How about California? I guess it hasn't dropped into the sea yet, since that was your original destination."

"No. But a major earthquake is due any time."

She laughed at that. "It's nice to know some things stay the same. What about the homeless? And the forests?"

"A coalition of government and private enterprise solved the homeless problem in the twenty-second century," Sebastian told her. "The forests, unfortunately, have gone. Although third-and fourth-growth forests were farmed, eventually the harvesting became too expensive, and wood products were replaced by superior amalgams."

"Oh, I hate that idea." She sighed and shook her head. "Well, we'll just have to change the future," she decided. "Have we had a woman president yet?"

"Five."

"Well, that's good news. What about the Boston Red Sox?"

"They have been on a several-solar-revolutions-long losing streak to the New York Yankees."

Another sigh. "Damn Yankees," she muttered.

"But they have a new owner, so fans are hopeful," Sebastian tacked on, in hopes of putting a smile on her face. His strategy worked.

"This is so amazing." She shook her head and looked at him, her eyes moving slowly over his face, as if memorizing his features. She pressed her hand against his cheek. "I like the beard you've got going on."

"In truth, I've been afraid of your razor."

She laughed. "Well, I still like it. Though I'd just as soon you not take it as far as one of those lumbersexuals."

"Which would be?"

"Guys who seem to be making a statement about re-claiming their masculinity by growing heavy, long, old-fashioned lumberjack beards. They cut down trees," she tacked on, in case he might not get the reference. "Lumber-jacks. Not all bearded men."

"I have no intention of cutting down a tree."

"Well, that's good news." She snuggled closer. "I never, in a million years, would have imagined that I'd be lying in bed with a Logosian astrophysicist."

Something belatedly occurred to her. "Your name. Is it really yours?" She hated thinking that she might have cried out a false name during their lovemaking.

"It's mine," Sebastian assured her. "Sebastian is my birth name. But when males reach the age of maturity, they are encouraged to choose a name they feel better suits them. My family name is Vardanyian. My father chose it because it's Logosian for Justice. He was a magistrate and later a diplomat."

"Why did you chose Blackthorne? The only other per-son I ever heard of with that name was the hero of *Shogun*. But you undoubtedly haven't read that."

"I have. My mother has quite an extensive library due to my father always bringing her antique books he'd find on diplomatic trips to Earth. But that's not why I chose the name."

Though, since he was both blessed and cursed with a memory that never forgot a thing, a quote from the book popped into Sebastian's head. When John Blackthorne was thinking that he'd left all his life's passion at the feet of his forbidden love. And how he'd never again know that spirit-joining ecstasy that had ignited them. And couldn't Sebastian identify with that?

There would never be another Kirby.

Therefore, once he left Rum Runner Island, he would never again know passion.

"That's a good assumption, though," he said, not wanting to dwell on that negative thought now. "And even more suitable given that the novel's John Blackthorne was shipwrecked in a strange land. But the true reason I selected it is because of an old movie I found in the archives when I was young and trying to learn about my mother's home planet."

"What one?"

"Butch Cassidy and the Sundance Kid."

"You're kidding!"

"On the contrary, I am every bit as serious as a Logosian Elder," he said.

"In the first place, that's not an accurate movie if you want to learn about Earth in the time your mother lived here," she pointed out.

"A fact I discovered for myself while watching it. But it was still very exciting. We do not," he admitted, knowing he could be accused of treason for talking negatively about his planet on foreign soil, "have a very stimulating planet."

"From what you told me about lovemaking, I figured that out all for myself," she said. "Give the place another two hundred years and you could end up like those people in the *Star Trek* TV show who lost their physicality and evolved into pure energy and pure thought."

"Organians," he said. "And the possibility has occurred to me, and some others considered to be more radical thinkers. But it's not spoken of except within very small circles and would undoubtedly take more than a mere two centuries of evolution to occur."

"I'll take your word for that. So, I still don't remember a Blackthorne in *Butch Cassidy*."

"There wasn't. But once I watched that movie, I became enamored with the idea of Butch Cassidy and searched for everything I could about him. Which led to my discovery of another film that suggested he'd changed his name to James Blackthorn and lived out the rest of his life in Bolivia.

"The government scribe who put my name change into the government database accidentally added an e at the end. Since dealing with bureaucrats can be a Hadean nightmare, I decided to leave it the way it was."

She laughed at that. "It's good to know that some things are universal. It's also interesting to know that you took a twentieth-century American outlaw as your role model. Though, I have to point out that Butch and Sundance were romanticized versions of the real thing."

"True. Yet against logic, the romance of their adventures appealed to me."

"They were rebels. So perhaps choosing Blackthorne for your name was your way of expressing your own inner feelings of frustration of living in a society that doesn't permit any rebellion."

He ran his hand down her hair and drew her close. "How do you know me so well?" he murmured wonderingly against the top of her head.

She looked up at him and smiled. "Simple. I love you. And," she reminded him, "I seem to be able to read your mind."

"Can you tell what I'm thinking now?"

She took a long time, pretending to look deep into his steady gaze. "You want to make love to me."

"That's very good."

"It was also easy," she said on a soft laugh. She ran her hand over the sheet that was tented over his lower torso. "Since your Logosian mind keeps sending the same message to your very human body."

Laughing, she pulled the sheet away and drew him to her. That was all either of them was to say for a very long time.

23

PINK FINGERS OF dawn were spreading across a pearl-gray Christmas Eve sky. Sebastian and Kirby were sitting at the kitchen table, watching a family of deer at the salt lick behind her house.

"I heard on the radio that syzygy occurs this evening," Kirby murmured.

Sometime, during the long, love-filled night, Sebastian had told her of Nate's belief that the upcoming arrangement of planets—lined up along the same radius and along the same orbital plane extending from the sun—could provide the optimum time for Sebastian's departure.

Kirby realized with a certain detached wonder that the idea of Sebastian leaving her was more shattering than the fact that she'd managed to fall in love with a man not only from another planet but another time.

"Yes." Sebastian couldn't look at her. His heart was already aching at the idea of leaving.

"So, we only have today."

"Not even that." He felt her intense disappointment. "I have to spend much of it in the lab."

"But I thought you and Nate had come up with the coordinates."

"We have. But now I have to come up with some way to boost my projection power. It's obvious that something about Earth's atmosphere or gravity is blocking my abilities. Ever since my arrival, I've been mindblind—"

"Not with me," Kirby pointed out.

"No." Sebastian smiled, took her hand, and linked their fingers together atop the maple table. "Not with you. But without a ship, my entire theory depends on my being able to achieve absolute astro-projection. As you saw earlier, I can no longer achieve the proper level."

"Does that mean you're going to have to call off the experiment?" *That you'll be forced to stay here? With me?* she wondered but didn't dare ask.

"It does unless I can get my hands on some diamaziman crystals within the next few hours," he agreed.

"Diamaziman?"

"A carbon-based stone whose atoms have been crystallized into a solid cubic pattern," he explained. "Blue diamaziman is preferable, because it possesses the impurity boron, which serves as an electrical conductor. On Logosia, such diamaziman is utilized to beam down visitors who do not possess the ability of astro-projection."

Remembering how many times he'd considered those individuals without such ability inferior, Sebastian felt humbled. And ashamed.

"There's nothing else you could use?"

"No." He frowned and dragged his hand through his hair. "It is, of course, possible to create diamaziman in a laboratory setting, by placing graphite, which is pure carbon, along with a metal solvent between tungsten-carbide pistons and subjecting them to a pressure of a million pounds per square inch, then heating them to thirty-five hundred of your Fahrenheit degrees.

"But your technology is behind ours. It would take at least a week to produce a usable diamaziman."

"And you don't have a week."

"No." The regret in her voice was echoed in his own heart. "I don't."

A silence descended. Outside the kitchen window, the birds had gathered for their morning meal. The cat sat on the windowsill, growling and batting impotently at the feathered visitors through the double-pane glass. Lost in her turmoiled thoughts, Kirby ignored both birds and cat.

"Wait here," she said finally. She rose from the table and left the room. When she returned, she was carrying a small gray box, which she held out to Sebastian.

"Maybe this will help," she suggested in a quiet voice.

He took the box and lifted the lid. Inside, resting on a bed of pearl-gray velvet, was a perfect marquise-cut blue diamaziman set in a platinum band.

Startled, Sebastian looked up at her.

"It was my engagement ring," she answered his unspoken question. "After my marriage disintegrated, I didn't want it. I walked along the beach, determined to toss the damn thing into the surf. But, being Yankee born and bred, I couldn't bear to toss away a valuable diamond, so I kept it."

"You could have sold it," Sebastian suggested. He ran his finger over the dazzling blue stone. "I imagine it is quite valuable."

"Probably." Kirby shrugged. "I considered that idea and rejected it." A soft, thoughtful look came into her eyes. "Perhaps, intuitively, I knew that someday I'd have a much better use for it."

He glanced around her homey, comfortably shabby kitchen, thinking that she could undoubtedly use the funds such a stone would bring.

"I appreciate your generous gesture, Kirby," Sebastian said, giving the stone one last look before closing the box with a snap. "But I cannot take such a valuable gift."

"It's only money," she argued. What she didn't say was that she'd given him something far more valuable. Her heart.

"Tell me about him," Sebastian said suddenly. "Tell me about the man who gave you this ring." Even in his own time, such a stone would be worth a virtual fortune. Sebastian tried to envision Kirby as a wife of such a wealthy man and failed.

"He was an actor. A big star, actually," she said. "On television. Movies." Something occurred to her. "His name is Steven Stone."

Sebastian knew exactly why she'd given him the man's name. "The name means nothing."

"Good." She nodded. "I'd hate to find out that such a lying rat had been able to maintain his popularity for centuries."

"I can't imagine you as the wife of a movie star," Sebastian ventured.

"Neither could Steven. We met when I was assigned to a security detail when he did a public appearance at a mall in Venice. He told me I was the most beautiful woman in the world."

"I thought you said he was a liar."

She shot him a quick, appreciative smile. "Flatterer."

"I find you the most beautiful woman in all the worlds I've ever traveled."

The compliment, like so many of Sebastian's statements, was simply, honestly spoken. It also went directly to her heart.

"Well." Kirby took a deep breath. "Anyway, the next thing I knew, I received an offer to act as a technical adviser on his series. I suppose I was flattered by his constant, unrelenting attention, or stardust got into my eyes, or I just liked the idea of seeing my name on the television screen every Wednesday night.

"Whatever, I finally agreed. At the end of that season, we were married." A soft shadow moved across her eyes. "Six months later, my father had his heart attack. I came home to Maine for the funeral. I returned to Malibu to find that week's romantic costar playing a starring role in my bed."

She shook her head with self-disgust. "Later I discovered that Steven had a reputation for bedding them all. The rest of the crew referred to the actresses as the flavor of the week." Her laugh was short and bitter. Like her marriage, Kirby considered.

"I was angry, hurt, and humiliated. So I returned home to lick my wounds. That's when I discovered I belonged here. So I stayed...."

"Now tell me about Zorana."

"She is a perfect Logosian," Sebastian said. "Calm, utterly logical, and unerringly precise. She is a time-management consultant."

"She sounds boring," Kirby decided.

Sebastian laughed at that. "She is. But we were matched at a very early age by our parents, so, until I disgraced her with my dismissal from the space council, neither of us ever questioned such arrangement."

Kirby knew that his alleged disgrace would immediately turn to galaxy-wide triumph when he returned to Logosia. Undoubtedly the utterly logical Zorana would be quick to change her mind about calling off their marriage.

"And now?" She had to ask.

"And now I know that I could never bond with her. Because my heart, and all my thoughts, will belong to you."

He looked down at the ring for a long, thoughtful time, then up at Kirby. "You realize that, without this diamaziman, I could not return to Logosia."

"Yes." Her lips were unbearably dry. She had to push the single softly spoken word past the lump in her throat.

"Then why?"

Tears stung at the backs of her lids, and Kirby resolutely blinked them away. "I understand your need to return to your own world, your own time," she said. "And if there's any way I can help, I will."

What she didn't tell him was that the thought of his molecules scattered all over space because he'd lacked the power to complete his projection was too horrifying to contemplate.

Sebastian studied her for a long, thoughtful moment. Conflicting emotions raged inside him.

Go. Stay.

Duty. Love.

Family. *Kirby.*

Logic warred with sentiment. His head waged battle with his newly discovered heart.

He wanted to promise that he would come back, but he didn't. His life was on Logosia.

She smiled, but her lips trembled, and the hot tears that had been threatening made her eyes glisten in a way that

Sebastian found more painful than any physical wound could ever be.

A single tear trailed down her cheek. When he tenderly brushed it away with his thumb, she choked back a sob.

"I don't want to talk anymore," she said in a frail, fractured voice. She looked up at him, all the love she felt for this man shining on her face, gleaming in her eyes. "Make love with me, Sebastian." She did not care how needy such a plea might sound; at this moment, she would have begged.

Sebastian needed no second invitation.

Hand in hand, they walked into the bedroom. And although she never would have thought it possible, this time the passion burned even higher between them and the hunger flamed even more intense.

And then, as if by mutual unspoken consent, they slowed the pace. If this was their last time to make love, they wanted to create a memory that would last throughout the ages that would soon separate them.

There were no whispered words of love, no wild, rash promises. They spoke with soft sighs and inarticulate murmurs. They spoke with touches, the brush of a fingertip along the curve of a lip, the press of a palm against warming flesh.

A wintry sun crept above the horizon, creating a misty glow and dappling their skin with frail, stuttering light. Kirby felt his hands slide over her, felt his breath warming her flesh.

"Would you do something for me?" she whispered.

His lips plucked at hers. "Anything."

It was not quite the truth and they both knew it.

"Make love to me the way you would on Logosia."

Startled, Sebastian braced himself up on one elbow. "You wouldn't like it."

"How do you know? If you don't try?"

"It's not nearly as fulfilling as the Earthly way," Sebastian argued. His body was aching to sheathe itself once again in her silken warmth. The purely mental sexual encounter he'd always found satisfying paled in comparison.

"Please?" She ran her fingernail down his chest and gave him a melting, sensual smile. "Just this once?"

Sebastian could deny this woman nothing. He was grateful that Kirby was too honorable to ask him to stay on Rum Runner Island, Maine, U.S.A. Because if she ever made such a request and looked up at him with those incredible blue eyes, Sebastian knew he'd never see Logosia again.

"All right. But don't say I didn't warn you." He gave her one last, long, deep kiss to satisfy himself, then said, "We have to kneel facing one another."

"On the bed? Or would the floor be better?"

Sebastian sighed. Sweet Valhalla, how he hated the idea of leaving the warm, love-rumpled sheets. "I suppose the floor would be a superior surface," he agreed.

"How do you do it on Logosia?"

"On a thin pallet on the floor."

"Well, then, the rug should work." She left the bed and knelt on the rag rug in front of the fire.

Grumbling, Sebastian joined her. The sensual mood, unsurprisingly, was gone, chased away with the need to explain the logistics of Logosian sex.

He knelt in front of her. "Now we touch palms."

"Like this?" She pressed her hands against his.

"Exactly. You must remember, although we're naked, to symbolize nothing between us, this will be purely mental, a melding of thoughts."

"I can't wait."

It was true, Sebastian realized with surprise. She was so excited she was trembling.

Sebastian had thought the experience would be typically passionless. He was wrong.

With only their fingertips touching, they tenderly explored each other's consciousness, their entwined thoughts exploring realms of sensuality beyond anything either of them had known.

The room became bathed in a warm, flickering glow. Swirling lights—royal blue, blazing scarlet, gleaming gold, and shimmering silver—surrounded them.

Incredibly, there was music, the sweetly poignant sound of the alto sax albums Nate liked to play in the lab, bringing to mind steamy nights and sensual summer days.

Three-dimensional images of them making love in myriad ways and places appeared. Together they watched themselves sitting in a meadow, surrounded by wildflowers.

Kirby was wearing a gossamer white dress made of some type of gauze, while he was clad in a flowing white poet's shirt and black pants reminiscent of a pirate's. Sebastian was weaving a coronet of sunshine-yellow flowers, which he placed atop her coppery head.

Then, slowly, they undressed each other, and as he laid her back among the flowers and slipped into her, the vision shifted, like the facets of a kaleidoscope, and they were lying on the deck of a tall-masted ship that was plowing through the waves.

They were in the midst of a squall but caught up in

their own passion. Neither noticed the bucking of the schooner, the pelting rain, the moaning wind. Sebastian was draping a king's ransom in ice-blue diamonds over her nude body while telling her how beautiful, how desirable she was and all the wild, erotic things he was going to do to her, and Kirby was saying *yes, yes, yes!* to everything.

And then they were lying on some golden beach, beside a blue lagoon, while gentle trade winds made the palm trees sway overhead. And they were making love—wonderful, glorious love—as the warm water lapped against the golden sand and the sun shone be-nevolently overhead, and when they climaxed together, their spirits soared away from their bodies on gossamer wings, flying directly into the bright and glowing sun.

And then they were back in her bedroom, and Sebastian realized that salty tears were flowing down his face.

He'd never felt anything like it, had never realized that it could be possible to experience such pure, sweet pleasure.

Together they lowered their hands, but not yet ready to draw apart, they linked their fingers and remained, bonded, mind and body and soul.

"I thought you'd taught me true passion earlier." Her voice was only a whisper but easily heard in the stillness of the room. "But I'd never, in a million years, imagined…"

"I know." He drew her close and pressed his wet cheek against hers. "I, too, had not known such complete ecstasy was possible."

The strength of the emotions they'd shared left them both exhausted. Arms wrapped around each other, they lay down on the rug and surrendered to a deep, blissful sleep.

24

ALL TOO SOON, reality returned.

Sebastian stood in the kitchen doorway, frustration etched onto his handsome face.

He'd invited Kirby—coming perilously close to begging—to return to the lab with him, to see him off. But she'd refused, saying that she wanted to remember him here, in her home, where they'd shared so much love.

"I hate leaving you."

"I know." Kirby was out of tears. All she had left was a terrible empty hole where her heart used to be. "But it's important that you return to Logosia and prove you were right."

He ran the back of his hand down her face. "If I could, I'd take you with me."

"I know. But you told me the diamond will only provide enough strength for one." She gave him a brave smile that wobbled. Then collapsed. "Damn. I'm sorry. I swore I'd wait until you left to cry." Turning away, Kirby buried her face in her hands and took several deep, calming breaths.

When she turned back to him, her expression was composed, although renewed tears shone wetly in her eyes.

"Have a safe journey, Sebastian."

For some reason he could not discern, her stalwart bravery, at a time when he knew her heart was breaking, made him want to weep like an infant.

"I will never forget you."

She took his hand in hers and pressed it against her heart. "Nor I you. Across time, I will love you."

"And across space, I will love you."

They could have been speaking their marriage vows, Sebastian considered. Their minds tangled, and he knew that Kirby was thinking the same thing.

Because the one thing that neither time nor distance could ever alter was that they belonged together. And they both knew that they would never forsake each other.

"I remember reading something once," Kirby said. "If two hearts are truly bonded, if two people are meant to be together, they will find each other. No matter what obstacles come between them."

Her hand tightened and her eyes grew moist again. "We *are* bonded, Sebastian. Hearts and minds and souls. And the only reason I can send you away, back to your home, is that I know, with every fiber of my being, that we will find each other again."

Logic told him that she was being an overly romantic female.

Sebastian's heart told him that she spoke the truth. That their love was timeless.

"We will be together," he agreed. "Someday. For always."

She bit her lip and refused to cry. Outside the open door, the waiting birds became more vocal, demanding their breakfast.

"For always," she whispered.

He drew her to him and they came together, body to body, mouth to mouth. His heartbeat was quick and hard against her as he succumbed to her softness, her strength. Her hands tangled in his hair as she submerged herself to his will, his tenderness.

And with one last reluctant, regretful touch of his hand to her hair, he was walking toward the shiny black snowmobile Nate had lent him.

Kirby stood at the window and watched Sebastian drive away. Back to his own life. His own time.

DESPERATELY TRYING TO keep her mind off what Sebastian and Nate were doing at the brain factory, after sending Danny out to patrol, watching for possible DUI drivers who'd begun celebrating the holiday a day early, Kirby spent the morning cleaning out her desk. She hadn't had the heart to do it before. Too many things that reminded her of her father, and how much she missed him, were buried in the bits of papers and various small treasures he'd saved.

She found memos he'd written to himself—domestic little notes reminding him to bring home milk or bread after work, forgotten immediately after having been written. There was a newspaper clipping from the *Rum Runner Island Yankee Observer*, detailing how a hometown girl, Kirby Pendleton, had been assigned to be a technical adviser on a television series in Hollywood. The article, written by Mildred Cummings, the *Observer's* long-time social editor, gushed effusively, making Kirby sound like a movie star herself.

There were other clippings regarding her work—specifically her apprehension of the Surfer Rapist, and an equal number relating Nate's various awards and achievements.

There were birthday cards sketched by her artist mother. After reading the suggestive, highly personal message her mother had written to her husband inside the first card, Kirby resisted opening the others. And although it did not come as a surprise to discover that her parents had remained very much in love both physically and emotionally during their thirty-five years of marriage, Kirby found herself experiencing a definite twinge of envy.

"Damn." She'd jabbed her finger on one of the trout flies her father had spent so many hours tying. When a tiny spot of blood appeared on the tip of her finger, she stuck it in her mouth.

And that's when she saw it. A vision appeared in her mind, a three-dimensional image so real that she felt she could reach out and touch it.

Sebastian was in danger. He and Nate were in the lab, the barrel of a gun pointed directly at them. As hard as Kirby tried, she couldn't see who was holding the gun.

After calling Danny on the radio, telling him to meet her at the lab, she ran out to the Jeep and raced to the wooded site. Although the temperature was in the low thirties, Kirby's hands were slick with sweat as they gripped the steering wheel.

She repeated Sebastian's name over and over, like a talisman. Like a prayer.

The odometer on the dash clicked away the tenths of miles. Unfortunately, the digital clock beside it was also rolling away precious minutes.

All the time, she tried to focus on the image, but it had faded away, like morning fog over the harbor. Fear coalesced into a tight, cold ball in her throat as she was forced to wonder if the reason she could no longer read Sebastian's mind was because he was no longer alive.

No! She wasn't going to allow herself to think that.

Her cell rang. Seeing Whitney's name on the dashboard screen, she hit the phone button on the steering wheel. "Police."

"Kirby, you have to come to the lab right away."

"I'm on my way. What's happening?" And, she wondered, could it have to do with this woman she'd never felt comfortable around?

"Look," Whitney said, "let's be honest. You've never liked me. And I've never liked you. But you have to believe me when I tell you that your brother's in trouble."

"Again, what's happening?"

"I'm not sure. But he and Sebastian sent everyone home a half hour ago. It was all so sudden, I left without securing the slides I'd been working on. So, I returned, and that's when I heard shouting coming from Nate's lab. And something about a gun. Which is why I left right away to call you."

"Okay." Kirby blew out a breath. This could be a trap. She'd known cops who'd been drawn into an ambush. But Whitney didn't sound as if that was the case. She sounded honestly terrified.

"You'd better go home, like they said."

"But—"

"If something bad goes down, you'll just be in my way. Neither of us want you getting shot, right?"

"You think it's that bad?"

"I think no one brings a gun to a tea party. Go home, Whitney. And whatever you do, do not go back in the lab."

"You'll call me? I do care about your brother."

"I'll call when the situation is taken care of," Kirby agreed. "Now get out of there before someone sees you. I don't want whoever is in there to know you contacted the police."

Not knowing what she was getting into, nor how many bad guys there were, given the size of her police force, surprise was the main thing Kirby had going for her.

"Okay." There was a pause. "Be careful," the other woman said.

"That's a given." Not wanting to tie up the phone any longer, Kirby ended the call.

Five minutes later, she stopped the Jeep in the trees, not wanting to pull up into the clearing right in front of the lab. She wished there was some way to sneak into the building. Unfortunately, Nate had installed a state-of-the-art security system, and the slightest attempt to break in would set off a series of computerized alarms.

"Hello. May I have your name, please," the computerized female voice requested as Kirby stopped in front of the door.

"Kirby Pendleton," Kirby obliged, hoping the bite of frustration in her tone would not screw up the voiceprint. "Police Chief Kirby Pendleton," she said, just in case the system would recognize rank.

"Thank you, Police Chief Kirby Pendleton," the disembodied voice continued, sounding less than impressed by any importance she might have in the community. "Now may I request a handprint, please."

Every nerve ending in Kirby's body was screaming as

she wondered what, exactly, was happening inside the building. But, knowing the futility of arguing with a computer, she placed her hand against the screen as instructed.

"Working," the voice assured her. "Scan completed. You may enter, Kirby Pendleton."

"It's about time," Kirby muttered as the door obligingly slid open.

"Have a nice day," the voice responded.

So far, so good. She was inside. Now all she had to do was find Sebastian and Nate and get them both out of here without anyone getting killed.

The building was strangely deserted. At first that puzzled Kirby, then she realized that Nate must have sent everyone else home in order to keep Sebastian's departure a secret.

Even as she tried her best to tread carefully, the heels of her boots seemed to echo noisily on the tile floor. As she headed down the hallway and up the stairs toward Nate's lab, Kirby wished that she possessed Sebastian's ability for astro-projection.

25

A T THE MOMENT, Sebastian wasn't projecting anywhere. In fact, he felt as if his boots were nailed to
the floor.

Having never been accustomed to violence on his own
planet, Sebastian found this entire scenario extremely
distasteful. And illogical.

"I do not understand how you believe you are going to
get away with this," he said, biting back his anger, instinctively knowing that giving in to his seething rage would
only make matters worse.

"It's actually quite simple," Fred responded with the
first smile Sebastian could remember seeing on his face. If
a rattlesnake could smile, it would look exactly like Fred
Simpson. "While I hold this lethal weapon on the two of
you, with Brian and Murph"—he gestured toward the two
men standing on either side of him, looking like muscle-
bound linemen flanking their quarterback—"will gather all
the data disks for the Way-Back Machine our boy genius
has created and take them out of here. Next they'll escort
you out to the secured van we have waiting.

"Then, unfortunately, some unstable substance is going
to leak out of the chem lab down the hall and explode into

a gigantic fireball that will level the laboratory.

"By the time they manage to dig whatever remains of Nate's body from the rubble, I'll be in Paris, sipping champagne on the Champs-Elysées."

"Who are you working for?" Nate asked, genuinely curious. "CIA? Some crazy terrorist group?"

He laughed at that, but the harsh sound held no humor. "I told my father that you'd never make the connection."

Nate's blue eyes narrowed. "Your father being Romaine Defour." It was not a question. Nate remembered his employer having spoken of having a son. A son named, *damn*, Frederic. "I should have realized." He shook his head in self-disgust. "I should have seen the resemblance."

"I don't look anything like my father."

"Perhaps not physically. But you both have the same glitter of avarice in your eyes." He cursed. "I should have figured it out."

"Oh, I wouldn't be so hard on yourself," Fred advised. "After all, you've been wrapped up in your work. Especially when your alien friend here arrived."

His eyes glittered with that very avarice Nate had accused him of possessing as he glanced over at Sebastian. "You're worth your weight in gold."

"Why are you doing this?" Sebastian asked. A white-hot rage was building inside him at the realization that the very same man who'd seemed such a harmless nerd was the person responsible for injuring Kirby. Although it took a Herculean effort, Sebastian forced it down. For now.

"Why, to advance the cause of science, of course," he said.

"Not to mention the dough involved," Nate added.

"Especially since your father lost his government funding."

"Because you stole his work," Fred snapped.

"The quantum jump time travel and antimatter work was always mine," Nate argued. "I created it, I nurtured it, I'm the one who did all the work. But your father was too greedy and too impatient, so he couldn't resist stealing the concept from one of his own employees, twisting the data to make it look as if we were further along than we were, then offering it to the highest bidder."

"You are so naive, Pendleton. That's the way the game is played," Fred ground out. "It all would have worked out if you hadn't blown the damn whistle."

"I wasn't going to let the Pentagon get their grubby little hands on my work and turn it into the latest high-tech war machine."

"Well, now you don't have any choice, do you?" Gesturing toward the computer with the pistol, he said to the larger of his enormous cohorts, "Tie these two up to keep them out of trouble, then start loading this stuff, along with Mr. Spock, into the van. We've wasted enough time as it is."

Sebastian exchanged a glance with Nate, who nodded imperceptibly. A moment later, all hell broke loose.

"What the—"

One of Fred's goons, the one who'd been about to tie the rope around Sebastian's wrists, gaped at the spot where his quarry had been standing. A second later, a hand pressed against the back of his head, and he crumpled to the floor.

At the same time, Nate lowered his head and rammed it into the stomach of the walking Coke machine headed his way. He was rewarded by a heavy *oof*, as the man's air was forced from his lungs. A moment later, Nate felt a bullet whiz past his ear and he dived for the floor.

"Damn it, Fred," he ground out as he rolled under a desk, "aren't you carrying this quest for knowledge a little bit too far? Whatever happened to the chaos theory? If you could solve the problem of climate change, you'd be saving the planet. That'd be a Nobel Prize for sure."

"That could take decades," Fred said. "Centuries. There's more immediate money in armaments," he said. This time the bullet splintered the wood only inches from Nate's head.

Nate cursed when he saw Murph was back on his feet and headed his way. He tipped the desk over, scattering papers. With an angry roar that would've done the Hulk proud, the man kicked the desk aside, shattering it as if it had been made of balsa wood.

But Nate had already moved on.

"You're not going to get away," Fred warned.

"I believe that's my line," Kirby said calmly, her Glock aimed point-blank at Fred. "At the risk of sounding clichéd, drop the gun."

Fred wasn't about to surrender yet. "Murph, get the damn alien."

"That's what I'm trying to do, damn it," he complained, furious that every time he neared Sebastian, the man would dematerialize, then pop up somewhere else across the room. Finally, frustrated, he charged.

Nate, crouched behind a bookcase, stuck out his leg. As he watched the giant go tumbling to the floor, he called out cheerfully, "Timber."

Fred, faced with the inevitable, obediently dropped his weapon to the floor.

Breathing again, Kirby whipped out her handcuffs and snapped them around his wrists.

Two minutes later, Danny arrived with the police van to pick up the unholy trio. As Kirby handed the prisoners over to her deputy, she gave into temptation and issued an order she'd been dying to say for years. "Book 'em, Danno."

SHE SHOULD BE ecstatic. After all, it wasn't every day the police chief of a quiet little island hamlet like Rum Runner Island had the opportunity to save her brother and lover from a potential murderer, not to mention the little fact that she'd kept a major scientific breakthrough from somehow being turned into yet another doomsday machine by war profiteers.

But she couldn't be happy. Because the one thing that hadn't changed was that Sebastian was leaving.

They were standing alone in the lab, hands linked, minds entwined.

"I thought you'd lost your powers," she said, seeking something, anything to say.

"I have, for the most part," he agreed. "But I believe you're right about the adrenaline rush. There's something very primitive about fighting for your life." But it had been more than that, he knew. Revenge had driven him. Revenge for Fred Simpson, aka Frederic Defour, having harmed the woman he loved.

"I don't imagine you have much opportunity to do that on Logosia."

He almost smiled. "No. So long as you stay out of the taverns frequented by outlanders, Logosia is unrelentingly peaceful."

"Violence is illogical," she agreed softly.

"That's the downside," he said. "But during my time on Earth, I have come to realize that absolute logic is not the utopia it is made out to be." He drew her close and pressed his lips against her hair. "Because of you, I have discovered that the very best things in life are sometimes the most illogical."

She smiled up at him through misty eyes. "Ah, we're back to me being an illogical female again?"

He traced her curved lips with his fingertip, appearing fascinated by their shape and silky texture. "No. We are back to how amazing you make me feel."

She wrapped her arms around him and wished she could hold him here with her forever. Wished that she could stop time. "That's better."

They stood that way, arms wrapped around each other, foreheads touching, for a long moment. Finally, accepting the inevitable, Kirby drew away, her eyes shimmering with tears. "I'm not going to say good-bye again."

There was an ache in his throat so large Sebastian couldn't swallow. And there was an enormous, gaping black hole where his heart used to be. "No. No good-byes."

And then his mouth was on hers, covering and conquering and creating a deep, aching warmth. It was not a kiss meant to soothe or comfort, but one born of raw and turbulent emotions.

On a soft sob, her lips parted in irresistible and avid invitation. His mouth was fevered with desperation, his hands rough with urgency. Swearing, first in English, then switching to Logosian, he plunged into the dark, frantic kiss, boldly taking what he needed, heatedly giving what she needed in return.

And then, before he dragged her down to the floor, he released her.

Shaken, Kirby stared up at him, wondering what kind of man possessed so much self-restraint he could put aside such fevered passion. Tense and wired and quivering like a plucked bowstring, she closed her eyes and struggled for control.

Then, she did the only thing possible. Biting her lip to keep from begging him to stay, she walked out of the lab. And out of Sebastian's life.

Nate was waiting for her by the Jeep.

"You really love the guy, don't you, kiddo?" he asked, his dark blue eyes filled with sympathy.

"Of course I do." She took a deep breath and scrubbed impatiently at the tears streaming down her face with the backs of her hands. "Enough to let him go."

"Does it help knowing that he loves you, too?"

She shook her head. "No. Oh, it probably will, one of these days," she decided reluctantly. "But right now, I don't think there's anything either you or Sebastian can say to make me feel better."

She lifted a hand to his cheek. "But thank you, Nate. You're a dynamite brother."

Her decision made, and wanting to leave before she weakened and changed her mind, she climbed into the Jeep and drove back to her office.

SHE COULDN'T THINK. After having the state police come and take her prisoners to the mainland, Kirby put Danny in charge for the remainder of the day and went home, where the twinkling white lights of the Christmas tree seemed to mock her, reminding her, as if she could ever forget, that Sebastian was somewhere out there among the stars.

Digging out her grandmother Pendleton's cookbook, she began to bake some cookies and cupcakes to take to Christmas dinner tomorrow. As much as she wanted to wallow beneath the covers until at least after the New Year, she knew that if she didn't show up at Emily's, her bossy big sister would come and get her.

Meanwhile, hopefully the concentration baking demanded would keep her from thinking about Sebastian. From wondering if he made it safely back to Logosia and hoping he'd remember her and what they'd shared when he did.

Three hours later, the kitchen was filled with smoke, and all she had to show for her efforts were a stack of what looked like flat charcoal disks and a muffin tin of charred, heavy rocks.

Deciding that perhaps the birds might not be too choosy, she took the cookie sheet outside.

That's when she saw him. Walking toward her in a strong, determined stride.

At first Kirby couldn't believe it was really Sebastian. It was undoubtedly a hologram, like the ones he showed her he could create from his mind.

Dropping the cookie sheet into the snow, she ran toward him, hurling herself into his firm arms. This was no hologram, she realized, as he covered her face with kisses. The man she loved was wonderfully, gloriously real.

"I should say I'm sorry." Tears of happiness streamed down her uplifted face. "But I'm not."

He buried his lips in her hair. "Neither am I."

"What went wrong?"

"Nothing went wrong."

"But you wanted to go home, to prove your theory worked."

"It's enough for me to know that it works," Sebastian assured her. "As for going home, that's exactly what I've done."

He cupped her wet face in his hands. "All my life, I've struggled to be a proper Logosian scientist. I've spent my entire life feeling like an outsider on my own planet, forced to suppress emotions that were inappropriate. But now, here, with you, Kirby Pendleton, for the first time in my life, I feel as if I'm exactly where I belong."

"For all time?"

"For eternity," he agreed. "I also have a new project I need to work on."

"What's that?"

"Lassoing the moon."

"Oh." She covered her heart with her right hand as the tears began flowing again. "You truly do love me."

"Of course I do. I would give you anything, Kirby. Just tell me what you want."

"You." She framed his beautiful face with her hands. "I want you, Sebastian Blackthorne."

"You already have me."

"As you have me," she responded, thinking they could have been saying wedding vows. But that was a discussion for another day. For now, she was going to bask in this glorious, perfect moment.

As they walked back toward the house, something occurred to Kirby. "Poor Nate must be devastated not to have had a chance to prove his theory."

"On the contrary. It went off like clockwork. In fact, your brother is undoubtedly having the time of his life."

"What?" Comprehension dawned. "Nate's gone to Logosia, hasn't he?"

"There was only enough diamaziman for one," he reminded her. "I trust your brother to rescue my sister and, if necessary, bring her and our mother here."

"Wow. Well, my brother has always accomplished everything he's set out to do."

Nine days ago, this idea would have been too incredulous to believe. How much had changed since Sebastian Blackthorne's arrival, which, although she'd never been a woo-woo type of woman, Kirby was convinced had been predestined. Even written in the stars.

"Nate on Logosia. Nearly two hundred years in the future." She shook her head. "You're right, he's probably in seventh heaven."

Kirby and Sebastian were almost back at the house when something occurred to her. "I hate to ask this, but what if Nate can't get back?" The thought was too horrendous to contemplate.

"He'll make it," Sebastian assured her with a cocky self-confidence that reminded her of her brother. "Rosalyn will help him. Besides, he has a date back here in two weeks."

"What's happening in two weeks?"

"He's agreed to be best man at our wedding. We decided that would be sufficient time to notify your mother and bring her back from Tahiti for the ceremony."

"Did it occur to either of you two geniuses that no one thought to ask me if I wanted to get married?"

He stopped in his tracks, obviously surprised. "But you

told me that you loved me."

"I do."

"And I love you." His brow was furrowed and a frustrated puzzlement darkened his eyes. "And we both agreed that we want to spend the rest of our lives together, so it was only logical to assume that you would want to get married."

The emotions were there, Kirby knew. She could feel them, warm and deep and rich, flowing from his heart. But his Logosian mind was still, and perhaps always would be, seeking logic, even in places there was none to be found.

After all, love, by its very nature, was illogical.

She did love him. All of him, his generous and caring heart, his body, even his sometimes frustrating, oftentimes intriguing mind.

"If you are concerned about my ability to provide financial support, you need not have any concern," Sebastian said. "Nate tells me that our work will bring in enough grant money to enable me to care for a wife and children, and I have no reason to doubt his accounting."

"Children?"

"I'm sorry. Am I taking too much for granted? About the children? Because if you'd rather not, you are more than enough to make me the happiest man on Earth."

"I've always wanted a family," Kirby said. "And the idea of making babies with you is definitely appealing. But"—she crossed her arms—"I don't need a man to support me. I'm perfectly capable of doing that by myself."

"You are very self-sufficient," he agreed amiably.

"I am," she agreed with a brisk nod of her head. "And if I marry you, it will be because I love you."

"I understand and appreciate the thought. However,

does the fact that you said *if*, rather than *when*, mean you have doubts?"

"Not a one," she assured him. "However, while I may not be looking for a breadwinner, I wouldn't mind at all if you wanted to take up the role of the bread baker."

He looked down at the charred crumbs scattered like chips of ebony over the white snow. The birds, chattering their disgust, pecked with obvious distaste at the results of three hours spent in a hot kitchen.

"I think," he decided, "that is the most logical idea you've come up with yet."

Kirby laughed at that. She'd never been happier. Which was totally illogical, since her twin brother was currently hurtling through space, headed out of the galaxy.

Reminding herself that Nate might be eccentric, but he wasn't crazy enough to attempt anything he wasn't truly positive would work, she decided to take Sebastian's word about her brother's safety.

She linked her arm through his. "Come on back to the house with me," she suggested. "We'll heat up some pizza in the microwave, and after dinner, you can spend the rest of the night convincing me of all the reasons I'm going to marry you."

"That scenario sounds most intriguing," Sebastian agreed. "Highly illogical, but definitely appealing."

"If you think that's illogical," Kirby promised with a bold, sexy grin, "just wait until I introduce you to the wonders of a bubble bath."

An erotic image shimmered between them. The sight of Kirby clad in those frothy bubbles made his blood turn molten in his veins. Metaphorically.

"I believe," Sebastian decided, "that perhaps it would

be most logical to skip the pizza for now. To save more time for the bubble bath."

"What a terrific idea." Kirby's smile widened as she thanked the gods or fates or whatever destiny had brought this wonderful man all the way across space and time to her. "Who'd ever guess that logic could be so much fun?"

Read on for an excerpt from **Somewhere in Time**, the second book in the Rum Runner Island series, on sale in January 2017, when Nate Pendleton finds himself in the adventure of a lifetime as he helps Rosalyn Vardanyian flee from the Logosian forces and discovers a woman worth fighting for.

THE MOON HAD begun to rise, casting a soft, rosy glow over Logosia. The inhabitants of the domed city were busy preparing for Truthfest, the annual observation of the arrival of the Ancient Ones. The two-week-long celebration was the one time in the year when even the most logical Logosians, aided by vast amounts of Enos Dew, tended to loosen the reins on their emotions.

The commuters were already smiling in anticipation. Their thoughts focused on the upcoming days, they failed to notice the sparkling bits of matter reassembling themselves outside the quartzalite windows of their speeding air shuttles.

"It works!" Nate stared around him in wonder. "Hot damn," he shouted, "it actually works!" He could feel the grin practically splitting his face in half.

A grin that faded when he realized that he was standing face-to-face with a pair of very large, very ugly men clad in black uniforms. They reminded him vaguely of Brian and Murph, although Fred's two henchmen had lacked the thick, leathery frontal ridge that ran along these men's foreheads. There was, however, the same primitive violence in their eyes.

"You are late," one of the men accused in a guttural language, which Sebastian's translator obligingly decoded.

Sebastian had assured Nate that since English was the chosen language of the terrans on Logosia, he would be able to make himself understood. "I got held up."

The men exchanged a look. "Truthfest is about to begin. We get paid overtime for holidays."

"Well, I'm here now," Nate pointed out.

With a shrug of his massive shoulders, the larger of the two men punched a code into what resembled a solar pocket calculator. The door panel behind him slid silently open. "Your prisoner awaits."

"Prisoner?"

Deciding that somehow he must have miscalculated and landed somewhere other than Rosalyn Vardanyian's home, Nate entered the gleaming white building. The door closed behind him, leaving him all alone in the foyer.

He was not alone for long. Two more men, twins to the pair outside the door and dressed in identical uniforms and knee-high black boots, entered the room with a rough, arrogant swagger. Between them was a woman who could only be Rosalyn Vardanyian.

Sebastian had told Nate that his sister was intelligent. And stubborn. As his appreciative gaze swept over her, Nate wondered why his friend had neglected to mention her beauty.

Her hair was golden-blond, arranged in a braided coronet atop her head. Although her body was reed slender, the clinging silvery-blue gown outlining appealing curves.

Her eyes were a tawny topaz, revealing intelligence and something else that strangely seemed to be disgust.

"So, you have finally arrived," she said. Her voice was soft, but there was an edge to it.

"Everybody certainly seems concerned about punctuality around here," Nate complained. "And I think you've mistaken me for someone else."

"Oh, I know exactly who you are." Rosalyn held out her hands, revealing the steel bands that encircled her wrists. "You're the man who has come to escort me to my execution."

Also coming December 13, 2016, *Finn*, the 7th book in the 7 Brides for Seven Brothers series:

Meet the Brannigan brothers! Seven sexy brothers who bring the heart and the heat! From bestselling authors Barbara Freethy, Ruth Cardello, Melody Anne, Christie Ridgway, Lynn Raye Harris, Roxanne St. Claire and JoAnn Ross comes a brand new contemporary romance family series: 7 Brides for 7 Brothers. You won't want to miss a single one!

FINN – JoAnn Ross

Finn Brannigan has a need for speed. Fast cars, fast jets, and the fast life that comes with being a TOPGUN naval aviator. He's flying missions over Afghanistan when his media mogul father dies unexpectedly, leaving Finn an airline in the wilds of the Alaskan wilderness. Which is a cool surprise, though he hasn't a clue what he's supposed to do with three small planes half a world away.

Nine months later, burned out from multiple deployments, Finn leaves the Navy and heads north to the Last Frontier to escape the world. But his planned isolation is blown to bits when a runaway bride insists he fly her to her planned honeymoon cabin located in his remote mountain town of Caribou. As the short Alaskan summer spins out, Finn finds himself wanting to slow the days down and savor every delicious moment with the free-spirited singer/songwriter who's made him feel alive again.

Tori Cassidy has had it with dishonest, cheating playboys. Alaskan bush pilot Finn Brannigan is exactly the kind of man she can envision building a life with. Hardworking. Honest. Ordinary.

There's just one problem: Finn is lying about who he really is.

Grab the rest of the series!
Luke – Barbara Freethy
Gabe – Ruth Cardello
Hunter – Melody Anne
Knox – Christie Ridgway
Max – Lynn Raye Harris
James – Roxanne St. Claire
Finn – JoAnn Ross

To keep up with publication dates, other news, and a chance to win books and other cool stuff, subscribe to the JoAnn Ross newsletter from her website at www.JoAnnRoss.com. Also connect with her on Facebook, Twitter, Instagram, and Pinterest.

Other Books from JoAnn Ross

The Shelter Bay series
The Homecoming
One Summer
On Lavender Lane
Moonshell Beach
Sea Glass Winter
Castaway Cove
You Again
Beyond the Sea (pre-publication title, A Sea Change)
Sunset Point
Christmas in Shelter Bay, November, 2016

The Castlelough series
A Woman's Heart
Fair Haven
Legends Lake
Briarwood Cottage
Beyond the Sea

River's Bend Series
River's Bend (Cooper's story)
Long Road Home (Sawyer's story) Pre-publication was Hot Shot

Orchid Island Series
Sun Kissed

7 BRIDES for 7 Brothers Series
Finn—7 Brides for 7 Brothers (Book 7), December 13, 2016

Rum Runner Island Series
A Place in Time, October 18, 2016
Somewhere in Time, January, 2017

About The Author

JoAnn Ross wrote her first novella—a tragic romance about two star-crossed mallard ducks—for a second grade writing assignment.

The paper earned a gold star.

And JoAnn kept writing.

She's now written around one hundred novels (she quit keeping track long ago), has been published in twenty-six countries, and is a member of the Romance Writers of America's Honor Roll of best-selling authors. Two of her titles have been excerpted in *Cosmopolitan* magazine and her books have also been published by the Doubleday, Rhapsody, Literary Guild, and Mystery Guild book clubs.

JoAnn lives with her husband and two fuzzy rescued dogs, who pretty much rule the house, in the Pacific Northwest.

Sign up to receive the latest news from JoAnn
joannross.com/newsletter

Visit JoAnn's Website
www.joannross.com

Like JoAnn on Facebook
facebook.com/JoAnnRossbooks

Follow JoAnn on Twitter
twitter.com/JoAnnRoss

Follow JoAnn on Goodreads
goodreads.com/author/show/31311.JoAnn_Ross

Follow JoAnn on Pinterest
pinterest.com/JoAnnRossBooks

Follow JoAnn on Instagram
instagram.com/joannrossbooks

CPSIA information can be obtained
at www.ICGtesting.com
Printed in the USA
LVOW12s1658240417
531982LV00004B/802/P